SET UP
Secrets and Lies in Zihuatanejo

A JadeAnne Stone
Mexico Adventure

ANA MANWARING

INDIES UNITED PUBLISHING HOUSE, LLC

Second Edition
Published by Indies United Publishing House, LLC

ISBN: 978-1-64456-434-9 [Paperback]
ISBN: 978-1-64456-435-6 [Mobi]
ISBN: 978-1-64456-436-3 [ePub]

Library of Congress Control Number: 2022931272

INDIES UNITED PUBLISHING HOUSE, LLC
P.O. BOX 3071
QUINCY, IL 62305-3071
www.indiesunited.net

Praise for Ana Manwaring's Series
JadeAnneStone Mexico Adventures

Kirkus Reviews
"With a likeable duo and a vivid, appealing setting, this adventure series is off to a promising start."

JC Miller, author of the bestseller, Vacation
A routine investigation takes a mysterious, chilling turn when JadeAnne is abducted at gunpoint then deposited in an opulent, albeit creepy manor. Moment-by-moment, her story unfolds in real time as she experiences the sights, sounds and myriad flavors of Mexico, the underworld of political corruption and high-stakes criminal activity roiling beneath the surface. When nothing is as it appears, and no one can be trusted, Jade's adrenaline surges—her mettle is tested. Told with humor and humility, grit and beauty, this page turner delivers.

Judy Penz Sheluk, Amazon international bestselling author
In her debut mystery novel, Author Ana Manwaring offers up more twists and turns than a Mexican rattlesnake. Fast paced, with well-crafted characters and a strong female lead, there's plenty to like about this world of power, politics, and Mexican money laundering. I especially enjoyed the strong sense of place, which Manwaring uses to great effect. Well worth adding to you TBR pile.

CT Markee, author of the Otherworld Tales, Irish/Abaddon Series
"...a fast moving tale of crime and danger in Mexico.... The plotline is devious and surprising. There are plenty of twists and turns in the story to keep you engaged. This is a complicated well-crafted story...I absolutely love the descriptions. It's a good read that I highly recommend."

COMING IN 2022

May 18, 2022
Book 2 The Hydra Effect
Revelations and Betrayal in Mexico City

August 17, 2022
Book 3 Nothing Comes After Z
Death and Retribution in Tepoztlán

November 16, 2022
Book 4 Coyote
Terror and Pursuit Across the Border

ACKNOWLEDGMENTS

I'm grateful to my parents who were readers and kept our home full of books. Even before I could read them, stories were my relaxation, my entertainment and my escape. I always knew I'd write novels in my future.

It was a future far, far away before I finished this novel, and it required much help along the way. My thanks go to my many teachers, particularly Brian Bolt and Guy Beiderman. Special thanks to my critique groups in all their configurations: First Drafters, Novelistas, Wordweavers and JAM. I'm ever thankful for my writer soulmates: Jeanne (JC) Miller and Mark Pavlichek of JAM for spot-on critique and pushing me to write well. A special shout-out to Kerry Granshaw who's been with me since my journey began and we founded Wordweavers. I couldn't do without Jan M. Flynn, my student turned colleague turned teacher for amazing critiques, or Kathy Rueve who convinced me to write in the first person. And heartfelt thanks to Malena Eljumaily for taking me under her wing and introducing me into Sisters in Crime Norcal.

Thanks to my editors, Jordan Rosenfeld, who set me on the path, grammarian Lorna Collins, mi maestra de español "Susanna Ackerman, for correcting the Spanish, and gun expert Clark Lohr, who explained what happens to your Prada bag when you put your Glock into it after emptying the clip. I appreciate your expertise.

And to my greatest champion, supporter and tech director, David. I can't express the depth of love and gratitude I hold for you. You've encouraged me in more ways than I can name."

DEDICATION

For Dr. John Hamilton Manwaring, M.D.
9/10/1919-4/11/1995

Dad, You encouraged me to travel and to read thrillers.
Look what happened.

Table of Contents

CHAPTER ONE

Jacked

July 27, 2007

A pair of headlights rushed my old VW camper, assailing me with their high beams. I moved over as far as the shoulderless causeway allowed. The vehicle pulled into the oncoming lane, honking furiously, but didn't pass.

"What the—? Pass, you idiot!"

Ahead, light strobed through the trees, and a bus barreled around the oncoming curve. It headed straight for the honking moron, and its brights reflected, blinding me through my side mirror. I tensed, gripped the wheel, and laid on the gas. The overloaded VW accelerated inch by inch while I rocked forward and back like a kid willing motion. "Go. Go. Go!" I yelled.

Just in time, the daredevil dropped back into the southbound lane of Ruta 200, and the bus roared past, spewing diesel fumes across the Mexican landscape on its route to "Cd. Obregon."

Stupid kids, I thought. But I kept my grip on the wheel and my foot to the gas pedal. Taking a missing persons case had seemed like such a good idea at the time—a working holiday, and a chance to take a good look at my life. Now I felt anxious as I drove south on the narrow, winding Pacific Coast Highway down through Michoacán on my way to Zihuatanejo.

Beep Beep Beeeep. The vehicle roared into the other lane again. Did the driver see something wrong with my camper? Lights out? Hatch open? Cargo falling off the roof? Through the mirror, I saw a white pickup. Colored lights set in the grille blinked back and forth—the kind that *camioneros* use to adorn their trucks. The honking became more insistent. BeepBeepBeep Beeep.

Pepper woke up from his nap on the back seat and growled at the side window, his hair standing on end. Confused, I toggled the lights off and on. They were working just fine. What did this asshole want?

BEEPBEEPBEEP—The cab pulled parallel with me, and two porky men waved frantically. I slowed down—there must be an emergency—until it registered they had baseball caps pulled low over their faces, and the driver even had a bandana tied like a western *bandido*. BEEEEP BEEEEP. I stiffened with fear. Why didn't I keep Pepper up front with me? Could they see him? The driver revved his motor and shot forward just enough to reveal a third masked man sitting in the back, pointing a mean-looking semi-automatic rifle at me. His brown belly poked out of his dirty, open shirt, and my headlights sparked off the thick gold chains he wore. Pepper went ballistic, clawing at the window with his forepaws and barking. I felt lightheaded.

Suddenly the pickup sped off around a bend, its taillights vanishing as quickly as its headlights had appeared.

My heart thudded fast in my chest. I scanned the forest for a break in the trees, somewhere to hide. What on earth am I doing in Mexico? I asked myself for about the billionth time since I'd crossed the border three days before. But now more than feeling lonely, I felt scared and pissed off. It was all Dex's fault.

Twilight faded into night too fast, and the forest turned to a black void. I wondered if I should stop and fish my gun out of its hidey-hole. I'd probably be safer if I kept moving. "Keep driving—don't stop. Just keep driving." A mantra against fear. Anyway, what good would the little pistol do against that rifle?

Truthfully, my feelings had morphed into edginess and irritation hours before. I hadn't had cell service or seen a road sign since Tecomán, and the few villages I passed were poor, sparsely-populated assemblages of huts and corrals, surrounded by plots hacked out of the forest and planted with scraggly still-green corn. Thin burros and even thinner children stared with large, sad eyes as I passed, posed like the ghastly velvet paintings in the tourist traps. Didn't anyone feed these kids? Cultivated fields stretched along the narrow littoral between mountains and coast. If the corn wasn't ripe, there were bananas, coconuts and mangoes, but all this bounty didn't help me relax—or put meat on those skinny little bones.

Pepper stopped barking but whined from the back, perhaps voicing my own question: Where did they go? The forest looked ghostly under the beams of my headlights, and I floored it when the road dipped down toward sea level. The camper shimmied, reminding me of my mechanic's warning, "If you're crazy enough drive in Mexico, drive slowly. The border will be dangerous, but don't stop for anything until you get to Mazatlán, especially not in the state of Sinaloa—not even for gas. And stick to the coastal route through Michoacán. It's safer." Well, call me crazy. But what did Ebbie know about fleeing armed Mexicans?

Keep driving, don't stop. Just keep driving. I turned off the heart-wrenching mariachi music playing on the radio. My mind raced. It's not my day to die, I told myself. Nothing is going to happen to me. Just keep driving.

Out of nowhere, the pickup reappeared and stopped in the middle of the highway, blocking both lanes. The fat guy in the truck bed sighted his weapon on me, and I exercised my only option. Gasping, heart hammering, I clamped my hands to the wheel to steady myself and braked to a stop. I took in a ragged, fear-filled breath. One, two, three, four. Hold, two, three, four. Exhale.

I thought about my gun again as the two thugs from the cab lumbered out of the truck. The masked driver positioned himself to my right and pointed his handgun in my direction. My legs ossified and clacked against each other with the tremors attacking my body. The other man came up to my window, and I smelled cheap tequila, tobacco, and rancid sweat—possibly my own. All I could think of was bad Mexican movies and guessed they didn't plan on showing me any "stinking badges."

"*¿A dónde vas, Señora?*" The man leered, a cigarette dangling from his pig-shaped face. He took a good look down my tank top and then glanced into the bus as he illuminated it with his flashlight. "*Quién está atrás?*"

"Good evening, Señor. I'm sorry, but I don't speak Spanish," I lied. "Is there a problem?" I strained to keep my voice steady.

"Where is your husband?" he demanded in accented English as his hand darted in the open window and ripped down the curtain. I cringed. Yes, the sixty-four thousand dollar question—where is Dexter Trouette? At least I still had Pepper to protect me, or would they shoot him? Me? I said nothing. Pepper growled.

"So, you are alone. El Patrón he is waiting for you. You must come." He turned to the other man who had moved directly in front of the bus and gestured toward the passenger door, "*Ábrela!*"

The thug promptly smashed the passenger-side window with the pearl handled butt of a small pistol. He reached in hesitantly, pushing cubes of broken safety glass out of his way. "¿*Muerde el perro*—does he bite?" He jerked his thumb at my growling dog. I let out a choked sound he took as "no." He opened the unlocked door then swept the map, guidebook, and a pile of CDs onto the floor and hoisted himself onto the red leather Cadillac seat Dex had installed in the bus. His stench overpowered the cabin. My stomach heaved.

"*Maneje*. Drive," he said, although the bandana made it hard to understand him. The sound of the camper door slamming was like the hollow clang of a prison door locking.

Choking back a mouthful of bile and a bellyful of fear, I slowly shifted into first gear and let out the clutch. The camper lurched forward then smoothed out when I shifted into second. Rivulets of perspiration coursed down my face and body. Pepper growled softly in warning. Well, I'd proved I was crazy enough to drive alone through drug cartel territory, but was I stupid enough to try and—and what? I knew I couldn't outrun the pickup even if I could get away, not too likely since the man pointed the small pistol at me with his meaty paw. If Pepper could make a direct hit on his wrist, he would have to drop the gun, but I wasn't sure the dog would be able to leap over the oak cabinet Dex had built. I signaled Pepper with a low whistle to wait on guard. He stopped growling, but I could see him in the mirror baring his teeth. The man yanked off the bandana and swiped at his neck as he jerked his head between me and the dog. I prayed. Wind whooshed through the open windows.

Home. The image came sharp and stinging behind my eyes: my houseboat, the Sarasvati, moored in the tree-shrouded cove at Varda Landing on Sausalito's waterfront, cool and silent in the fog.

The pickup turned into an almost invisible break in the forest, and I reluctantly followed at the insistent prodding of the man's gun. I felt like a sheep going to slaughter—

hopeless, dead.

We arrived at an electric gate, which opened to allow the two vehicles through and closed rapidly in a shower of sparks. The forest pressed in on the lane and closed up behind us as we drove through. Unlike the highway, this private road was smooth, hard-packed sand without ruts or potholes, better than my parking lot at home. No light shone. It was impossible to see anything beyond the small bubble we traveled in.

Eventually the trees began to thin and drop away. The evening became brighter. A skunky odor I hadn't smelled since college poured through the windows and I sneezed. The sneezes roused me from the torpor of fear I'd slid into and I began to notice my surroundings. If Dex couldn't magically rescue me, I'd better pay attention.

We drove along a farm track beside cultivated fields of pot. The black shadow of the forest ringed what I estimated to be two or three acres of budding marijuana. The redolent smell of the crop covered the stench of sweat and I took a deep belly breath, letting it out slowly and completely to the count of eight. My taut muscles loosened slightly, but I couldn't shake the thought that I'd never see Dex again. Why hadn't I believed my mechanic? He'd warned me. Michoacán was a prime marijuana growing state and filled with dangerous roadblocks, weapons, and hot tempers. "If the Federales don't kill you while trying to rob you, the *narcotraficantes* will—just because they can." I blinked back the hot tears spilling onto my cheeks. El Stinko sneered.

The lane curved up around the edge of the field and back into the forest where it joined a wider road paved in red brick neatly laid in a herringbone pattern and cemented in place. Everything looked hyper-clear to me. I noticed details such as the tin roofs on the well-lit compound in a small valley below the road. I noticed men with rifles outside three large buildings that looked like warehouses. Beyond the buildings, I could make out a barn and what I thought might be a stable for horses or tack rooms. I smelled a chicken coop as we skirted the compound and circled through gardens illuminated by the rising moon. Silhouettes of coconut and banana trees lay beyond the kitchen gardens, and the steep mountains to the east looked like black shadows against a star-studded sky.

We arrived at another gate set into a high stone wall topped with broken glass. The gate, black metal wrought into a serpent motif shined with gold accents. I didn't see who opened it, but the pickup continued inside and my captor waved me on. We pulled up in front of an apricot-colored Mediterranean-style house with more iron grillwork on the lower windows. I couldn't get a good look at the place because the pickup eased to the curb, and El Stinko motioned with his gun to pull in behind it.

Fatso, with the semi-automatic, remained in the truck bed, but the driver got out, strode to the smashed passenger window, and said something too low to hear. My captor jumped out of the bus and scuttled around to my door, waving his little girlie gun at me.

The driver bent into the window and ordered, "*Bájate*,"

El Stinko yanked my door open and half-dragged me from the bus. He marched me around the vehicle to the sliding door, gripping my arm roughly, but lowered his pistol.

"Open it," he barked in Spanish.

I didn't really have a plan, but I saw opportunity cracking open. We'd make a run for it. I whistled two notes and pulled down the handle, ducking to the side while the door slid open on its track. Pepper flew at the man's throat, knocking him over. The gun fired, the man screamed, and we all hit the ground. Pepper lunged at his throat a second time. El Stinko let go of me to fend off my dog. I rolled under the bus and watched in horror. The man's neck was coated with blood. His breath gurgled through the punctures. When he tried to get up, he collapsed onto his ugly face. Three more shots rang out. The driveway filled with shouting and running feet, clattering across brick and stone. I braced myself, expecting to see my beloved Pepper in a bloody heap.

CHAPTER TWO

Five Star Holding Cell

Pepper's warm tongue bathed my face but the whimpering woke me up. Mine? Had I passed out? A sharp ache seared my scull and diminished to a hot, dull throb. I ran my fingers over my scalp and felt a nasty egg where I must have hit something when I rolled under the bus.

I heaved onto an elbow and looked around. We lay on a bed topped with an eyelet cover and fluffy pillows stacked against the brass headboard. How did we get here? I sat up and hugged my dog. Tears welled and spilled down my cheeks.

"They didn't kill you, Peppi," I whispered. I felt his body for injuries and found none, thank God. He grinned and wiggled onto his back. "No time for pets, Pepper. We've got to get out of here."

I scuttled off the bed, wincing at the pain in my head, and edged toward the door, Pepper at my heels.

"Of course. It's locked. Come on, let's check the window."

The floor-to-ceiling multi-paned windows opened easily onto a narrow balcony overlooking a courtyard. A tiled fountain splashed water into an illuminated pond whose surface shifted black and golden with, I supposed, large carp. The courtyard overflowed with colorful flowers and tropical plants but I didn't see any people.

I gasped at the profusion of red-lipped "Dianne Feinstein" orchids and the yellow oncidiums I grew in a hothouse on the Sarasvati. The stone benches and statuary scattered about looked like pre-Columbian artifacts by the light of candles flickering in terracotta wall sconces. Groupings of *equipal* furniture, made of pigskin and split bamboo, clustered under a colonnade.

I breathed in the smell of paraffin and smoke and the subtle scent of night blooming jasmine that sweetened the waxy air. The lighting might have enhanced serenity and romance if this were a honeymoon, but in my situation, I felt sick. Strains of Beethoven's "Moonlight Sonata" floated up from some interior room. My sister used to play that piece on the piano before she died. My parents wanted me to play, too. Or learn ballet and tap like Mom. But I couldn't do it. I always failed. I wasn't like that mom, and I never knew my real one. I'd felt like a prisoner in a luxurious jail then, too.

Pepper guarded the balcony from inside the bedroom, and I sat down and leaned up against the wall to consider our predicament. I didn't see any immediate escape. We'd risk breaking our legs if we jumped to the floor below. Besides, we'd still be in the house.

Damn that Dex. Okay, it was as much my fault as his that things had cooled between us, but instead of running off on silly investigations, he should have stuck around and attended to our business. I doubted I'd have taken the case if Dex had stayed home instead of chasing sunken treasure with his Army buddy Penn, on what he claimed was a salvage job. Or whatever he was up to. I'd heard it all before, how he and Penn were "this close" to diving a Spanish Galleon laden with Mexican gold. I'd stopped listening. Dex's scuba diving was just one more thing I didn't fit into.

SET UP

Pepper whined. My heart hammered my ribs. "What is it, boy?" I whispered. He poked his nose into the cramped balcony and clicked the baseboard with his toenails. I reached through the window and gave him a pat. "Just thinking about Daddy," I said. He sighed and plopped down onto the tiles.

My family disapproved of Dex. So what was new about that? Mom dubbed all my boyfriends, "not our class of people". Okay, my judgment of men lacks malice—so sue me. But Dex proved them right, running around Baja California, alleging he was on a case, one without billable hours to pay Waterstreet Investigation and Marine Salvage's high Sausalito rent. Classy or not, I had a lot of my life tied up with Dex—seven years. Ever since grad school.

That was the problem. I'd been stuck in the office doing boring reports and feeling sorry for myself. I could still picture the fog hovering over Mt. Tam like a thick, grey pall. God, I hated that damp chill. As usual, I closed the office windows, and I clearly remember wishing I were somewhere warm—like in Mexico with Dexter—when the client showed up and interrupted my meditation on the mountain. Everything had been wrong. It was after hours, he skulked in with a briefcase full of cash, and said his wife was missing in a foreign country. What had I been thinking? My mother was right; I was wasting "that expensive education" as the managing partner of WIMS. I should have gone into insurance. No one kidnaps an insurance broker.

The leathery scent of the pigskin sweetened by the night jasmine wafted on the air and reminded me of the client's cologne. I pictured him in his well-cut suit, reeking of something expensive. His face boyish and full. Intelligent, deep blue eyes twinkled even in the dimly lit corridor.

"We're closed," I had yelled. "Come back during business hours." Our hours are posted on the door.

"I-I need the services of a private investigator.

11

Immediately. It's my wife. She's lost."

Lost? That was curious and I hesitated a beat too long. "What do you mean—lost? We don't handle domestic problems."

"She's gone missing in Ixtapa, Mexico."

Mexico. A parade of images passed through my mind: sun, sand, margaritas, and plates of fresh fish smothered in salsa, mangoes on sticks, greasy pork tacos eaten under palm-thatched roofs, and tropical rhythms keeping time with the crash of the surf outside my hotel balcony. Ixtapa. I could visit my best friend, Sally, at her place in neighboring Zihuatanejo. I was gaga over vacation possibilities and thrilled by the scent of investigation. After all, I had trained as a journalist.

I unlocked the office door and ushered in the client.

Matching my grin, he introduced himself. "Daniel Worthington, President CalMex Federal Bank."

"HQ recommended your firm to me," he continued and described an investigation my predecessor had conducted as I led him to my office. CalMex Fed was a San Francisco-based bank.

"Mrs. Pistolesi retired. I'm the managing partner now." I gestured to the settee. "Have a seat. May I offer you a cup of coffee or a drink? We have scotch or rum."

"Thank you, a Cuba Libre—make it a double, Miss–"

"Stone," I replied from the bar, stirring the rum and cokes. "We're out of limes, sorry."

The music beyond the balcony changed to a Mozart piano concerto and brought me back to my incarceration. I checked my watch. No one had entered the courtyard or appeared in a window or on another of the balconies across the way for over an hour. No one had even come to check on me. The evening cooled, and I shivered. I wasn't sure how much was from the long drive, my tumble out of the VW, or the cold hard tiles. Or maybe because I was clenching every muscle in my body.

Did Dex wonder where I was? Obsessing again, locked in a room I didn't know where, and all I could do was think about my failing relationship. I said a silent prayer that Dex would turn up in time, well armored. But could he find me? GPS on my cell phone like in a thriller? Surely he worried. I had missed our scheduled call. But had the person who kidnapped me called for ransom? Narco kidnappings had become common. I shuddered. WIMS didn't have much by way of liquid assets. My stomach somersaulted. Would he ransom me?

Gasping through a panic attack, I clawed my way to my feet on the narrow ledge and lurched back through the window into the bedroom. My bladder about to burst, I found the bathroom. I'd take a hot shower, if there was hot water, and try to make sense of my abduction. A shower might shake off the prickly feeling that someone watched me.

"Hey. Hey. My dog needs to pee. Let me out of here." I looked around for a camera. Nothing. Poor Pepper was going to have to hold it or break all his puppy training.

I tried to relax in the endless supply of hot water. So why did the thugs smell like dirty sweat socks? My few cosmetics and toiletries nested in cupboards and lined the counter, completely creeping me out. I slipped on a white terry robe I found hanging on the back of the door, but the tantalizing smells of food led me into a dressing room where my suitcase had been unpacked, and my own clothes hung in a massive, carved wardrobe. A very high-end hotel or a serial killer cliché? Whichever, I didn't plan to stick around to find out. I dressed in black pants and a dark shirt with long sleeves, determined that somehow we were going to get out of there, and I'd better be able to fade into the shadows.

But first, we'd eat. I found a glass-topped rattan table set with platters of cold meats, cheeses, and fruit covered in plastic wrap. I lifted the lid on a chafing dish and steam rose from a portion of chicken poblano. Someone had come in while I showered. The service would have been five-star in a hotel. Impeccable. Worthington had been like that, including his pale, well-manicured hands visible as he hoisted his briefcase onto my desk. I pictured the tidy stacks of crisp one hundred dollar bills. It was right out of the movies. Or was it?

My stomach growled, and I turned to a sideboard displaying fresh baked breads, a sweating pitcher of iced limeade, and a bottle of Vino Tinto Bodegas de Santo Tomás Barbera 2005. "From the vineyards of Baja California," I read off the label. I reached for the limeade, sat down at the table, and noticed the initials LAS entwined within serpents, similar to those I had seen on the entry gates, monogrammed on the white linens and the silver. This LAS person complemented his English bone china with a blue bowl of violet-speckled sprays of phalaenopsis floating like little moths over lacy ferns. The rich can afford to live graceful lives. But these rich, where did their money come from? Worthington was a banker, presumably an upstanding citizen. This LAS character grew marijuana. Was my retainer the wash cycle for some drug business? A little late to worry about it. I hadn't had any problem taking the retainer then. Lacking in moral fiber, my dad would say. I felt like I had a tight band around my head.

Pepper had already found a plate of cooked meat and a water bowl placed on a plastic mat in the corner. The scene came right out of Hitchcock. Should we eat? My stomach knotted itself in a drawn-out growl.

"Pepper, they're probably poisoning us, but it looks good, and I'm starving, aren't you? We better eat and get our strength up. Then we're out of here."

Pepper thumped his tail against the floor and tucked into the meat. I spread my napkin across my lap and helped myself to the poblano and some fresh pineapple, topping it with salsa verde and a mound of cilantro. If this were going to be my last meal, I wanted to enjoy it. I sniffed at the food and took a tiny bite. I didn't taste anything bad and felt no adverse effects after several moments, so I dug in.

The food was delicious, but I paced myself and chewed each bite slowly just the way my doctor said I should, thinking about Worthington. He hadn't seen his wife in three weeks—over three weeks. What kind of marriage was that? He hadn't even seen her, but had his secretary track down her Visa charges in Ixtapa, "Ten thousand pesos spent at Christine's, the disco in Hotel Krystal. It's possible her card was stolen, but she hasn't called me in more than two weeks, and it scares me." His laugh had sounded forced.

I poured a glass of wine and finished the last bite of my chicken. Heck, I worried when I didn't hear from Dex every day.

It had been hours since I'd lunched in Manzanillo, and I still had room for more. I loaded up my plate with another serving, this time tender roast beef and a slice of Muenster-like cheese to fill the fresh telera sandwich roll from the sideboard. I finished off my meal with a Mexican-style sweet roll slathered in soft butter and mango jelly then shoved the plate away and tossed my napkin onto the table, sated.

Why hadn't Worthington notified the local authorities? After spending $800 in the disco, I figured Mrs. Worthington was shacked up with some hot tamale beach boy and having the proverbial ball—or worse. Mexico had become the kidnapping capital of the world.

"Let's get out of here, Pepper," I said.

Nothing had changed in our room. The door remained locked, and I couldn't find an escape route besides jumping off the balcony, which still landed inside the courtyard. If I didn't break a leg, Pepper surely would. I couldn't do that to him. Grabbing a pillow off the bed, I dropped it onto the balcony and plopped down to think.

A clock chimed one, and my head drooped, but I was afraid to go to bed. I ran through my meeting with Daniel Worthington again.

"They—I, uh, I prefer, in my position, you understand, to locate her privately. I'm prepared to pay whatever you ask. Please, Ms. Stone. I'm certain something has happened to her."

I thought he'd been pleading for his wife, and I'd allowed myself to be suckered in. I asked if he'd received a ransom request and noticed a distinct tic in his right eye. He'd hung his head and shook it. "No, nothing. Please, Miss Stone, find Lura." Idiot! I'd believed every word after his voice caught in that sob and look where it got me—locked in a pot grower's guest room in cartel country.

"WIMS doesn't negotiate kidnapping and ransom releases," I'd told him. I wrote it up in the contract too. If Mrs. Worthington was being held by a cartel, could I terminate the investigation and still bill for the balance? I should have paid more attention to my Business Law class.

He'd dabbed at his eyes with a handkerchief and inclined his head slightly. I reached over and laid my hand on his sleeve, a gesture of comfort, and punched a button on the small tape recorder I kept on my desk. "Now, tell me everything you can about your wife's disappearance."

The piano music had long ceased and the soothing gurgle of the fountain stopped, waking me. I might as well get into bed. The courtyard remained empty and dark, most of the candles burned out, and the electric light had been turned off. When had that happened? I had to stay awake and be ready to fight or run if it came to it.

SET UP

"Pepper?"

He woofed from the other side of the window. I checked my watch. It was two-forty. The night sky lit up with stars, and the humid air smelled of salt and growing things. I stood up and stretched before settling back down to keep myself awake by identifying constellations above the open courtyard.

I'd listened to the interview tape I made of my client several times on the long drive from Sausalito to this cell and could clearly conjure up Worthington's voice. Had my kidnappers found it?

"Lura, Lura Laylor is my wife's name. We've been married for five years but she wouldn't change her name. When I was transferred to Mexico City a few years ago, she took a job out of San Francisco with HandiMex Imports, as a buyer." He'd stopped talking for a moment. "It's an important position for her. HandiMex is the largest importer of Latin American goods to the U.S." I pictured how his grin had faded to a look I couldn't read. What was he hiding? He said they didn't live together, but vacationed every month at one of Mexico's myriad of exclusive resorts. Sounded fun, but not how I pictured my marriage with Dex, whenever that happened. The last vacation—the tenth through the fifteenth —they'd stayed at Las Hadas in Manzanillo before a trip to their property at Cuastecomate south in Jalisco. Near Barra de Navidad. I remembered the sign and a turn-off I passed yesterday, a million light years ago. From the highway, Cuastecomate hadn't impressed me. I didn't see why anyone would go there. But now I questioned why I hadn't. The woman might be at their property. I might have found her and avoided being hijacked off the highway.

Worthington made it sound like a tropical paradise complete with the unspoiled white sand beach, thatched *palapas*, and island music. He'd rambled on about a group of folks playing Jimmy Buffet tunes on steel pans or something. I hadn't kept up with his tale, too many names, but I had detected a slight change in his voice when he mentioned a man named Medrick—and saw that tic again. He paused in his story and sipped from his drink, gazing out my office window where the lights of Mill Valley twinkled up the slope of the mountain. I'd felt a chill run through me. I knew the banker was hiding something under all his talk. Yet here I am. Serves me right.

I woke up again, close to dawn, cold and stiff from sleeping on the cramped balcony, my head still pounding, and Pepper patiently guarding me. He would protect me to death, but was death outside the door? I was determined to get out of there. It was so late, everyone would probably be asleep, and we could tiptoe out the main door—if we could get to the first floor. But where would we go? I prowled around the suite again, looking for anything to tell me our location. I poked into drawers, the closets, and I even crawled under the bed. Finally, I opened the sideboard where we had eaten. It overflowed with books, magazines, and a photo album. I sank down into the chair at the table and flipped the album open. There were pictures of workmen and a construction site with the ocean in the background. As I turned the pages, I watched a building being built. No captions or time stamps, but toward the end of the book I was startled to find a shot of a hotel—the Hotel Krystal. It was the ribbon-cutting ceremony and a smiling Daniel Worthington and his petite wife, Lura Laylor, flanked the man with the shears. Unlike the photo Worthington had given me in my office, they weren't mugging for the camera in swimsuits, but I had no doubt who they were. Something stank. I'd been played.

Noise came from the bedroom, distracting me from my discovery. Clutching the album to my chest, I scurried in. A small, dark girl of about twelve, carrying an envelope on a platter, bobbed to me and said some words in a strange language while depositing the envelope on the bureau. She fled when she spied Pepper, her long shiny braids streaming behind her. I listened to her footfalls slapping along the gallery. The girl's appearance surprised me. I mentally kicked myself for missing a chance to escape through the open door. It locked again—I tried it— although I hadn't seen a key or heard a click.

Shrugging off my annoyance, I picked up the apricot-colored envelope. My name was written calligraphy-style with ink and sealed with a gold wax seal embossed with the initials encircled by the serpents. I popped open the flap with my finger and scanned the message written on the deckle-edged writing paper:

> Dear Señorita Stone,
> Welcome to my home. I will send for you at half past six. Please be ready to join me in my morning swim. Breakfast will be served in the courtyard at eight.
> At your service,
> Leopoldo Aguirre S.

This Aguirre person sounded civilized, but the note clearly wasn't an invitation. I now had a name to go with the initials, LAS. I looked at the photo again. The man cutting the ribbon must have been Leopoldo Aguirre S., but what did he have to do with my client and his missing wife? Was Aguirre the "hot tamale" in the photo? The man appeared attractive enough, and Lura Laylor leaned into him, grinning in a way that might be read as flirtatious. Somehow, though, it didn't stack up. Also, if Worthington knew this guy, then why hadn't he checked with Aguirre for information about his wife?

The nasty tune that I'd been had played again through my mind. I tried to ignore it, but it hummed along anyway.

Had I been set up? I couldn't imagine why. I didn't know these people, but it was hard to believe it a coincidence I had been abducted off the highway by someone the client knew. I guessed I'd find out pretty soon, since I was to be ready and swimming in forty-five minutes, according to a glance at my watch. I imagined swimming under the armed guard of fat walruses with drooping mustaches, and sniggered. I should have been concerned, not making jokes. It wasn't funny, but I was tired and feeling stupid. And a little hopeful. We'd get out of the room.

"Peppi, are you up for a swim?" The dog rolled his eyes and wagged his tail at the sound of my voice.

"Okay, if you're up for it, let's throw on our suits and lace up the Nikes. Maybe we'll be able to make a run for it."

Pepper grinned and thumped harder.

CHAPTER THREE

Morning Swim

July 28, 2007

Punctually at six-thirty a knock sounded on the door. I waited by the window. Pepper strained at his leash.

"Yes?" I called out.

The door opened and the dark-haired girl gingerly stepped in, curtsied, and gestured for me to follow her. She was dressed in a costume of bright pink satin with puffed sleeves and a lacy white apron. Her hair was now plaited with narrow ribbons and neatly tied together at the ends.

"Where are we going?" I inquired in Spanish.

The girl looked at her dusty, sandaled feet and mumbled something in the strange language I had heard earlier. Eyes cast down, she hurried into the gallery leaving the door open but keeping well ahead of us. She glanced nervously back at Pepper as we made our way down the long, dimly lit corridor that circled above the open courtyard. Portraits of somber men and severe women lined the walls between the several closed doors we passed. The heavy wooden benches reminded me of the antechamber in an old country courthouse where petitioners and lawyers awaited

21

appearances or verdicts. I expected Atticus Finch to pop out through a door. The tile floors gleamed and resonated with the rhythmic tapping of Pepper's toenails; I made a mental note to have them clipped as soon as we got home.

At the end of the passage, we turned a corner and descended a narrow staircase into a small room filled with open shelving stocked with hats, boots, sports equipment, towels and all manner of sports shoes. A few low, hand-hewn benches scattered about and a pair of shining silver spurs hung over the back of a caned chair. The girl pushed open a heavy door, letting the brilliant morning sun flood in. Pepper strained at his lead. The poor boy needed to pee. I released the button and let Pepper run into the small walled garden to the length of the retractable leash. He sniffed out a suitable bush, lifted his leg then settled behind it, tail up, back to us humans.

I thought the little girl was terrified to see the dog on such a long lead, and was surprised when she whispered, "¡Vamos! No hay tiempo. El patrón waits. He is angry when we are late."

His business done, Pepper happily sniffed and marked the garden, and he looked disappointed when I reeled in the leash. The girl looked up at me with a faint smile and nodded toward a gate set into the high wall, obscured somewhat by a vine with long, tubular orange and yellow flowers resembling oversized honeysuckle. She was about to speak when a man's voice said in perfect English softened by Spanish consonant pronunciation, "You may release him. He will want to acquaint himself with the smells of my dogs. This is their garden."

Pepper and I turned in unison toward the sound of our kidnapper's voice. A low growl gurgled up my dog's throat. The little servant shrank back through the garden door. I tightened my grip on the leash, making no motion to obey the man's request as he stepped around the corner of the house and into view.

I checked him out as he approached: tall with the lean physique of a swimmer. His tan was deep and he radiated vitality. I would describe him as polished, even in swim trunks—manicured hands, trimmed moustache and sideburns, white, even teeth. Streaks of silver shot through his dark hair, the only hint of his age. Even in his swimsuit, I recognized him from the ribbon ceremony photo.

"I'm sorry. It is so rare that I have a visitor to my remote valley I have forgotten my manners." As he moved forward along the glaring crushed-shell path, he slipped off his dark glasses and stretched out his hand in greeting.

"May I present myself? I am Leopoldo Aguirre Sotomayor, *a sus órdenes*." He inclined his head and clicked his bare heels with archaic European formality. "And I know from your papers that you are Miss JadeAnne Stone of Sausalito, California. You are not married, you entered Mexico at Nogales on July twenty-fourth, and you are driving a 1969 VW camper alone with a highly trained dog. I want to know why you are here."

I clamped my teeth together and frowned. Aguirre didn't seem to notice.

"You must not be aware, Miss Stone, of the dangers to a woman traveling alone in my country."

He spoke with a slight smile as though all these facts amused him. From the crow's feet around his eyes, I pegged him to be closer to fifty than forty, but I never was very good at guessing people's ages.

I didn't reply and hoped that my P.I. license and permit to carry stayed safely hidden in the bus. They would certainly have raised some questions with Aguirre. Tit-for-tat. Aguirre had raised some questions with me. But if he already knew who I was, well, I'd figure that out later.

"Ah, a quiet one. Let us see if you have more to say over breakfast. But first, our swim." He took my arm, dug his buffed nails into the muscle, and propelled me through the garden gate and into a sandy track toward the gentle roar of surf. Pepper strained to break free, softly growling.

"Let go of me. I can walk just fine by myself." I struggled to pull away from Aguirre but he gripped tighter. "Ow. You're hurting me. Am I your prisoner or a guest?"

"You must forgive me, Señorita Stone, but I am concerned for your safety here." He clamped my arm harder yet. "Some of my men are not pleased with your attack on my foreman last night—"

My knees locked and I stumbled, "My attack? Your foreman kidnapped me at gunpoint."

"—and I fear you may try to run away and become lost in the forest where these men may find you." He continued to drag me along the path. "Do you know what happens to women who shoot men in this country?" He glared at me. I stumbled, my running shoes softly thudding on the packed sand.

"Who did I shoot?" I looked at the ground, avoiding his gaze. "I don't carry a gun."

Had Aguirre's men found the little pistol with the scrimshaw handle hidden in the bus? I hoped not. Dex had made such a big deal in giving it to me after our former associate's incarceration last year. Anyway, I like the Semmerling LM4 because it's light and feeds from a magazine inserted in the grip like a semi-automatic. I'd spent hours at the Bullseye Indoor Shooting Range. I wished I had it. As if reading my mind, Pepper snarled at Aguirre.

"Keep that dog away from me." He flinched, and I slipped out of his grip, but Aguirre let it be. "Do you know he almost ripped Enrique's throat out? I had to airlift him to the hospital in Colima at great expense to me, and great anguish to his wife and children. He, what do you call that beast? Oh, yes, Pepe—like a *burro*. Pepe would have killed him. Geraldo was about to shoot the animal when I came out of the house with my dog trainer."

"Enrique is the fat, smelly thug you sent to kidnap me? You should teach him to wash." I shuddered with disgust.

Aguirre smiled that half-smile again. "You have to forgive our country ways. We live in a warm climate, and there is little water."

"You mean you need your water to grow marijuana."

"Yes, of course. You passed through the fields. I've insisted that our guests be escorted through the main entrance, but the men continue to take shortcuts. Your hypocrisy amuses me, Miss Stone. You Americans 'just say no' and continue to buy, buy, buy."

I ignored the jab. "You have a dog trainer? Is he the one who came into my room? Did he tranquilize Pepper?"

"Yes and no. He had no need of drugs. He's a skilled handler, and your dog is well-trained."

I thanked God for small mercies.

The path opened to the sea. The beach blinded me after the dappled shadows of the forest. I shaded my eyes against the glare and searched for an escape while Pepper tugged on the leash, anxious to be free. A couple hundred yards to the north I saw a small river delta, what in California I'd call a creek. I made a mental note to get the name of the river as I scanned the area for men with rifles lurking in the undergrowth.

Aguirre jogged down to the water, throwing off his sandals and towel. He dove under a wave and surfaced on the other side, swimming a strong Australian crawl.

"The temperature is perfect," he shouted. "Join me."

It was another of his polite orders, and shivers ran across my skin. This guy creeped me out. Something was wrong with him, but I couldn't sort it out in my dull, tired mind, and I didn't see any obvious escape. I dropped my towel, kicked off my shoes and trudged through the sand to the waterline. I tested the foamy current with my toes. It felt silky and lukewarm as I waded in, but swimming took too much effort. My body felt battered, slow. Pepper, though, bounded around my knees happily.

Waves rolled lazily into the cove, breaking close to the shore, indicating deep water very close in. The waves washed along the curve of the cove before sluicing back out into the next breaker. There might be a riptide. I'd better be careful. I could see the brown line, which marked the silted path of the freshwater creek emptying into the Pacific. Slipping under a cresting wave, I breast-stroked underwater for a few yards. Resurfacing, I gulped for air. I was close to Aguirre, and we paddled idly between swells.

The tepid water soothed me, and I began to enjoy the swim despite my fear. Crystal-clear blue sky hung above the thick green forest that reached up from the narrow strip of sand to a jagged and mountainous skyline. Streams of hazy sunlight flowed down the canyons, and pools of brilliant light heated the beach and the banana groves as day crept into the cove. Breathtaking.

"It is going to be hot today." Aguirre broke the moment's peace. "I apologize for my men. They are ignorant and crude. I instructed them to invite you to stop in for a visit, not to abduct you with violence. They know I enjoy visitors, especially beautiful women."

He's got to be kidding—beautiful women? "Why me? Why did you bring me here, Mr. Aguirre?" Various possibilities stroked through my mind—none of them pleasant.

"It is very lonely on the coast. My beloved Maria and our children were killed in an automobile accident on the highway," Aguirre's voice thickened, "three years ago."

A twinge of sympathy stabbed at my heart as I flashed on the roadside shrine I'd admired along the cliffs of Ruta 200, but I quickly pushed it aside. Aguirre was a player. He had to be conning me.

"I don't buy it. People don't kidnap tourists off the highway for company. Why am I here?" I sculled rapidly to keep my head well above the waterline and scowled at my kidnapper as a swell raised us up to its peak. I panted with exertion and nagging fear.

Aguirre glared back, a cold, hard stare. We sank into the glassy trough. I felt chilled to the bone.

"You tell me, Ms. Stone. Women don't drive thousands of miles alone in dangerous foreign countries for vacations. Why are you here?" His eyes narrowed, face twisted to a menacing sneer.

A Mexican standoff. I'd been manipulated. Why did these men, Aguirre and the banker, want to find Laylor? I kicked away from him. Why was I in the water with this man? He could reach out and drown me with no effort.

I cleared my throat, steadying my voice, "What happened to her? Your wife, I mean."

His tone softened, "She was taking Polito and Elizabet shopping in Colima. Mari lacked confidence behind the wheel and was driving in the middle of the road, according to the bus driver who hit them. He claimed he would have driven over the cliff and killed all his passengers if he had moved any more to the right. He killed my beautiful wife and my two children sleeping in the back. You know the spot. You stopped there and admired the shrine. You prevented your dog from disturbing that sacred place."

Aguirre had surveillance at the roadside shrine.

"So you expected my arrival?"

Aguirre didn't answer, but the quiver at the corner of his mouth and the sudden pulsing at his temple told me there was something more he wasn't telling, and it had nothing to do with his family. Somehow this suave narco knew I was coming. He'd make a poor poker player, I thought.

"Where on the coast are we exactly, Señor Aguirre?" I probed while I edged further away from him.

"Almost fifty kilometers north of Playa Azul and one hundred fifty kilometers south of Manzanillo. The creek you see entering the bay…" he gestured northward as we topped another swell "…is Río Carrizal. The land of my grandfather is marked by trés ríos." He circled his hand. "Río Cachan to the north, south to Río Balsas, into Presa del Infiernillo, the little devil's ditch."

A gull cried and I shivered but plunged on. "And was your grandfather also a *narcotraficante*?"

His lips flattened. "You Americans. Always making jokes with sarcasm. No, my grandfather was a poor banana farmer who barely had enough to feed his family."

Aguirre's eyes looked into the distance just beyond the breaking waves while we continued to tread water in silence. I felt my energy dissipating into the silky, cool ocean. Maybe Aguirre's plan was to let me drown myself. I choked on a mouthful of seawater and coughed.

The sound of my sputtering brought Aguirre back. "My father was also a farmer, but had a visionary outlook. He left his home and disappeared into La Capital for many years, but his love for the land and the sea drew him back when my grandfather was about to give up."

"What do you mean?" I tired rapidly, but Aguirre didn't react.

"You see, by this time the demand of the hippies had become great for the Acapulco Gold. Ruthless men flooded into the area, buying or stealing the fertile land of Michoacán to grow this new cash crop. Bananas had lost wholesale value in the market because the American company, Chiquita, monopolized the growers along the Caribbean and stopped buying Pacific bananas. The 1960s were hard times." He paused to catch his breath.

"So your father started growing pot."

"Under my father's management, our farms prospered and expanded."

"Where were you? Behind the barn smoking the shit?" I couldn't help myself. Dad always said I'd dig my grave with my tongue and, well, I aimed to make him right.

Aguirre glanced at me with a look of distaste. "My mother didn't like the country and kept us in La Capital for school. For the first few years, Rosario and I only visited during school holidays. When we were ten and twelve, Father hired a teacher, and we moved to our plantation. My grandfather and I became very close. I am a simple farmer at heart."

"A simple farmer grows bananas, not illegal drugs." I shoveled another foot deeper into my grave. I turned toward the beach.

Aguirre's voice rose a notch. "We save the bananas for the house and the workers. With the money we earn, we send our bright young people to school, and our workers are paid a good wage. They have medical attention and modern conveniences in their homes. No one is forced to work here. Mine is considered a model farm. You must join me in a tour of our operations after breakfast. I will be making an inspection and meeting with my foreman. You will come along. And, please, Señorita Stone, call me Polo. I want us to be friends."

I looked over my shoulder at him. Was this guy out of his mind? As if he were my buddy, not my kidnapper. "Señor Aguirre, as your invited guest, I'm sure you'll understand I was expected to arrive in Zihua yesterday and must be on my way." I started swimming toward shore.

He swam with me. "Please take my warning as concern for your safety, Señorita. The forest is dangerous here. Without my protection, there are those who will be happy to…"

"So this is a charade," I shouted as hysteria took me over. "I'm not your guest, am I? What do you want with me?"

I ducked under a swell, made a few powerful strokes, sloughing off the panic, and then let the current carry me until I was deposited in the churning eddies at the junction of the incoming and outgoing waves. Staggering to my feet, dripping and breathless, I waded onto the now completely sunlit beach. Aguirre's head bobbed beyond the swells.

"Pepper. Come, boy."

Pepper bounded down the beach from the cool shade of the banana grove, yelping and gurgling like a happy pup. I picked up my shoes and towel and ran as fast as I could into the shade. The already-hot sand burned my tender feet. Settling under a tall coconut palm, I contemplated our escape and watched Aguirre finish his morning swim.

We returned to the house in silence and retired to our separate rooms to change. Under Aguirre's order, we breakfasted in the courtyard at the long table visible from my balcony. A cream-colored cloth intricately embroidered with fanciful, brightly colored creatures topped it. Shocking pink napkins rolled around the engraved silverware marked our places. Once we were seated, the little girl and an older woman, also dressed in shiny satin topped by a stained plaid pinafore protecting her ample bosom, stepped out of the shadows to serve the meal. The girl poured fresh mango juice into cobalt blue glasses while the older woman passed painted clay bowls brimming with refried beans, white rice, and a pewter platter laden with fried eggs layered on tortillas and some sort of soft green leaves that gave off a pungent aroma. Fresh red sauce with a sprinkle of white crumbled cheese topped the concoction. Aguirre heaped his plate with mounds of food, adding sliced fruit and more salsa from the dishes on the table.

He opened a basket and the scent of the hot, steaming tortillas made me salivate. I wasn't sure how I'd gotten hungry again. Aguirre tore small triangles off his tortilla and scooped up his food. I followed his example and set about eating my second breakfast of the day. For prison, the food was great.

"This is wonderful. What do you call this dish?" I rudely asked through a mouthful of the spicy mixture.

"Huevos rancheros. Don't you eat it in California?"

"Not like this. What is the herb—this large leaf? We don't have this, that's for sure."

Aguirre thought for a moment. Then he spoke in Spanish. "Elena, what is the herb in this dish?"

The stout woman slowly approached the table. "Yerba santa," she said, keeping her head bowed. The woman's manner reminded me I was dining with a criminal who was feared by his servants, kept a company of armed thugs to protect his interests, and was arrogant enough to hijack tourists off the highway to fill his empty life. Shivers ran down my spine, and Pepper whined quietly. That is, if this was a random hijacking.

We ate in silence for a few moments while I contemplated the possibility that Aguirre planned to keep me. How could it possibly be? It just didn't add up. I heard laughter and the strange language deep in the house, probably the kitchen. It quieted, and then I heard muffled laughing coming from the upstairs wing opposite mine.

"Wait, Ani. I'll be right back." It was a woman's voice, and it was in English. I looked up in the direction of the sound in time to see a petite blonde rush out of one room and into another. For a fraction of a second, our eyes locked. My heart raced and my huevos rancheros threatened to come back up. Lura Laylor.

Aguirre acted oblivious to Laylor's intrusion into our breakfast. I ate on autopilot, one hand on Pepper, my touchstone. The food tasted like cardboard as my mouth went dry. My hijacking hadn't been random. What is she doing here? What am I doing here? My mind screamed. Was Lura Laylor another "guest?" Aguirre's back faced her wing, and for all I knew, he missed Lura's quick change of rooms. One thing was clear: Lura Laylor was not locked in. Could Aguirre be her "hot tamale?" My mind spun like a whirligig in a squall. I gripped the seat of my chair under the tablecloth.

"Señor Aguirre, how close are we to Zihuatanejo? I'm supposed to meet a friend."

"It is another two hundred kilometers."

"That far? How long will it take me?"

Aguirre put down his fork and signaled for the servants. The woman whisked the empty plates through a swinging door while the girl poured coffee into mugs, placing one at each of our elbows. With a clumsy curtsy, she left the sugar and creamer on the table and backed away through the same swinging door.

He called after her in rapid Spanish, "Take a plate to the Señora and tell her to keep it quiet up there."

He turned back to me. "You are going to Zihuatanejo? I am fond of the area. Ixtapa means 'where there are salt lakes' in Tarascan, the language you hear spoken by my servants. It is very old. Anthropologists say it was contemporary with Náhuatle, the language of the Aztecs."

"Yeah?"

"I have business in Ixtapa, the resort area just to the north. In fact, my holdings include a hotel and a construction company there."

The photo from the album flashed to mind.

"I've stayed at the Riviera del Sol, but I didn't like Ixtapa very much, too touristy, and way too expensive." I knew my tone sounded disagreeable. "Not to mention the mosquitoes pouring out of all those salt lakes." I paused to sip from my mug. "Which hotel?" I asked, knowing what he'd reply.

"The Krystal."

CHAPTER FOUR

Farm Trail

I have the notion I'm supposed to do something to earn my money—Dad's work ethic. He'd be proud. Either by coincidence or design, I had found the missing wife. My firm would look great. That is, if I wasn't murdered before I collected the rest of the fee.

I waited for Aguirre and his farm tour at the front door. I hadn't even arrived in Zihua, and I'd completed the investigation: Laylor found. But I didn't have time to worry about it because Aguirre pulled up in a Jeep, hopped out, and held my door as he guided me into the passenger seat. Pepper jumped in the back, and we jostled up the hill.

Aguirre kept up a narrative about the estate and its agricultural operations as we circled through the compound. I saw gardeners and cowboys, but the armed guards were gone. In a paddock, a cowboy broke a wildly angry bay as several hands looked on. It reminded me of visits to my uncle's ranch when I was a kid. Aguirre and I stopped to inspect a barn and one of the warehouses. The horses were magnificent and the warehouse held only feed. I wondered what was in the other buildings. I was right about the pigs and chickens, they stank in the hot air.

Back in the Jeep, I saw fields bursting with corn, beans, and tomatoes, rows of bright flowers, squash, and Nopal cactus. Workers raised their heads as we passed but quickly lowered them again. The looks of fear I saw on the weathered faces struck me hard.

We dipped down the shell-lined road into the orchards on the lower end of the pot fields. Aguirre lectured on the benefits of modern farming methods and agricultural economics, justifying his illegal activities. To hear him tell it, he was doing the world a favor. I considered my own checkered past and had to agree with some of his points. At least he didn't appear to be involved with cocaine. Or was that just a romantic notion I had? Aguirre's armed thugs weren't pets. They were rough, violent men, and I felt certain Aguirre was up to his eyeballs in the drug trade.

Lost in thought about my chances for escape, I missed some of what he said about the village we entered.

"…and the people hold town meetings there." He pointed to a low cinderblock building groaning under the weight of the red and orange bougainvillea climbing over it. "They elect their own *alcaldes*—town leaders. All the adults can vote, just like in the United States. It's a democracy, you see. What the villagers decide, my corporation abides by. See the school over there?" He gestured to another low building shaded by a huge tree several doors beyond the meeting hall. "I built that." He slowed the vehicle, parking under a spreading jacaranda. The sound of children's voices speaking in unison drifted out of the open windows.

"All my children go to school until they are twelve. Those who pass the exams go on to high school, even to university, at the expense of my corporation. Others I send to trade schools, especially in agriculture and construction. If a man does not wish to work on my farm, he can apply to one of my many companies in another industry. I'll show you." He hopped out, slamming the Jeep's door behind him. The voices went silent.

I clambered out behind him, nodding in understanding—a company town. "What about the girl who came to my room? What are you doing for her?" I came around the vehicle to stand by him. I wasn't seeing the utopian society. He referred to "his children." Aguirre bred his own workforce?

His cell phone rang, and he stepped away to answer. He spoke quietly in English, but I couldn't pick up more than a word here and there although I tried. Instead, I took in the village. Scrubbed-clean adobe and cinderblock homes clustered around a tree-lined plaza with ornate iron benches placed in the shade at intervals. The church, which dominated the square with its red-domed roof and bell tower, contrasted with the backdrop of green mountains. The town market occupied a bulldozed space next to the church and opened onto the plaza. It looked dead. A few vendors sat by their wares, but the main activity of the village surrounded the water pump. Women, several with tiny babies bound to their backs in their shawls, clustered, gossiping and filling buckets and containers. Some washed laundry in the square rather than haul the water home, I assumed. Villages this small didn't usually pipe water into the homes. The children, too young to attend school, played in the water.

"Lura. Talk to Grijalves if you won't listen to me." Aguirre's voice suddenly rose. "Worthington may be your husband, but I assure you he is—" He whispered something I couldn't hear. "*Te lo juro*, I swear it." He hung up, turned, and smiled at me.

Obviously he knew Lura was married, but that wouldn't preclude an affair. Who was Grijalves? Would Aguirre divulge information if I asked? I doubted it. Well, why not? He probably wouldn't let me go, anyway, after he'd hijacked me off the highway and showed me his illegal operation. I wondered if he would introduce me to Lura. I considered telling him what I was really up to.

"We have to return to the house. Some business has come up," Aguirre announced, rushing his words.

"An emergency? Is there something I can help with?" I asked with my most sincere smile, hoping he'd reveal some useful information.

"No." He gave me a mean, squinty look then spun around toward the Jeep. He caught himself and smiled back at me. He said more kindly, "No, Miss Stone, I'm sorry. It was some bad news to do with one of my concerns in Ixtapa. I must leave immediately. The best way you can help is by packing up your things and joining me in the helicopter." He wasn't asking.

"Oh, I'm so sorry. I was enjoying the tour. I would love to join you," I lied, "but as you know, I have Pepper and a vehicle that also need to get to Zihuatanejo." I talked too fast.

"It is a long and treacherous drive along Route 200. It will take you hours. I would be a poor host, Señorita, if I allowed you to leave my protection."

"Didn't you say it was only a few hours away?"

"I will arrange to have a man drive your combi to your apartment in Zihuatanejo. Your dog can fly with us." Aguirre stared down at Pepper with a look of utter abhorrence. Pepper responded by curling his lip into a silent snarl. Aguirre jerked away, and I struggled to keep a straight face.

"I'd rather drive, Señor Aguirre. I want to see the scenery. This is such beautiful country. Why don't I come for dinner when I arrive, and you can tell me more about your operations?" I asked, sounding insincere even to me as we clambered back into the Jeep.

Once we settled into our seats, I asked, "Señor Aguirre. Again, am I your prisoner? Because, if I'm truly your guest, you'll let me make my own way. I've managed to drive from Sausalito to Costa Allegre, and I'm sure I can drive another four hours." He glared at me, but I rushed on, "That is, if I'm not invited to stay here another night." I realized with Aguirre out of the way, I had a shot at talking to Lura and getting some questions answered, like, what was her husband up to?

He put the Jeep into gear and drove on without speaking. We turned off the road onto a track hidden by undergrowth. It appeared to follow more directly back to the house, but was in need of repair and not much traveled. I mentally recited lines from a famous Frost poem I had loved in school:

> *And both that morning equally lay*
> *In leaves no step had trodden black.*
> *Oh, I kept the first for another day!*
> *Yet knowing how way leads on to way,*
> *I doubted if I should ever come back.*

Tree branches whipped over our heads, and bushes scraped the sides of the Jeep as it bounced along the overgrown track. Several half-hidden shacks came into view. I smelled wood smoke, burning chilies, and tortillas baking. This didn't look like a model village. Rounding a bend, a clearing opened where three tin-roofed shacks clustered next to a split-rail corral containing a goat and her two kids. A large black pig wallowed in a patch of sun that warmed a muddy depression at the edge of the trees.

Near the shacks, an old woman dressed in yellow satin and a filthy pink pinafore squatted in front of a wood fire, heating tortillas on a flat pan. The smell of coffee boiling in a blackened aluminum percolator permeated the air. The woman ignored us and continued to cook, while a pack of unhealthy-looking mongrels raced alongside the Jeep, yapping and snarling at the tires and our legs. Aguirre kicked one away from his door opening, "*Pinche perrito pendejo. ¡Véte!*" He reached under his seat, produced a pistol, and aimed into the pack. There was a blast and a terrible squeal as one yellow mutt ran off into the forest howling and spraying blood behind him. I gripped my seat. If he'd shoot a dog so easily, well—I didn't want to think about that.

The sharp sound dispersed the pack of dogs but gained the attention of four men who filed out of one of the shacks, each armed with a rifle and wearing a western-style straw hat. Aguirre stopped the Jeep, and three of the men walked over. The fourth took up guard position by the door of the shack and blocked a fifth man when he loomed on the threshold. He stared at me from inside the doorway then raised his hand in the salute my dad always used. I shivered. Like on Dad's, a snake undulated down his arm.

"Hi, boss," a guard said in Spanish, nodding his head toward the shack as a skinny, older man with a scruffy beard and aviator glasses under a cap pushed passed the guard. "He's losing some cash in dominos. José, there—" He tipped his elbow toward the armed man by the door. "—been the big winner this morning. We didn't expect you so early. What's up?" He eyed me suspiciously.

I shifted in my seat and looked over the thug's shoulder at the man losing at dominos. He smiled at me and my heart fluttered. Tachycardia. Was I about to have a heart attack? I pressed on my chest and the arrythmia slowed to normal. Was I reacting to this old guy?

Aguirre replied, "I've been called away. I want you to keep him here, but no rough stuff. I want him in one piece. Do you understand me? Do not harm him in any way. I'll be back in a day or two."

"Sure thing, boss. He ain't goin' anywhere. Enrique gonna be all right? That the dog?" The man paused, thrusting his chin at Pepper, eyes gleaming. "I'd a killed that monster, if it was up to me. I'd a killed them both. She's a looker, though, boss." He leered at me with his tongue hanging out. "We get to keep her?" The three men laughed.

The prisoner lunged into the clearing as Aguirre

backhanded the man across the jaw. "*Cállete*, you ignorant *burro*. Listen up."

The men abruptly stopped laughing. Jose blocked the man from coming closer to the Jeep.

The one Aguirre had hit gave me a long, murderous glance then turned away sullen-faced. The domino player smiled at me again, kindness, or concern, radiating in his expression. *How weird.*

"We've got a problem. I need you, Antonio." Aguirre singled out a stocky young man wearing a faded shirt and dusty tooled-leather boots. "You'll take the truck and follow my guest—" He shrugged in my direction. "—to the turn-off to Playa Azul. Wait at the house for my orders." Aguirre glared at the man as he stood holding his hat in his hands, not moving. "Go. ¡*Véte!* Now." Antonio backed away from the Jeep, put on his hat, and took off running into the forest.

"What about me, boss? That dumbass can't find his way around a tortilla," said the first man, snickering with his remaining companion. "Shouldn't me and Memo go...."

"Do not presume to give me advice, *pendejo*." Aguirre raised his hand again. The man ducked and backed away. "Get back to work. Memo, get in the Jeep."

The third man jumped in and arranged himself as far away from Pepper as he could. He sat stiffly with his limbs held close to his body and eyed Pepper with nervous glances. Did the idiot think it would prevent Pepper from biting him? Pepper leaned over and started sniffing, growling slightly until he sneezed, spraying the man with a load of dog slime. I was the one sniggering now.

Aguirre shifted into first, and the Jeep eased back onto the track and into the trees. He clearly didn't know I understood Spanish and heard he'd ordered his man to follow me in the truck when I left. I wondered why he gave that order. To protect me or kill me on the lonely road? Beads of sweat pricked my skin. I ran my hand across my brow and wiped it on my cutoffs. If he wanted to kill me, why not just lock me up here with the prisoner losing money at dominos and let the thugs have their fun? My stomach lurched like I might puke. I would have to do some fast thinking. Somehow, I had to make Lura Laylor a part of my escape from this drug boss. Aguirre didn't seem to be holding her. The phone conversation made it sound more like he was advising her.

Thinking about the case calmed me, and I'd cooled down by the time we came out of the forest into the bright sun. I thought about what I'd just seen. Was the prisoner in the hut part of the problem Lura called about? This prisoner had money coming from somewhere to pay his gambling debts and was not in a hurry to escape, or was too disingenuous to create a diversion to confuse the guards. Aguirre's men didn't seem to have half a brain between them. Deep into considering the possibilities, I jumped when Aguirre spoke.

"You may leave in any manner you wish, Señorita Stone. You American women are too independent. You don't know what it is like outside of your country. You all think you can go anywhere, live how you want. You think that men will treat you with courtesy and respect. In my country, men still own women and you and—" He stopped talking, making a show of navigating around a fallen tree. "—and your countrywomen come here flaunting your wealth and your bodies and wonder—" He faltered. "It would be best if you got on a plane and went home."

Is he referring to Lura Laylor and me? Did she leave while we were out?

"Aren't you worried I might tell the authorities about your pot?"

"No. Who will you tell? I am the authority. I am the elected Senator of the State of Michoacán."

"You're a senator?" My voice rose an octave.

Aguirre turned a sour look on me. "Yes, and I sit on the board of directors of a respected philanthropic organization with President Calderon. My companies finance schools and hospitals for children. I am leading Mexico into a bright and prosperous future where all Mexicans can get an education, work, and be free of the tyranny of both our own government and our powerful neighbors to the north." Aguirre glared at me. I wondered at his hypocrisy in sitting on a board with the president who declared war on El Narco when he took office.

"But you see, Miss Stone, the provinces in Mexico are still run like your Wild West. *Bandidos* might try to steal my crop, or *federales*, acting under pressure from your government, may try to shut me down, but no one will care if I shoot trespassers. Money buys power, and a name that goes back to the Revolution buys respect."

He maneuvered the Jeep around another fallen tree and laughed, a hollow sound.

"Run to your DEA if you want. They won't touch me." Aguirre finished speaking as we came over the rise and saw the house below. My combi, as he called it, was parked in the driveway. I grinned. A big weight lifted out of my chest.

"You are welcome to stay as long as you like. When you are ready to go, Antonio will see you to the Playa Azul turnoff in the truck. Once you are in the State of Guerrero, Ruta 200 becomes a toll road, and you should be safe enough. I will be staying in my penthouse atop the Krystal. Do not drive after dark, Señorita Stone. Do you understand me?"

"Thank you, yes, Senator. If you are sincere about the invitation to look you up in Ixtapa, I'll be pleased to dine with you." I'd shifted gears. My journalistic instincts, although rusty, said Aguirre knew plenty about Worthington, and I wanted his information.

We arrived at the house, and Aguirre dropped into

41

neutral, letting the motor idle. Pepper leaped from the Jeep, and Memo swiped the perspiration from under his hat band, a relieved expression on his face.

"Miss Stone, I apologize again for the unconventional meeting we have had and for the uncouthness of my men. You *gringas* may be bold and brazen, but you are interesting, not to mention beautiful." When he smiled, I noticed what an exceptionally attractive man he was, but aren't all weirdo cons?

"I await your call. My contact information will be prepared for you. Good luck, Señorita, and be safe. *Hasta la vista*—until we meet again." Aguirre inclined his head in parting as I climbed down, and roared off toward the airstrip with Memo hanging on to the roll bar for dear life.

CHAPTER FIVE

Kitchen Confidential

The front door swung open as I reached for the knob. A houseman clad in loose-fitting white pants and shirt beckoned to me until I passed into the entry hall. Creepy. Obviously, Aguirre had ordered the staff to keep an eye on me.

Inside, the same pink stone trimming the exterior of the house formed a floral pattern on the floor. High, leaded windows flanked the heavy carved door, and a black iron lamp, perforated with colored glass, hung from the high ceiling on a heavy black chain. I found myself alone and inspected the artwork displayed on the walls. I really hadn't seen too much of the entry, passed out as I was when they carried me in, but I still didn't understand why Aguirre hadn't just had me killed. Or why he'd brought me here in the first place. I prodded the lump on my head. Embarrassed, I pulled my hand down and pretended to study the next painting. I felt that way you feel when you're caught picking your teeth or wiping your nose on your shirtsleeve and glanced around looking for video cameras.

I recognized pieces from Zuñiga's "Market Women" series, a show I'd seen on a trip to Mexico City. I liked the tension in the one that depicted two women without goods sitting in front of a wall, the taller wrapped in a black blanket and the other wearing a pink dress. Both looked dejectedly out of the frame. They'd probably had a bad selling day or been ripped-off. Maybe they had a big decision to make, run away from abusive husbands, or like me, a creepy narco-lord toyed with them.

I could get in my bus and race for the border, or stick around and put Lura Laylor into the hands of the client paying my invoice. My choice. I already had fifty thousand dollars secure in the bank. High-tailing it out of Michoacán probably would be the smartest move. I'd be safe at home in Sausalito, but at the price of failure. How would I prove myself to Dex and get out of that boring office? More importantly, how would I prove myself to me?

A door slammed somewhere above us. Pepper nudged me. I realized I stood in the middle of the hallway staring into space. I took a look around and noticed a dark wooden console positioned against one wall displaying various pre-Columbian artifacts many made out of copper. I'd heard transporting artifacts across the border was illegal and wondered if Mexican citizens could own them. There must be quite a trade in antiquities here. Who was allowed to dig them up? Did it really matter? What was I going to do?

I sucked in a lungful of humid air and held it, letting the images of home, Dex and my experiences at the Aguirre farm swirl across my vision. What should I do? What should I do? I blew out my breath to the count of eight. And like a human slot machine, the reeling images thunked to a stop in the pay line: two deep breaths, a lemon, and a second spin.

I relaxed and made myself at home to explore, hoping I might run into Lura Laylor. Like on a TV quiz show, three doors led from the hall. I opened the door on the right. A winner. The grand living room. Again, the art and artifacts impressed me. An antique writing table and low shelves containing old books and copper figurines sat near a set of French doors opening to the courtyard. I bet myself that the small canvas hanging above an inlaid chess table was an original Frida Káhlo, a still life with fruit and a fat little ceramic dog. I'd seen it on exhibit at San Francisco's MOMA.

The spotless room smelled of lemon oil and academic dust, but the lack of personal items and photos made it cold. The sound of my shoes echoed from the stucco walls. I tried a small door tucked into a corner and found myself in a narrow hallway in front of a powder room. Its cream-colored tiles soared with blue-painted birds.

"Who uses monogrammed towels anymore?" I asked Pepper, who had slurped a drink out of the toilet and dripped onto the polished tile floor. I grabbed a hand towel off the black iron rack and mopped up. Ignoring my mother's voice nagging me to put it in the hamper, I guiltily dumped the towel into a corner for the servants to pick up.

The hallway turned to the left and revealed another door, but it was locked. Aguirre's office? I leaned against it and pressed my ear to the smooth wood. I could hear the clicking of a keyboard. Who? I searched for surveillance cameras and hoped that I couldn't be seen, then I edged along the wall trying to determine the room's dimensions. I made a mental note to get my set of lock picks out of the combi. Once I had the lay of the house, I'd break in, but first I'd check for a courtyard door.

I didn't really know what I hoped to find beyond additional proof that tied Worthington, Lura Laylor, and the senator together. Maybe something would pop out to give me a hint. I couldn't shake the frightening notion that my presence in the house was more than coincidence.

More artwork lined the hallway. Wealth had its benefits.

All the work appeared original, but I didn't recognize many of the signatures. Aguirre might like to invest in emerging artists. I did, but even my emerging artists' work hung prominently in the Sarasvati, not tucked away in a back hall.

An archway led into the colonnade encircling the central courtyard. The interior room didn't have windows or another door but I spied a stairwell mounting to the second floor near where I had seen Lura. I'd just go on up and knock on her door. I didn't see anyone to stop me.

Pepper took the lead, bounding up the stairs. As we reached the landing, Pepper's hackles rose, and he began to growl. I looked up to see a man with a rifle and crooked teeth grinning above us. I whistled a note and Pepper stopped. The grin faded as the man raised the rifle and took aim at my dog. My heart stopped beating for a moment, then thundered into action as I screamed, "Pepper, come," and plunged back down the stairs to the courtyard. I flattened myself against the wall out of sight of the gunman and gripped Pepper by his scruff. My free hand felt around me for something I could use as a weapon and closed around a heavy ceramic candlestick from a shelving unit. I'd see the gunman at the bottom of the stairs before he saw me. But the man's footsteps rang off the tiles in the opposite direction with the echoes of his nasty laughter.

We fled back to what I thought would be the main entry but landed in the formal dining room. The luscious light-filled room with its delicate furniture upholstered in gold and apricot damask reminded me of rooms I'd admired in Architectural Digest. Those rooms had been honestly earned. The opulence in this house was a lie. But for the moment this was sanctuary.

I slumped against the doorjamb and exhaled a breath I hadn't realized I was holding and patted my dog. Life-sized apples and pears blown in gold crystal filled a Murano-glass bowl and dominated the sideboard. My stomach growled. I pushed through a swinging door into a well-stocked pantry that smelled of silver polish and the ubiquitous burned chilies. Distinct and comforting, the sounds and smells of cooking wafted through an open door opposite me.

"This case is bad for my blood pressure," I whispered to the dog. He looked at me and then at the kitchen door and wagged.

"Oh, you want to check out the kitchen? It does smell good. Okay, let's do it."

Conversation stopped the moment we entered. Two women, an old man, and the serving girl stared at us. The serving woman from breakfast rose from her seat at a wooden table and began to speak rapidly in Tarascan, waving a wooden spoon in my direction. The young girl chopped bundles of green-topped onions with a large cleaver on a rough round of tree trunk and kept her eyes cast down, but translated the older woman's words into simple Spanish.

"My grandmother says you must leave. No guests or dogs come to the kitchen." She paused to listen and formulate her thoughts. "My grandmother says dinner— *comida*—is at two o'clock. *La cena* will be at eight. She wants to know if you will eat in the courtyard or in your room."

I smiled at the older woman. "*Muchas gracias, Doña.* Your granddaughter is a lovely girl. I would prefer to eat in the courtyard. Will Senator Aguirre's other guest, Señora Worthington, join me?"

I hoped this was the name Lura was using, and my guess was confirmed by the uneasy glances that shot between the staff. The girl hung her head closer to the onions, and the grandmother launched into an excited debate with her thin, wiry coworker. The old man sipped coffee from a clay mug and punctuated the discussion once or twice with a low utterance. His battered straw hat sat by his elbow, and his faded western shirt crackled from starch and pressing as he moved. The women seemed to be influenced by his comments, and after a short exchange, fell silent. The man then said something to the girl.

"My grandparents say that you must leave right away. You are in danger."

The grandfather looked kindly at me. "I heard about how you were brought here and how your dog almost killed Enrique." Pepper pricked up his ears and wagged.

He spoke as one unused to talking, making each word succinct and clear through his heavily accented Spanish. He glanced at Pepper and continued at his measured pace. The wiry woman lifted the lid on a pot and a blast of rich meaty steam billowed into the air. Pepper licked my hand.

"I heard some men talking at the airfield after *el patrón* left. They are angry about Enrique. They want you to pay. It will look like an accident."

My heart pinched in my chest and my knees turned to rubber. "Does Aguirre plan to kill me?" I fought down panic as my blood raced. A trickle of sweat slid down my back. Pepper leaned into my thigh and looked up at me.

"Who knows the mind of *el patrón*? He has changed since the death of his wife and children." The old man went back to his coffee.

The girl pushed aside the chopping block and wiped her weeping eyes with the hem of her apron. Tension hung heavy in the tropical heat. The grandfather studied each of the women and then spoke in their indigenous tongue.

Another debate took place. I felt uncomfortable. The grandmother shook her head, and the cook's voice rose. She spoke rapidly, gesturing wildly. They all looked at me. The women argued against whatever the old man wanted. He remained calm, and in several minutes the argument died down.

Finally, the grandfather took a draw off the mug his wife had refilled with steaming cinnamon-scented coffee and looked at me with wise eyes.

"Cook—" He leaned his head in the direction of the wiry woman whose short black curls popped from under a faded Raiders cap. "—was waiting outside his office this morning and listened as he used the telephone." He looked at the cook.

"I took the weekly menu for his approval. Señora always took care of this until she died, poor saint." The cook gazed over at a small shrine by the windows and crossed herself. "*El patrón* insists on approving the menus himself." She frowned. "He shouted at someone."

"What was he shouting about?" I interrupted.

It took the cook a moment to respond. "The banker."

"What does this have to do with me?"

She shrugged and looked at the old man, who also shrugged.

I gritted my teeth. These people knew something, but to get the information was like moving a stubborn mule when it was happy standing still. My mind raced. That lemon again. Worthington. I waited to see if the servants would divulge anything else.

"Cook said el patrón was very angry. He shouted that *la mordita*—a bribe—could not change his mind. He would not vote against the interests of his people. I know little about the government, but I know all Mexicanos must protect my country's petroleum from *el norte*." Grandfather finished his baffling speech, pushed away from the table, put on his hat, strode to the outside door, and stumped off around the corner.

He reminded me of a bantam rooster strutting with his hens. It was clear the interview was over. I thanked the women for their kindness, *"¡Qué amables!"* I showed myself out of the kitchen through a door, which linked to the hallway leading to the "dog garden." I had an hour to wait before *comida*, a meal I hoped to eat with Lura Laylor, presuming that she was still in the house. Had she been the one in Aguirre's office?

What did Grandfather mean "vote against the interests of his people", and what did oil have to do with it? I pushed open the metal door and let Pepper into the walled garden. A small glass-topped table sat in the shade of a late-fruiting mango tree, and I seated myself out of the hot sun. Raucous barking suddenly erupted from the direction of Aguirre's kennels. I glanced in the direction of the noise. The dogs fought a fierce battle at the kennel fence behind the hedge. I didn't bother to call Pepper. It would be over soon enough, and he would trot back with a grin on his face, his back hair standing on end and his tail held high.

Everything around me shouted power and control. I'd seen wealth and how it made people on both sides act. The kids I'd visited after school had servants. I'd been adopted into a well-to-do family, but I didn't fit in. I was the weirdo girl in high school. The one no one talked to. It was then I developed a knack for figuring things out. I let my mind wander among the perplexing events of the last eighteen hours and forgot about my growling stomach. I pulled a little notebook and a pen out of the bag I carried everywhere. Mexican oil policy was not part of my lexicon. I jotted the word "petroleum" and underlined it, then wrote down everything I knew about oil that could have anything to do with this case, which wasn't much. Worthington, wife, Aguirre, marijuana, bribe, oil.

I listed the facts I knew under that heading:

- Worthington, banker
- Wants to find wife Lura Laylor
- Last known whereabouts: Hotel Krystal
- Aguirre, owner Hotel Krystal, grows marijuana, senator
- Lura, buyer for a Latin American importing firm. HANDIMEX.

- •Worthington, Laylor, and Aguirre well-acquainted
- •Aguirre, convince Laylor about Worthington?
- •Aguirre to vote on something/ petroleum industry?
- •Aguirre on the phone talking about "the banker"

Wait a minute. Worthington is threatening Aguirre and/or Laylor. I was sure of it. I brainstormed every theory I could think of, relevant or far-fetched, and started connecting facts with lines and circles. Pepper, back from his visit to the kennel, settled down on the grass nearby to chew a stolen bone.

Lost in concentration, I pictured the photo Worthington had produced when he hired me, of Lura and friends at Mom's Café in Cuastecomate. Aguirre was the headless man sitting under the *palapa* at the top of the photo. It was his monogram ring I'd seen, not a camera light leak. I added: Worthington—liar, to my list of facts.

I began writing a narrative from my notes:

Whatever is going on started about three years ago: Worthington became bank president for CalMex, Mexico City. Lura Laylor took her job with HandiMex. Aguirre's wife died in an accident. Aguirre was a senator when his wife died. Was he elected in the same election as Calderon?

I paused to think. *No, Calderon took office in December last year*. I remembered the news, demonstrations. The opposition said he stole the election.

I wrote:

> Is Worthington connected to the…. the what? Something to do with PEMEX. Has Worthington tried to bribe Aguirre for a vote? But what does it all have to do with narcotics trafficking?

"So who is the bad guy here?" I asked the birds and insects. I needed to talk to Dex.

I stood up and stretched. Dinner would be served in fifteen minutes. Pepper and I ambled back to our room to freshen up. I watched the wing opposite mine for any sign of sound or movement, but the house posed like a tomb. I knew the kitchen operated, but I felt uneasy in the silence.

I quickly changed into a fresh sundress and washed my face and hands, then grabbed Pepper's bowl. We slipped back out into the corridor, but we walked away from the stairs and toward Lura Laylor's room. The corridor turned at the narrow end of the building. As we rounded the corner, another man stepped into my path and barred the corridor with his outstretched hands. He growled something I took to mean, "Go back. You are going the wrong way," and I felt it was wiser to follow his directions than send Pepper to his throat, although Pepper growled, ready for a command. Turning the other cheek, so to speak, seemed the more neighborly action. I whistled Pepper down, smiled at the man, and wished him a good afternoon. We took the stairs he pointed out and went down to dinner.

Aguirre sure didn't want me to meet Lura Laylor.

CHAPTER SIX

Lura

Laylor didn't show up for *comida*, but I hadn't really expected her to. The grandmother served me a dry vermicelli soup as a starter, plain but very tasty. Then came a plate of delectable *chile rellenos* drizzled in spicy red sauce, Mexican rice, and a pot of refried pinto beans that were positively fluffy. The serving woman filled my glass from a pitcher containing a dark red beverage. It tasted like a sweet fruit punch. Finally, a plate appeared with cheese slices and slabs of fruit jelly, which resembled thick fruit leather. I didn't want any coffee but took a small clay cup of Kahlúa and contemplated the events of the past twenty-four hours while I sipped the sweet liquor. What would Dex think of all this? I needed to find my cell phone. I prayed it hadn't been stolen and I could connect to whatever service Aguirre used, but grimaced, dreading the roaming charges I was sure to incur.

My server did not return from bussing the table, so I excused myself and found a tiled bathroom near the dining area. I washed my sticky fingers and went back to exploring the mansion, poking into the rooms I encountered along the colonnade. A plasma TV screen dominated one wall of a room filled with comfortable-looking upholstered furniture and a fireplace. I didn't know it got cold enough here to need one. A state-of-the-art stereo system and an impressive collection of CDs and DVDs filled built-in cabinets on the facing wall. I dialed the radio but only received a static-filled Banda station on the AM band. Not my style. Give me tropical salsa. I smiled to myself and gave my hips a little roll. Look out Ixtapa discos. Well, if I made it to Ixtapa. What if I were trapped in this beautiful house forever, a Twilight Zone episode? Pepper jumped up on one of the couches and groaned as he settled down for a nap.

"Hey, dog, don't get too comfortable."

He whacked his tail against the leather a couple times and sighed. I turned to the floor-to-ceiling windows, pulling aside the dark linen drapes to look out to a garden enclosed by the high, vine-covered wall I'd seen in the dog garden. The expanse of lush water-hogging lawn irritated me. The bland but pleasing vista revealed nothing. Pretty much the story of the entire house: pretty, opulent, empty and totally creepy. Way too much like the house I grew up in. Well, except for the armed men at the top of the stairs.

Somebody here played games. The adjoining room contained a pool table, electronic game paraphernalia, a laptop computer, and a small bamboo bar with six high stools. Instead of plush furniture, cane and rattan "lanai" furniture scattered across the bare tile floor. Nothing interested me. I hastened back to the courtyard, Pepper clicking along by my side. He wasn't letting me out of his sight. I didn't think he much liked the place. Maybe he felt like I did, afraid any moment all hell would break loose.

I fidgeted, running my fingers across picture frames and giant planters. It was too silent in this house: no settling creaks, no refrigerator hum, not even the fountain tinkled into its basin. I tensed for the trap I thought certain to come. Another rifle-toting guard? Or worse? My teeth ached from clenching. I'd be seeing my dentist for cracked molars when

I got home. Time to get my gun. I pushed through a set of double French doors into a passage opening onto the veranda I'd glimpsed from the TV room. Maybe a gate opened to the driveway.

Enormous Talavera pots of elephant ears and bird's nest ferns lined the hall with more copper figurines in shadow boxes displayed along the walls. I determined to ask Aguirre about them when I got to Ixtapa. I bet he stole them, tomb robbing probably a popular sport of wealthy men in a country where the bulk of antiquities still moldered away under the jungle.

The same style *equipal* furniture I had seen from my balcony decorated the veranda as well as a wet bar. It appeared better stocked than most restaurant bars in Sausalito. The swimming pool lay to the right of the veranda, surrounded by more thirsty lawn, which sported white iron furniture with yellow-striped cushions. A well-tanned woman reclined on one of the lounges, her hair tucked under a large-brimmed straw hat. She held a pink iced drink in her hand. I couldn't see her face.

"Make yourself a drink," she called out in English. The same voice I'd heard this morning coming from the second floor gallery.

I twitched with excitement as I made my way across the lawn. "Hi. I'm JadeAnne Stone." I extended my slightly trembling hand to shake Lura's.

"I'm Polito's cousin, Lura Aguirre-Worthington, but call me Lulu. Everyone does." She grinned up at me, her eyes shrouded behind dark glasses. "You must be the poor unfortunate—Enrique is a pig. Even when we were growing up, he was the one who tortured small animals and birds. He's been in trouble. Polo went out on a limb for him and bought his freedom. You'd think he'd have a little more gratitude." Lura's words gushed out like water through a break in a dike.

"What a beautiful dog. You can thank him for your life. Enrique is deathly afraid of the brutes. One of Uncle's guard dogs attacked him when he was young. He tried to steal something out of one of the storehouses. I never knew what. Well, Enrique got what he deserves, if you want my opinion." She stopped talking as abruptly as she'd started.

"His name's Pepper." I flashed hand signals to the dog. He sat down, gave a soft woof, and reached his paw out to Lura in greeting.

"Oh, how adorable," she squealed. "Does he do tricks?"

I commanded Pepper to perform. He rolled over and played dead, sat up and begged, and disco danced on his hind legs, panting heavily in the hot sun.

"Lura, would you excuse me for a moment? Peppi needs water."

Lura sat up. "There's a bucket behind the bar. Here, I'll show you. My drink is warm anyway. Let's call for my man and have him make us something."

At the bar, Lura rang a small bell, while I filled the bucket with water and ice cubes from the bar refrigerator. Pepper gave a grateful sigh when he finished drinking and plopped down on the cool tile floor for a siesta. I glanced toward the pool and wished I could swim some laps. My body felt knotted up. I needed exercise.

A handsome, muscular serving man appeared and asked what we wanted. He was dressed in loose-fitting white cotton pants and a tight black t-shirt, which read "Star Wars" in faded type. It showed off his well-defined physique.

"I'm tired of Cosmopolitans. What do you like to drink?"

I asked for a beer.

"I'll have a beer, too, and Aníbal, go ask Goya for a plate of *botanas*. I love her *tamales*, don't you?" She switched between Spanish and English easily. Aníbal handed us beers from the refrigerator and went off on a quest for food, proving that his backside was as exquisitely formed as his front side.

Lura lowered herself gracefully to a lounge chair close to the edge of the veranda, which caught the slight breeze. She stretched out her slender legs and pointed her dainty, polished toes. She could be the cover of Travel and Leisure.

"Did you have lunch? I asked the kitchen people to invite you to join me." I tucked my own bare toes out of sight under my chair. Scents of jasmine, roses, and plumeria drifted in the air, and tiny yellow warblers twittered in the bougainvillea.

"No, I didn't feel like eating," she said. "Now I'm hungry, though. Anyway, they never mentioned it to me. Typical of the serving classes. They have the minds of *burros*. I would have enjoyed dining with you. I'm so curious to know what you are doing here, and coming all alone. Aren't you afraid to drive? I mean, with what's going on and all. It's a war." She stopped talking and studied me for a moment. "I could never drive here except to travel between D.F. and Acapulco on the *autopista*, I mean toll throughway. You came right through the heart of the two worst cartels. I looked at your *combi* when Polo brought it up from the garage. Do you sleep in it? It has everything, doesn't it?"

She was talking avbout my VW bus. "Yeah. I've been staying at trailer parks. I'm spending two weeks with my old friend, Sally. She lives in Zihua, and I never get to see her. I planned a week on each end to explore the coast, but maybe driving wasn't such a hot idea." I'd started to perspire and fanned my face with my hands. I hoped it was the hot afternoon and not because of my half-truth about Sally, but it was safer to let people think someone waited for me. I shot her a piercing glare, daring her to comment. Her "Polo" put me in this mess. Or maybe blame should go to Lura's husband.

Lura smiled and ran her hand across the damp slick of her forehead. "The humidity does it. The air is only about eighty-two or so. The heat's why they take siestas here, you know."

"I should be used to humidity. I live on a houseboat, but it's nothing like this." I yawned. "Sorry, I'm a bit tired from all the excitement. Didn't you say your last name is Worthington? That's an English name."

"My husband's ancestors were originally from England, but he's American. We met at UCLA and later lived together for a number of years in Palo Alto while he finished his MBA at Stanford. My family had a fit, but what did they expect? I was raised in Southern California, and I'm more American than Mexican."

Well, that accounts for the American accent. But what accounts for the difference in name? "Stanford? I wonder if we were there at the same time? I was in Journalism. Do you live in Mexico now?"

"No, actually, I live in San Francisco. My husband, Daniel, is the President of CalMex Federal Bank in Mexico and lives in Mexico City. I took an apartment in San Francisco when he came here to be close to the headquarters of the company I work for. I'm a buyer for HandiMex. It's North America's largest importer of Latin American goods."

"That must be tough. Don't you miss your husband? Do you ever see him?"

"Danny and I adore each other, but we live very differently. Our marriage has strengthened since we stopped spending so much time together." She chuckled, no sarcasm or irony in her voice

"Absence makes the heart grow fonder?" I laughed too, and wished it was the same way between me and Dex. Absence was making Dex's heart forget me.

"Something like that. We spend a week together every three weeks or so. I'm on vacation right now, but Danny has important meetings going on with some Japanese businessmen, I think, and couldn't get free. I hadn't seen Polo for ages and thought I'd drop in." Apparently Lura stuck to as much truth as possible, too, because her story matched Worthington's except for the part about his meetings. Maybe Worthington knew his wife was visiting her cousin and lied. Why? And if she were a liar too, did she know her husband hired me to find her?

Aníbal's return distracted my attention. I had trouble taking my eyes off him although I pretended I was transfixed by the tray laden with tiny corn husk-wrapped tamales and wedges of quesadillas oozing white oily cheese and herbs.

"Gracias, Aníbal. Did you get yourself something?" Lura picked up a wedge of quesadilla and popped it in her mouth. "Have you tried these *epazote quesadillas* yet? Goya puts a dash of *habanero salsa* in them with the *epazote*. I don't know what kind of cheese she uses. I can't live in Mexico. I'd get too fat!"

"What's *epazote*?" I tasted the cheesy sandwich. "Mmmm. Different. Is that bitter taste the *epazote*?"

"Yeah. It's an herb to help digestion, very strong and pungent. It grows in dry regions, but loves the damp banks of rivers. At least in California it does. I've seen it on the Russian River. Do you know that area?"

Lura Laylor gets around, doesn't she? I wonder what she was up to between college and marrying Worthington five years ago. "Sure, I've spent a lot of time there. What part of the river do you go to?"

"Guerneville. Friends of mine have a house there. This was way back when. Twelve years ago, can you believe it? Where does the time go?"

Lura's houseboy, Aníbal, popped the caps on another round of Victoria, the lager brewed in Mexico City, and whisked the empty quesedilla tray away. I hoped Lura might drink too much and divulge some useful information. She gossiped about her family, her work, her youth, but never mentioned anything about why her husband might be looking for her.

"My work sometimes takes me to remote places," she said. "I've traveled on foot and donkey-back when necessary." She told an amusing story about searching for mescal stills in the high valleys of Oaxaca. Lura claimed to be one of the top buyers, able to ferret out unique items and negotiate low prices, not really Fair Trade, but from talking with her, I believed if there were rarities or bargains, Lura would have been the one to find them. Under her ditzy façade, I saw a tough woman.

When she excused herself to use the bathroom, I had a moment to consider a new perspective. Was Worthington after Lura because she had something of value? Aguirre might be protecting her. That's what his side of the phone conversation had sounded like in the model village. The proverbial light bulb lit up.

Pepper stood, stretched into a downward dog pose, shook out his hind legs, and came over to poke me with his nose. I ignored him. He poked me a few more times and started a little dance with a lot of wagging, batting me with his muzzle until he had my full attention. "Peppi, are you hungry, boy? We'll get your dinner soon. Now go away." The dog sighed and plopped down on the floor again.

I gazed into the garden while Lura was gone, thinking about the odd events of the afternoon. According to the grandfather, something big was about to happen in Mexico. Worthington and Aguirre obviously had something going on, but I couldn't connect Lura on the lam with Worthington lobbying her cousin. Drugs seemed so much likelier.

"What is it with Mexico's oil?" I asked the garden. I remembered reading something about Mexico's oil industry on the Internet. PEMEX—*Petróleos Mexicanos*—had traditionally been a closed corporation controlled by the

Mexican government, Mexico's "cash cow." But the profits had been collateralized in case of default when the U.S. provided the $50 billion Emergency Stabilization Package after the 1995 peso devaluation. So Mexico didn't own its oil. What did that mean?

The report had gone on to say that Mexican oil production peaked in the 1990s. Experts claimed Mexico's production and reserves would decline so low Mexico might default on either the big ESP loan from the decade before or NAFTA, the 1993 North American Trade Agreement. Both big deals for the U.S. So what would an American banker want to gain from an importer of tchotchkes and mescal or a pot-growing Mexican senator?

Lura flapped back to the bar, her sandals slapping her heels. Pepper poked his nose into her belly ring. She cackled and pushed him away. I'd never made it to the bus for my gun and needed to look for my cell phone. Now seemed like a good time to excuse myself.

"Pepper, leave her alone. Sorry, he's being a total pest. I have to get the dog food out of my bus and feed him."

"Okay, it's getting late, anyway. I think I'll go change. Would you like to meet here at seven and go watch the sunset with me? You haven't seen anything like it. I know a place out on the point where I sometimes see the green flash. You know about that?"

"Of course, it's that brilliant light that flares just as the sun drops below the horizon. They say you can see it from San Francisco's Cliff House. It has to do with the salt particles in the air." I smiled. "I'll see you at seven then."

As I stepped out the massive front door, rays of late afternoon sun spotlighted Dex's bus, illuminating every smear of rust, every dent, every pit in the finish. It looked cheap and shoddy against the lovely façade of the house, but

I had the feeling that the shell of this home, just like the shell of my parents' lovely home in Mill Valley, hid something rotten. For most of my life, I thought I was the spurious secret, the product of a Chinese hooker co-ed and an American GI. Or that's what my mother once said. Dad insists that she was a student, and they loved each other. Dad claimed he died in a Viet Cong attack, and I ended up on the PAN AM flight to Seattle during Operation Babylift.

From early childhood, I'd learned to cope with the emptiness housed inside my adoptive parents' home, but I left as soon as I turned eighteen. First to college and grad school, then to one under-employment after another until I met Dex. Finally I fit in. At least until things between us changed. I crunched across the crushed shell driveway and opened the bus.

Everything in the bus looked intact, but something about this visit to the Aguirre farm felt off. Everything was too easy. I'd been led here. But by whom? Worthington couldn't have engineered my abduction by Aguirre's thugs, unless, of course, the two men were in cahoots. It nettled me. Why would Aguirre go to so much trouble? Or Worthington? What did I know that could be useful to either man?

Aguirre had replaced the smashed window, and my cell phone remained on the sticky mat installed on the dashboard. He'd even thought to put the sunshade in the windshield, after a wash and vacuum. I checked the phone for messages. None. My throat constricted and my mouth tasted like dust. Dex wasn't on his way.

Clenching my abdominals, I fished the Semmerling from its hidey-hole, dropped it into my bag, and went on with my inspection. Armed, I blew out the breath I'd been holding. I couldn't trust Aguirre. He let it slip that he had surveillance at his wife's shrine, and I knew he had an electronic lock on my door, now turned off, but I wouldn't take chances. I swept the interior for listening devices. Nothing.

I climbed up the ladder Dex had installed to reach the baggage on the luggage rack and checked inside the footlocker bolted to the roof. I'd stored the dog food in it, and I filled Pepper's bowl. Finally, I sniffed at the bottle of propane secured on top used to fuel my camp stove, but didn't smell leakage, nor did the long hose appear to be damaged.

I mentally checked off my gear:

> *Honda generator
> *ice chest
> *sheets, towels, pillow, and cases
> *sunglasses
> *iPod
> *stove
> *backpack
> *diving gear
> *camera
> *table and chairs

Shadows lengthened across the driveway and dry leaves rustled in an afternoon breeze. I hurried to finish; I didn't want to be late for my date with Lura. And Aníbal. I couldn't see any bombs, cut brake lines, or other signs of tampering in the engine or under the bus, but what did I really know about it?

Satisfied that I couldn't find anything unusual, I climbed into the driver's seat and turned the key. The engine sparked to life and settled into an even putt-putt as it idled. Maybe I should run back into the house, grab my stuff, and make a run for it. But I'd never make it through the first gate. There were men who wanted me dead.

I grabbed the bowl of dog food off the seat, my cell phone from the dash, and locked up. The temperatures had cooled down in the late afternoon, and Pepper busily chased after noises in the forest. I could hear him crashing through the underbrush and yipping in happy pursuit of some creature. I whistled, and soon he showed up, his muzzle covered in dirt.

"Ah, digging, I see. Do you want your dinner?"

He woofed.

We returned to our room. Pepper ate his kibble with gusto. I cooled off in a tepid shower and changed into a pair of black low-rise capri pants, a lacy cotton tank top, and hot pink kitten-heeled flip-flops. I wasn't sure why I was dressing up to stroll down to the beach with Lura. The servant, Aníbal, flashed into mind. He oozed sexiness, and I imagined burning my fingers against his taut, cafè-au-lait colored chest. I tossed on several glittering crystal bracelets, drew my hair back into a severe ponytail, added big silver hoop earrings, and studied the effect. I needed a touch of makeup, and added smoky charcoal mascara and fuchsia lipstick while considering my face in the mirror. I was getting some color, my skin radiated. Satisfied with my appearance, I dialed Dex.

The cell phone had plenty of charge and range here in the house, but Dex didn't answer. I left a message saying I was visiting in Michoacán with my new friend, Lura Aguirre Worthington—aka Lura Laylor, and listed the coordinates Aguirre had given me. I left the same message on the home service and at the office in case he called in for his messages. Hearing Dex's voice on the machine made me sad and a little guilty about admiring Aníbal. Not that there was anything to feel guilty about.

What would Dex make of the intelligence I'd collected? More importantly, what would he suggest about the warning the old man had given me? Now that I had Lura, I needed to get to Ixtapa and put Aguirre under surveillance. I was not going to accomplish it if his thugs ran me off the road and I lay dead in a crumpled mass of steel on a lonely beach two hundred feet below the highway. What could I do about that?

I believed the grandfather. Pepper trusted him, and he

had every reason to keep quiet, but it made no sense. I was no threat to Aguirre. He had been clear about that. Now I was "best girlfriends" with his cousin and, ironically, I liked her. Was she in danger too? Maybe I should tell her Worthington wanted to find her.

The proverbial light bulb lit up. Lura was curious about traveling in the combi. She could come with me. Aguirre wouldn't have his cousin run off a cliff. The question was: how would I convince Lura to drive with me?

CHAPTER SEVEN

Mexican Families Are Dysfunctional Too

Lura carried a seagrass basket packed with what turned out to be a bottle of Chardonnay from a Baja winery, three glasses, and a selection of small pork-filled turnovers with salsa for dipping. Aníbal carried a large flashlight. He had thrown on an oversized plaid shirt and wore running shoes instead of sandals. I was sorry to lose sight of that magnificent body, until he leaned down to take the basket from Lura's hands. He had a gun tucked into his waistband. Lura isn't safe here, either?

Lura, on the other hand, was dressed in a sleek pair of white silken trousers, a silver bustier, black jeweled wedge sandals, which added at least three inches to her five-one frame, and a black shawl with long fringe. Her jewelry looked genuine. The wild poodle do of unruly curls framed that huge, slightly lopsided grin she always wore. I envied her upbeat outlook on life. Easy to be happy with a handsome hunk attending your needs. I imagined Aníbal on the Sarasvati.

Lura linked her arm through mine. "Ready to be awed by Mother Nature? C'mon. Let's go."

"I've got to change my shoes. I can't hike in these." I

looked down at my pink sandals. "You?"

"Mine are full of sand down by the gate. I left them this morning. Hurry up. We're in the tropics. The sun goes down quickly."

We sashayed arm-in-arm to a gate in the wall. I hadn't noticed the gate before, but I hadn't noticed the gate in the dog yard, either. Losing my edge.

Lura slipped on a pair of Keds while I tied my Nikes. Aníbal held the gate open, and we passed through, onto the track leading to the beach. I caught Aníbal's clean, musky scent as I brushed by. Lura didn't give the guy a second glance, if that was possible. Me? I couldn't keep my eyes off him and had a burning urge to put my hands all over him. Whoa, Nelly.

It was darker in the woods than I expected, but brilliant golden rays of late sun penetrated the dense canopy, slanting at a low angle and puddling on the track where we walked.

"We better get a move on or we're going to miss the event," Lura called back as she sprinted onto a bisecting path that ran south, parallel to the beach. Aníbal and I raced after her, kicking up a low-flying spray of sand. Running felt good. I hadn't exercised enough in the past few days and my muscles needed to loosen up. Pepper, in heaven, bounded forward and back along the path and in and out of the woods. I loped ahead of Lura, my feet barely touching the hard-packed sand, and raced for a few hundred yards before I sagged down to the ground at a fork in the path, panting. Pepper appeared ahead of me, as usual, and Lura came puffing up in a few moments. Aníbal, handicapped by the picnic basket and the weight of his gun, brought up the rear. It occurred to me that he might be her bodyguard. Maybe he'd guard my body if I played nice. He handed around a bottle of water from the basket.

The promontory loomed to the right. We took the fork which led in that direction and climbed the hundred feet to the pinnacle, reaching a spot facing west toward the blue Pacific Ocean. Twelve square-hewn rocks set in a circle around a firepit filled a clearing about twenty feet from the edge of the cliff. We took seats on the outer edge of the circle and gazed at the gold ball of fire sinking toward the horizon. A bold riot of oranges, reds, and pinks colored the sky. In the distance, puffy cumulus clouds looked like mounds of spun gold. The foam on the surf lit up in a rosy hue and the tide washing back into the swells reflected the shifting shades of the sunset. We all held our breath as the sun disappeared, waiting for the flash of green.

"One, two, three," counted Lura.

The sun dipped over the horizon, leaving a brilliant green flash in its wake.

"Wow. Incredible! I saw it," I said.

Aníbal smiled and nodded. Aníbal understands English? He glanced sideways at Lura then busied himself opening the wine and arranging the snacks on one of the flat rocks.

"Did I tell you? I've been coming here every summer and Christmas vacation since I was a little girl. This is one of the most beautiful sunsets I've seen."

She leaned toward me and gently rested her hand on my arm. A sweet and sincere smile replaced the grin. "I'm glad that I've had the opportunity to meet you, JadeAnne. I like you, and I apologize for my cousin's rude behavior. Polo can be a real dick. He does things just because he can." A troubled look clouded her eyes.

Aníbal handed out the wine, and I raised my glass to Lura. "I like you, too, Lura. I hope we can become great friends. Here's to you, a gracious hostess and a fabulous conversationalist." We clinked glasses and sipped our wine. For a moment, I forgot my case and the dangers lurking around us, and allowed the warm fuzzies of new friendship to lift my spirits.

The colors of the sunset darkened. Oranges changed into

reds, pinks to purples, and the sky above them deepened into cobalt. We nibbled on the tiny tamales and pupusas arranged on the plate while Aníbal tossed some of the meat turnovers into the air for Pepper to catch. They liked each other, too. I regretted I was going to betray Lura in the end. Either I would turn her over to Worthington and receive the balance of my fee, or I would turn Worthington over to the authorities, or worse. Whichever way, Lura probably wouldn't want to be my new best friend anymore.

Aníbal refilled our glasses, and we sipped in companionable silence for a few more moments. The colors quickly faded to night and the mosquitoes and gnats crowded around us in the still dusk.

"Let's get out of here." Lura waved her arms to ward off the bugs.

"You didn't put on bug juice?"

"Yeah, I did, but bloodsuckers have always loved me. I'm sweet and tender. Unlike Aníbal, who is never bothered by any bloodsucking fiends."

"Oh, not even the human kind, like Enrique and his buddies?" I wedged my toe into the thin opening. Lura and Aníbal laughed.

"Aníbal, you understand English."

"*Sí*, señorita, I espeak some *inglés*. It would be hard to do my job when we are in the States if I didn't espeak *inglés*."

"Aníbal lives in San Francisco with me. His family has always looked out for my family. Aníbal, can you remember trying to follow us up here when you were about three? He was so cute. My cousin, Polo's sister, Rosario, and I loved to dress him up like a little doll."

At the mention of Rosario, Aníbal's face darkened.

"Lura, may I ask a personal question?" I changed the subject.

"Sure. What?"

"Doesn't Polo's occupation bother you? Doesn't your family disapprove?"

"Of a politician? Heavens no."

"No, not his political career his…"

"Oh, you mean the marijuana?"

"Yeah."

"Of course. My father hates it. Grandfather originally wanted Dad to take over the farm and sent him to UC Davis for an Ag education in the '50s. Dad was no farmer and didn't really get along with my grandfather. He transferred to UC and switched his major to pre-law. He'd never have gotten into the drug business. He's totally conservative." Lura recounted her family history as we tramped back down the trail.

It was getting dark, and the sounds and smells of the forest intensified. I was glad Pepper was along. "So then what happened?"

"Dad met my mom in college. She was the first of her family to go to school. Her parents are Irish. My name, Lura, comes from the song "Too-Ra-Loo-Ra-Loo-Ral." She and Dad married, but she missed her family, so they settled back in L.A. where they went to UCLA Law School. Mom still practices trust and estate law. She never took Dad's name, preferring her maiden name, which I also use."

I smiled to myself in the dark. So the name, Lura Laylor, was no mystery after all. Things always had a way of revealing themselves. I hoped there would be enough time to uncover the answer to Worthington's complicity in what was developing into a plot.

"Mom loves it here. She even learned Spanish. We kids came every summer, and she and Dad both came at Christmas."

Lura told a complicated story about her family and Aguirre's father, Tito, the family dilettante.

"So, how did a dilettante turn things around?" I asked.

It was completely dark on the path. Lura and I walked arm-in-arm, following Aníbal who lit the way with the flashlight. The night sounds surrounded us, audible below Lura's voice.

"Well, he didn't, not right away. Had some money of his own from our great-grandfather, Buendía. When he was seventeen, he took off and didn't come back until the early sixties."

Aníbal interrupted, his exaggerated accent gone. "When Tito *regresó* he claimed to have a degree in Agribusiness from UNAM." How did Lura's man know this?

"He met my Aunt Lidia at a student party in Coyoacán," Lura interrupted, "a district of Mexico City that used to be considered very bohemian. All the writers, artists, anthropologists, scholars, and thinkers lived there. My aunt is a niece of Frida Káhlo."

"Frida Káhlo. No kidding. Wow." I remembered the small painting I'd seen in Aguirre's living room.

"Yeah, and it didn't hurt Polo's political career. The family has money, as you might guess." She paused as we passed single file through a narrow section of the dark path.

"So Frida Káhlo's niece is Polo's mother?"

"Uh-huh. But Lidia was never really interested in living in what she called 'the provinces' and stayed in the capital. Polo went to the best schools, associated with the best people. My aunt saw to it until sometime in the late '60s, after Uncle Tito and Grandfather were rich men."

Lura stumbled over a root, and I gripped her arm tightly to keep her from falling. "Didn't you say you grew up in Marin County?" she asked. I nodded, and she continued, "You must remember hearing about the infamous Acapulco Gold. Well, it wasn't from Acapulco."

We rejoined the main path and it became easier to walk, but the story got stranger.

"Polo was my grandfather's child, a farmer in his soul,

71

but he was also his father's son, shrewd, ruthless, extremely intelligent, and never satisfied with what he had."

Aníbal snorted. "That's for sure."

"Shut up, Ani. I'm telling the story. Rosario, poor girl, was a beauty, but she lived in Polo's shadow. They were four years apart, Tito and Lidia's only children. Rosario was twelve, Polo was sixteen, and I was ten when she died in a raid on the fields."

"A raid? By the government?"

"No one will talk about it, so I'm not totally clear myself. Rosario was shot to death—murdered. Anyway, Aunt Lidia left and never came back. She blamed Uncle Tito, but he blamed Polo and completely shunned him. The family sent him to California, to boarding school. He was depressed, angry, unpopular, and miserable."

"He still is. Really, the asshole has to hijack a woman just to get a date." Aníbal forced a laugh.

Lura kicked some sand at him. "My dad took responsibility for Polo. He was like our brother and was my favorite human being. I had such a crush on him."

So Aguirre was protecting her, but from what?

We arrived at the gate as Lura finished the story. Aníbal held it open while we changed shoes and tottered through to the bar for an aperitif before dinner. Lura sang at the top of her lungs, "Too-ra-loo-ra-loo-ral, Too-ra-loo-ra-li, Too-ra-loo-ra-loo-ral. Hush, now don't you cry." Lura's voice was loud, if not on pitch.

"Come on you guys, sing along."

We joined the chorus. "Too-ra-loo-ra-loo-ral, Too-ra-loo-ra-li, Too-ra-loo-ra-loo-ral, That's an Irish lullaby." Pepper started a singsong howl, making us laugh until tears ran down our faces.

"Aníbal, now look what you've done. You've made us all cry with your *burro* voice." She imitated a braying donkey.

Aníbal laughed harder, brayed too. He danced across the tiles to the bar, exciting Pepper. He let loose with a piercing howl, and with toenails tapping, danced little circles around Aníbal. The sight was too silly for words.

"Hand me a tissue, won't you, Hon," Lura asked Aníbal. He passed a box of Pañuelos from under the bar and turned to me.

"Hey, good lookin', can I buy you a drink?" he joked in a sexy voice.

"Only if you have a friend for my sister," I shot back.

He poured a round of Herradura Reposado and three narrow shot glasses of something resembling tomato juice from a fat green glass pitcher he pulled from the refrigerator.

"What's this?" I asked.

"*Sangrita*," he answered.

"Sangria? I thought that was wine punch."

"San-gri-ta," Lura enunciated. "It's a typical tequila chaser. You drink it before a meal. It's made out of chile and grenadine—hot and sweet, just how I like my men." She laughed and reached over the bar to pinch Aníbal's cheek.

"Ouch, Lulu!" He pulled away grinning.

"Okay. Am I missing something here? I thought Aníbal worked for you or something. You two just don't act like employer and employee." Not to mention the fact that he's completely proficient in both Spanish and English, and knows your family history like it was his own. "I'm confused," Damn, he's the hot tamale. Well, duh.

"Let's drink our toast, and then I'll finish the Aguirre Story—Legends of Us All over dinner. Aníbal, you're eating with us, aren't you?"

"Yes."

"Good. Then I propose a toast to our new girlfriend, JadeAnne Stone and her little dog, too." She cackled wildly. "No, seriously. To us. May our journey be filled with laughter and never stop being an adventure." She gulped down her tequila.

"To us," Aníbal and I echoed, shooting back our drinks.

"I have a proposition. Let's all go to Zihua together tomorrow. We can caravan. Aníbal can drive my rental, and JadeAnne, you and I can go in the combi. We'll have lunch and a swim in Playa Azul if the sun is out. How does that sound? Ani?"

It was the answer to my prayer. "Great idea."

"I'm in, but you have to let me check out the combi, too, Lura."

"Here's to a Grand Adventure." Lura raised her Sangrita and drank it, slamming the glass onto the bar. Aníbal drank next, and I followed suit.

A shadow crossed the wall behind the bar. I tensed instinctively, but Pepper remained calm. It was the serving woman. Aníbal smiled and greeted her in Spanish, calling her Grandmother. I wondered if that were some sort of traditional name people used for the oldest woman? She said something back in her native Tarascan, and Lura made a face.

"Elena, speak Spanish," she demanded.

Elena gave Lura a sour look, and announced dinner in Spanish. We followed her through the passageway to the courtyard. I took Lura's lead and stopped to wash up in the guest bath, and then we seated ourselves at the table. Elena served a light supper of chicken-filled *caldo* Tlalpeño, tortillas, sliced cheeses and meats, and cold tuna-stuffed *poblano chiles*. The tuna tasted fresh.

"I didn't finish our family's history," Lura said between mouthfuls. "Aunt Lidia refused to join her husband, but the Church didn't allow divorce. Tito was lonely. Elena and her husband, Tanok, have been with Grandfather from the time they all were kids. They were the only ones Pepper allowed near you last night, you know. Tanok carried you up." She explained how Pepper and I got to the room.

"That's amazing. He's trained to protect me if I'm down. How did Tanok get near me?" This is why he talked to me in the kitchen.

"He's a marvel with animals. Always has been. They, Tanoc and Elena, had a beautiful and wild daughter, Anahí. Dad said Tito and Anahí fell in love in kindergarten, but Elena and Tanok never could tame her. They weren't going to let their wild daughter disgrace their name and convinced Grandfather to send her away to school when she showed too much interest in my uncle. It's another story no one talks about." She took a bite of cheese and sipped the wine Elena sullenly brought to the table. I wondered if she spoke English, too.

But the story was getting pretty clear. Aníbal was Anahí's. That made him Polo's half-brother and Lura's cousin. How cozy. I ate some more soup and noted Elena's disapproving scowl when she looked at the cousins.

Lura went on with Anahí's sad story. She died in Mexico City. Aníbal squirmed in his chair and grunted in reply to her questions. Elena, hovering in the shadows, fumed. Perhaps it isn't wise to wake the dead.

Elena stepped out of the shadows and asked Lura if we wanted dessert. She answered no, but asked for a certain wine. When Elena brought the bottle, it turned out to be a late harvest Riesling, smooth and very sweet. I sipped it while I considered the fate of the Aguirres. This family was more dysfunctional than my own. I really couldn't take anymore and stopped listening. Anyway, these people were very odd, and again I felt like I'd stumbled into a Hitchcock film.

I needed a dose of reality and checked my watch. It was ten o'clock, time for the news.

"Would anyone mind if I go in and watch the news?" I asked. "It's been a week since I've caught up on what's going on."

"Good idea. Let's." Lura got up from the table and headed toward the veranda. "Who wants something from the bar?"

"Not me," called Aníbal.

"Is there a tamarind soda?" I asked.

"I'll look," she said as we left the table and Elena began to clear.

Aguirre received about two hundred stations by satellite. Aníbal found CNN, and we watched clips of the democratic presidential debate recorded for YouTube, mostly a "town hall" where Hillary Clinton and Barak Obama disagreed about the war in Iraq, and we learned Microsoft had conquered China during Bill Gate's visit. Hillary wasn't my choice, but was America ready to elect a black President? I liked what Obama had to say. Maybe a majority of the U.S. voters would too.

"Let's get the local weather. I want to know what we can expect in Playa Azul and Zihua," I suggested.

"Yeah. We should watch some local news for a while."

"But it will be in Spanish," Aníbal argued.

"So? You speak Spanish, right?" Lura baited him.

"I was thinking about JadeAnne. Don't get sarcastic with me, Lura."

My eyes wanted to close. Lura sloshed and slurred her words. I doubted I'd be able to keep up with her in a drinking contest. Aníbal switched to a station out of Acapulco which broadcast news. The weather there was looking exactly like the weather here. He scrolled through the menu looking for something closer and finally found a broadcast that included Zihuatanejo and Ixtapa. A pretty weathercaster with a ridiculously low-cut blouse told the viewing audience it would be overcast in the morning but would clear toward midday, and the temperatures would range from a low of seventy-eight to a high of ninety-two. The water temperature in Zihuatanejo Bay would remain

89.9 degrees, and a 5-mile-per-hour wind would come from the northwest. I yawned, ready to go to bed.

"In the Capital today, police arrested protestors gathering illegally on the Plaza of the Three Cultures in the historic Tlatelolco district," the TV newscaster announced. "The protest was against the anticipated PEMEX privatization bill currently under discussion in Congress. Protesters allege that privatization will open Mexico's petroleum industry to foreign profiteers who will plunder Mexico's reserves, leaving them depleted and Mexico bankrupt. Televisa Channel 9 reporter, Antonio Lopez, talks with Oil Industry Economist, Roberto Sanchez."

I sat up at full attention.

"Financial analysts predict Mexico's oil production will be in big trouble in a few years. What is your outlook, Mr. Sanchez?"

"Antonio, the solution isn't simple. PEMEX needs investors for the continued development of oil reserves. Without investment, our reserves will run out on the current mining schedule."

And an American bank would stand to profit from privatization. American investment in Mexico's oil would be inevitable and could make Worthington's career.

We all watched the broadcast intently. Aguirre must have told Lura her husband had attempted to bribe his vote. It was clear how Aguirre planned on voting. But what was Worthington's threat to Lura? Why didn't I see it? Lura seemed to be a straight-up kind of person, happy, funny, positive. Why did Aguirre say Worthington was not to be trusted over the phone? The Aguirre family had a lot of bones in its closet. Maybe it was some old business. Or Worthington could have threatened Aguirre. Well, all I can do is wait and see what will unfold. I've got Lura.

CHAPTER EIGHT

Who Are These People?

July 29, 2007

Contrary to the weather report for Costa Azul, the day dawned bright and clear. I had a more difficult time than usual getting out of bed, which I attributed to my foggy head —too much wine and tequila the night before, something I'm not accustomed to. I imagined Lura had quite a headache. Pepper was ready for his breakfast and morning run. I pulled a pair of shorts over my Speedo and slipped into running shoes, then dragged my hair into a ponytail. The house was silent and no guards lurked in the shadows as we headed toward the back stairs. A pair of handsome Labradors and a slender boy of about ten greeted us in the dog garden.

"Buenos días. What beautiful dogs. What are their names?"

"Mole and Ole' Yeller. Yours?"

"Pepper. I'm JadeAnne." I held out my hand to the boy.

"Luis Miguel." He shook my hand.

The dogs busily sniffed and wagged. Mole flirted with Pepper coyly. I let him go. "I'm going for a run on the beach. Want to come?"

"Okay. I have to walk the dogs anyway." He grinned, high-fiving me.

We jogged to the gate and onto the track to the beach. The dogs ran ahead, crisscrossing the path, yelping and barking in pleasure. I scanned the ground as I ran and noticed some very large pawprints in the sandy soil. They ran parallel to tracks, which could have been made by boots and headed away from the house. I assumed that this was a night watchman and one of Aguirre's rottweilers.

The boy, a fast runner, had no trouble keeping up with the dogs. He jabbered over his shoulder to me as he chased them back and forth in the dappled shade of the now-familiar forest track. We arrived at the beach in a few minutes and sprinted down to the tide line. I decided to jog to the promontory and back before taking a swim. Luis Miguel stayed behind to play in the sand and throw sticks for the dogs.

The morning was lovely. I made it to the point and skirted along the cliff to the top of the beach at the edge of the forest. An outcropping of rock marked the path to the lookout, and I stepped up to check it out. On the far side, the grass was trampled and a couple of stubbed-out Delicado butts lay in the damp sand surrounding a small pool of stagnant water under the edge of the rock. Footprints. In one very damp spot I could clearly see the impression of a boot, matching the partial prints along the track. They appeared fresh, and they'd be gone after the next high tide. The trail we had taken to Sunset Point was clearly visible from this vantage. The hair on my neck prickled.

Someone watched us.

I retraced my steps around the outcropping, rejoined the path, and hiked up slowly, looking for signs of disturbance in the dense growth. The trail was too rocky to yield clear prints, although I could see impressions of sports shoes here and there in soft spots. At the top, I inspected our sunset-viewing area. Nothing appeared sinister, just the impressions of our shoes, Pepper's pawprints, and the hum of insects and surf in the warm air.

I went into the trees and continued the search. Not far from the circle, I found a fallen tree. The limbs offered enough protection for an intruder to watch the circle undetected. With good hearing, he could have listened in to the chatter, too. I smelled the unpleasant odor of stale cigarette smoke and spotted another Delicado butt. I thrashed back through the undergrowth to the cliff. How had a man in boots, smoking cigarettes, managed to follow us up this cliff without anyone, especially Pepper, noticing him? Was this why Aníbal came armed? The sounds of laughter and happy yelps from the boy and dogs playing on the white beach in the sun belied the hidden threats of this place.

Refreshed from my exercise, I sat down to hand-squeezed orange juice and a carafe of *café de olla*. The cook brought in huevos mexicanos and a stack of steaming tortillas. Aníbal joined me before I finished, and helped himself to the platters the little maid left on the table. She appeared nervous when Aníbal came in. They conversed in Tarascan for a moment, then she retreated from the courtyard as quickly as she could get away. I let it pass and finished my food.

"I'll see you both in the driveway at ten, okay?" I said.

"Yeah, if Lulu is ready. I got the rental packed with my stuff while you exercised." How did he know? "Lulu hasn't stirred, as far as I can tell, and probably will be late. She was pretty drunk last night."

"I figured. How long does it take to get to Zihua? I don't want to be on the road after dark again."

"Not too long, I could make it in three and a half or four hours, but I know the road. Your camper? I estimate five hours. Lulu mentioned lunch in Playa Azul. It's the armpit of Costa Azul, in my opinion. That means three o'clock earliest if we drive straight on from lunch." He turned away from me. "I don't really want to go to Ixtapa, JadeAnne. My brother hates me. I'm uncomfortable around him. It's just as bad here. My grandmother doesn't approve of me." He looked a bit sheepish.

"Aníbal, you don't need to tell me your personal business, but if you want to talk later, I'll be happy to listen. I've got to go up and pack." I backed toward the door. His confidence embarrassed me.

At ten o'clock, the sun beamed down on the brick driveway and waiting vehicles. The rental turned out to be a new VW Beetle painted sunflower yellow with a Puebla license plate. Lura was not in sight. I used the extra time to stow my clothes and Pepper's gear. I double checked the tell-tales and was satisfied that the vehicle had not been touched since my inspection the afternoon before. Pepper jumped in and settled himself on the back seat, letting me know he was ready to roll.

I walked back to the Beetle where Aníbal sat in the driver's seat, studying a map and making notes on a pad. He tucked the tablet into his pocket when I approached, jumped out of the car with the map, and spread it out on the hood. He pointed out our location and the route to Ixtapa where Aguirre would put the cousins up in his penthouse at the Krystal. I planned to go on to Sally's.

Zihuatanejo/Ixtapa was in the state of Guerrero. The state line cut across some of the Aguirre holdings near the Highway 37 turn-off to Uruapan, Pátzcuaro and Morelia. From 37, Ruta 200 became a toll road, and I hoped we would make good time. The last 50 kilometers of the coastal route to Lazaro Cardenas looked safe on the map, but old

Tanok had warned me to be careful on the cliffs near the turnoff. I debated telling Aníbal what his grandfather had said.

Lura's grand entrance into the driveway settled the debate. She was decked out in a hip-hugging, white pleated mini-skirt and a pink tube top under a lacey midriff-baring tank. She wore orange flip-flops decorated with pink spider chrysanthemums and carried a matching pink python Prada bag. Her pigtails bushed out from under a wide-brimmed straw hat with a pink polka dot band and a hot pink floppy flower. To complete her look, a pair of pink sunglasses studded with rhinestones hung from a jeweled chain around her neck, a twist of pink pearls on her wrist. She carried a laptop-sized silver satchel over her shoulder. Elena struggled behind her lugging a heavy yellow portmanteau and a red hatbox.

"Hi, guys," she called out. Her wide smile took over her face and lit up her ocean-blue eyes. "I'm ready."

Aníbal gazed at his cousin with his jaw hanging open.

"What? Don't you like my outfit?" she asked, still grinning.

We both laughed. "No. No. It's fabulous, Dahling. I just love your shoes." Aníbal lisped and wiggled his butt. "It's just—Lulu, where do you think you're going?"

"I'll go change, then," she snapped.

"No-o," Aníbal and I cried in unison.

"You look fine. But the combi is so funky—full of dog hair. I'll toss a sheet over your seat. We need to get going." I thought her cousin might not come after us, but the fashion policía certainly would.

Aníbal took the luggage from his grandmother and tossed it in the trunk of the Beetle while I covered the passenger seat. When everything was ready, he handed Lura up into the bus, and we took our places. Aníbal, familiar with the way out, took the lead.

The stone wall and wrought iron gates adorned with the Aguirre serpent logo at the main entrance didn't surprise me. Nor did the surveillance cameras mounted to watch the comings and goings of traffic on the property and the highway. Aníbal took charge of closing the gate after we passed through and made sure no one was following us while I had the combi pulled over. I was certain we were being watched, though. Lura seemed oblivious to the cameras or any potential danger as she flipped through my CD collection and found some music she liked.

"Kirsty MacColl. I love her. I didn't know anyone else knew about her. She died in Mexico in a boating accident some years ago."

"Yeah. Sad story. What a loss."

The music started, and she punched the player to the second cut. We looked at each other as I put the bus in gear, eased off the clutch, and turned onto the highway, taking the lead. "In these shoes?" we sang along. Lura kicked up her flip-flopped feet and shook them in the windshield.

Rolling, everything felt lighter. Lura and I sang and chatted through the CD, although I still kept an eye on the mirrors for anyone following us, and prayed Aníbal knew to do the same. I was careful to stay alert to turnouts and breaks in the trees. This was Aguirre land. They didn't need to follow the highway, but surely Aguirre had called off his gang. He wouldn't kill Lura or Aníbal, would he?

The CD ended as we neared the turn to Playa Azul. The highway rose up onto steep bluffs overlooking the ocean, and the bus moved slowly. Lura swapped Kirsty for The Iguanas.

I'd set the side mirrors to see far behind the combi since I couldn't see anything out of the rearview because of the no-see-um netting. The yellow Beetle kept a close distance behind us. A green van materialized behind Aníbal in the curvy road, coming up on his tail quickly.

I slipped my gun out of the side pocket where I'd stashed it while packing and slid it under my thigh. I prayed Aníbal could handle whatever would happen and turned to what was in front of us. The road had narrowed. On one side there was a hundred foot drop and on the other, a steep road cut. If the combi was forced off the road and down the cliff, we would die. If I hit the bank, we had a chance. Dex had installed front seat airbags in the old bus when they first came on the market. I pulled over to the left. Any Culiacán-bound buses would have to swerve around us. I wondered if this was how Aguirre's wife and children died.

Lura hummed along with the music and rummaged in her little python-trimmed bag. She pulled out a slim lipstick tube and flipped down her visor to use the mirror. She angled the mirror and brought the tube toward her lips. Her humming changed into low singing but the CD drowned out her words. She grinned at me and pantomimed singing into a microphone. This woman was a real piece of work. I checked my mirrors. Aníbal followed closer now, with the green van on his tail. He held one hand up to his mouth as though he, too, were singing into a microphone.

It dawned on me, "You're talking to Aníbal."

Lura's grin widened. "Watch ahead. We'll keep an eye on the rear. Smart move, staying over like this."

The combi rounded a blind curve. Ahead, a turnout was partially visible.

"JadeAnne, Ani says there's a hidden clearing through that turnout where we can hide." She pointed ahead. "He's slowing down to let us get away. He can outrun the van once we've disappeared."

I skidded off the pavement onto the sandy shoulder, following Lura's directions, and almost collided with Polo's grey pickup coming around the bank toward us. The vehicles swerved away from each other. The combi fishtailed in the loose gravel and swayed precariously. The pickup smashed into an abutment shoring up the highway cut and stopped. It was too late to hide. The yellow Beetle rounded the curve with the van next to it trying to force it off the road. I stepped on the gas, hoping to make it to the trees at the far edge of the clearing. I could use the hill and the bus as protection. We slid to a stop in a billow of dust.

"Get out. Run into the trees," I ordered Lura. "I'll cover you." I pulled out the Semmerling.

Lura's grin got wider yet. "With that? Let's use mine instead." She yanked a ten millimeter Glock 29 out of the Prada bag and flung herself out the door and under the vehicle. She was barefoot. I whistled for the dog as I dove out my door and scooted along the ground to the rear of the bus. Pepper jumped over the seats and was by my side in a flash.

"Run for it, Ani. We're good. Both armed," Lura shrilled into the radio.

The Beetle passed the turnout, zigzagging to keep the van from pushing him off the cliff. We heard the sickening crunch of metal-on-metal as the van started to push the VW toward the drop. The Bug's motor whined, and we cheered as the little car shot ahead. The van swerved over the edge. We heard it crash down the cliff and thud onto the sand.

"Ouch." Lura crawled out from behind the tire. "Ani, are you okay?" she shouted into the two-way radio. "And you, JadeAnne?"

"I'm fine," I replied. My heart raced and I sucked my lungs full of air to slow it down. "Lura, where did you get that gun? For that matter, where did you get that little two-way?"

"Oh, a girl has to look out for herself, you know." She batted her long eyelashes.

"Should we go check on the grey truck?"

"Why? They would have killed us. Why should we save them?"

I had no answer. We dusted off and got back in the bus. I started the engine and pulled back to the highway. The music stopped, and the only sounds were the old motor putt-putting and the faint rush of wind and whoosh of the ocean through the window. Then a motor revved, and I heard a sharp popping noise. Lura leaned out her window, leveling her gun at the oncoming truck while I stepped on the gas. The overloaded bus lumbered through the bumps and potholes, slowly gaining speed. Lura shot out the window, but the truck stayed behind to the left while it gained on us.

"Down Peppi! Down boy," I screamed. He obeyed my command just as I heard bullets pierce the bus. I punched the gas pedal once more and jumped forward with the help of gravity on the downgrade. Once we cleared the truck's fender, I veered the bus left to cut it off and prevent it from pushing us over the cliff like Aníbal had done. The road straightened out, and I could see Aníbal ahead. Lura was speaking rapid Spanish over the radio. The shots continued. I feared what would happen if a bullet hit the propane tank on the roof. Or the reserve gas can mounted on the back.

"Lura. Do you see smoke behind us?"

"The gas can? No, it hasn't been hit yet." Her grin was gone, and I noticed she had a streak of crank case oil on her cheek.

The pickup was gaining again, but the shots had stopped. It pulled out to the right of the combi. Lura leaned back out the window, pointed the Glock, and squeezed the trigger once and then again. The truck went out of control a second time. It landed upside down against some trees partway down the cliff.

Lura's grin was back. She brought her gun inside and blew away the imaginary smoke. "Do we have any water aboard? I need to tidy up my face." She took an embroidered handkerchief out of her bag.

Handing over a water bottle, I asked, "Lura, where did

you learn how to shoot like that?" I was shaken, but she was completely cool, acting like nothing had happened.

Aníbal waited by the Beetle in a turnout. An abandoned-looking silver car parked at the edge of the forest beyond him. I pulled over. My legs felt like Jell-O as I climbed out of the bus. I still clutched my gun, and it felt heavy in my tremulous fist. It didn't matter how often I saw violence, I would never get used to it. I checked the damage to the bus while I steadied myself. There were nine bullet holes low on the driver's side. The shooter had aimed at the tires.

"*Burros. Pendejos.* Assholes. Ani, they have rocks for brains. All that idiot, Geraldo, needed to do was plug the gas tank she's got mounted on back, and we would have been Cheech and Chong—up in smoke." No one laughed.

"Lulu, who were they after? JadeAnne?" Aníbal asked the question I was thinking. "Do you think Polo knew about this? He is going to be pissed off when he learns about his truck. And who were the jokers in the green van?"

"You mean you didn't recognize any of them?" Lura looked dumbfounded. "They were too far back. I couldn't see their faces."

"No. I only recognized Smith and Wesson. I got a little nervous there for a moment. I think you've lost your security deposit on the Beetle."

"Yeah, I think you're right." Lura turned to look at the crumpled side of her rental car. "How will I explain this?"

We laughed this time. "Okay. That was some excitement to work up an appetite. I'm starving. Let's get this circus moving and get some lunch. We're only a half hour out of Playa Azul."

"Armpit of the Blue Coast," Aníbal mouthed to me.

"I heard that."

No one but Pepper gave a second glance to the silver Nissan pulled over just beyond the VW.

87

CHAPTER NINE

Under Surveillance

Hotel Playa Azul merited two stars but billed itself as four. The property was pretty enough, but the late 1960s architecture with garish fraying orange and yellow plaid Danish Modern put me off. I never liked God's Eyes, which adorned the walls, and still think potted sago palms and saw palmettos are boring. When the day manager, an obsequious twenty-something pest, showed up to greet us and practice his English, I agreed with Aníbal's negative assessment—a pit. I would have called it tacky, not an armpit, but that would have been splitting hairs.

Lura loved it. She loved acting loud and obnoxious, calling attention to us. She played the quintessential ugly American, braying over stupid jokes told by the manager, demanding attention from the entire dining room staff, ordering and changing her mind repeatedly. She even had the gall to send one of her dishes back to the kitchen because, "I don't like it." Despite our attempts to calm her down, Lura just got louder.

"What do you do, Aníbal?" I tried to make small talk.

"I work for a think tank out of D.C. We come up with ideas for trade agreements and advise the policy makers."

"D.C. I bet it's exciting if you like politics. I watched West Wing occasionally."

"Ani hates politics. He thinks they're boooo-rrringgg," Lura sang out and laughed loudly. She glanced around the room smirking at the annoyed looks on the faces of the other diners.

"Well, what about you, Lura?" I prayed she'd lower her volume.

She sighed dramatically and turned her smile on me. "What? Oh, school? UCLA."

"She asked what you studied, Lu." Aníbal's tone sounded exasperated. He turned to me and added, "Industrial Design and Marketing."

Lura stuck out her tongue at him. "Ani, I'm right here." She winked at me over her crooked smile. "Yeah, I stayed on for an MBA in International Trade too, but emphasized Import/Export. Ani doesn't actually know anything about buying and selling, the dummy."

"So you two understand this business about the oil? Who buys Mexican oil? Do we?"

"Oh, not PEMEX again. I'm sick of it. It's all Poli talks about." Lura rolled her eyes and folded her arms across her chest, frowning. At least she shut up.

"Polo sees privatization as the road to bankruptcy for Mexico. But typically, many see it as a quick fix to Mexico's financial problems and a potential 'get rich quick' scheme for them. It could be a really good move; it would mean outside money."

"If you're going to talk politics, I'm going to the bathroom," Lura whined, the leg of her chair sending up a squeal as it scudded across the tile floor. She flip-flapped across the dining room, leaving her barely touched enchilada congealing on the plate.

"So, as an economist, what do you think Mexico should do?"

"With investment, Mexico could explore for oil, then mine it effectively, and do it right for a change. If she could sell off PEMEX, make a bundle, and fifteen to twenty years later nationalize the oil industry again, she'd reap the profits of the dwindling supplies free and clear."

"You mean, if there is more oil under the ground," I added.

"Yeah, if it's mined right, or if the greedy bastards don't make off with the profits, investments, and assets."

"I bet that's a big if." I took a bite of my rubbery *chile relleno*. "Why is she acting like this?"

"I guess she's pissed our cousin tried to kill us—or you, maybe. She's letting off steam. Lura's a drama queen, or hadn't you noticed? Look around. We're the only Americans in here. It may be ugly, but it's considered a very nice resort for middle class Mexicans, the best hotel here. So Lura comes in and acts low class to go with the classless hotel. She can be irritating, and once she's made up her mind, there is no changing it. It makes my job hard."

He studied the room. Alarm played across his face.

"JadeAnne, don't you think she's been gone too long?"

"Is there any possibility there could be more guys following us?"

"I wouldn't be surprised if Geraldo radioed back to the farm before they crashed. We would have been smarter to get a move on to Ixtapa. We're losing our lead."

"Well, I'll go look in the bathroom. Wait. Why don't you try to raise her on the two-way?"

Aníbal pointed to the Prada bag sitting on the table. I hoped she'd left the Glock in the bus.

I scraped my chair back and got up. Job? What do these people really do? I picked my way through the crowded room. I was anxious to get to Zihua, reunite the Aguirre family, and get to Sally's apartment where I could go online and do a little research. Lura had killed two men today without batting a mascara-enhanced eyelash. She and Aníbal were too well equipped and worked too smoothly together to be a family on vacation.

I flashed to the image of Aníbal grunting while he lifted Lura's valise into the Beetle after Aguirre's serving woman, Elena, half-dragged it from the house. They were in it together, whatever it was. Before I went online, I had to get into that suitcase. Whatever Worthington was after must be in the valise. Money?

When I didn't find Lura in the ladies' room, I took the opportunity to slip out to check on Pepper. The combi baked in the semi-shade of a hedgerow of queen palms, which accented taller coconut palms towering over the parking lot. I let Pepper out.

"You need a drink, don't you boy?"

He smiled, tongue lolling. I poured him a bowl of water and opened the hidey-hole where I stored my set of universal keys. Maybe I would break into the Beetle's trunk while I was out there. No, without knowing exactly where Lura was, I couldn't risk it, but I added the picks and universal keys to my purse. Since the Mexican women in the restaurant all had their little yappers with them I assumed Pepper would be allowed too, and went back to the table with Pepper prancing at my side.

A chorus of little dog voices rose up as the Mexican ladies' shih tzus, cockapoos, beagles, bichon frisés, and ugly, hairless xoloitzcuintlis complained and tangled in their mistresses' legs. Pepper grinned and sat at perfect attention by my chair.

To my relief, Lura had returned to the dining room. Wearing nothing but a miniscule black and gold bikini, she laughed and flirted with a balding older man by the patio door. She waved to me and leaned in closer to the man. He looked like he had just seen the pearly gates open. A woman, presumably his wife, watched from her seat at a table close by, her expression suggesting if he kept up his current course he'd be passing through those gates at any moment. Lura laughed and whispered something to the man.

The wife gracefully got to her feet and strode toward her husband with that murderous look in her eye reserved for naughty men. Lura laughed again, gave him a big smack on the cheek, and excused herself in garbled Spanish, leaving the man to the wrath of his wife. Lura threw a wink at us and scooted off to the pool.

"She was getting her suit and towel out of the rental and changing for a swim," Aníbal offered in explanation of Lura's long absence.

"What suit?"

He laughed. "You should see the other one she brought. JadeAnne, I'm thinking that Polo wasn't behind this. Maybe Geraldo decided to get some revenge on you for his brother. Enrique had to have surgery to reconstruct his throat where Pepper tore it open yesterday. He will live, but his life is not going to be the same. Grandfather warned me that the men had planned something."

"He told me, too. I feel responsible for what happened." I hung my head for a beat then looked Aníbal in the eye and took a gulp of air. "But not too responsible. I didn't go looking for Polo's thugs to hijack me." Contrition colored my voice. "I'm sorry for involving you two, though."

"Don't worry about it," he said.

"When Lura suggested we caravan, I was all for it, expecting Polo to call off the jackals. I can't imagine he'd harm Lura." I challenged him. "Would he?"

"Let me get this." He reached for the check our waiter had deposited onto the table.

"Would he, Aníbal?" I wasn't going to let him change the subject this time. "What's really going on? I heard Polo on the phone with Lura's husband. Why would Polo warn her against him? I'm certain Worthington has tried to bribe Polo, but Lura? It's only fair I know what danger we're in."

"Worthington's a pawn. He's a wuss, a wannabe. He thinks he's some sort of player because he owns a bank," Aníbal blurted out in disgust. The air crackled around him. "He's going down. Polo is pissed. Polo wasn't behind this. It was Worthington. I told you, I didn't recognize the van or the men in it. They weren't Polo's."

"So what's Worthington up to?" I asked.

"Something to do with financing for U.S. investment in the Mexican oil industry. He's been lobbying for privatization of PEMEX for a couple of years and is after Polo to spearhead his campaign. He wants Lulu to convince Polo, but she won't."

"I don't see what this has to do with men in green vans shooting at us."

"Well, Worthington's contacts have plenty of resources. He even stooped to bribe Polo with money. Christ. Polo is richer than God. A half a mil? Chump-change. What could that mean to him? Danny is an ass."

This explained everyone's interest in the newscast but still didn't shed light on the shootout. "Well, that's a story." I smiled at the waiter who sidled up to the table, obviously wary of Pepper.

"Can I bring you anything else?" he asked.

"No, thank you. Keep the change." Aníbal handed him the check. The waiter bowed and backed away several steps, then turned and fled.

Aníbal thought for a moment. I listened to the dampened drone of voices in the dining room. Maybe all the cotton string God's Eyes worked as baffles.

"Do you remember years ago when Mexico nationalized the banks?" he asked.

"What a mess. My family had friends who lost a lot."

"So you remember a decade later when Salinas de Gortari turned around and sold the banks back to the private sector. Of course, only days after he left office, the peso devalued and the country practically went bankrupt." He gave me a complicit look. "Gortari left the presidency a rich man."

Aníbal sipped the last of his coffee and tossed his napkin onto his plate. "Let's get Lulu and go. It's getting late."

We got up from the table and almost escaped the day manager.

"Was everything to your liking?" he fawned.

We made some polite noises, assured him the mediocre meal was terrific, and said we'd be back soon. Pepper, tired of waiting, tugged on his leash and woofed. The manager blanched and scurried off. We bolted to the pool where Lura lounged in a floating chair, a pink tropical drink in one hand and a paperback novel in the other. Her oversized sunglasses prevented me from reading her expression.

"Lulu. Let's go. It's late. There's a pool at the Krystal."

"Hi, Ani, JadeAnne. Get your suits on. The water is divine."

"No, you get your bare ass out of the pool now or we'll leave you here—without your suitcase," Aníbal replied. Sunbathers stared at us.

"You're such a grouch, Ani," she said through her lopsided grin. "Okay, I'm coming. Let me finish my drink first."

"No. Get out now. Christ, you are such a *tzcuintli*."

Lura stuck her lip out in a pout and looked toward the back of the patio before she paddled her way to the steps. I glanced back, but she handed me her drink, and I missed what she saw. Aníbal snatched the half-empty glass and deposited it on a busboy's tray.

"I want you sober and dressed, Lulu. Go put on a pair of pants and shoes." Aníbal's tone said *don't mess with me*. She wrapped herself in her towel, trailing us to the cars. He opened the trunk, and Lulu pawed through her yellow bag until she found a pair of denim shorts, a t-shirt with "New York" on the front, and her Keds. I tried to see into the bag without being too obvious.

"I'll be right back." She meandered to the ladies' room.

"I'm taking Pepper for a quick walk." I released him from his leash. We jogged to the beach.

I felt my cell phone vibrate in my pocket. I stopped and whistled to the dog.

"Dex."

"Yeah, it's me. Where are you?"

"Boy am I glad you called. I'm in Playa Azul on the beach."

"Jeez, JadeAnne, you're supposed to be working."

"On the beach walking the dog while we wait for 'our friend' to change out of her bathing suit and get ready to push on to Zihua."

"You found her?"

"You won't believe what I've been through in the last three days. Look, I can't explain now. Armed men are lurking along the highway gunning for one of us. We aren't sure who. And my client may be one of the bad guys. Can you call tonight at eight and have me paged at Hotel Krystal? I might be in the penthouse. Say I'm a guest of Senator Aguirre. I'll get your number and go to a safe phone to call you back. If you can't reach me, call the consulate. And Dex? Where the hell have you been?"

"Drinking with Guinn in Bahía de los Angeles. Who is this Aguirre character?"

"He's our client's wife's cousin. They ran to him for protection."

"They?"

I felt my face flush. Dex would see right through me if I mentioned Aníbal. Luckily I caught sight of Lura through the palms. "I gotta go now. Love you, bye."

I didn't want to hang up but did, and jogged to the parking lot. Pepper glanced back at the beach, disappointment written all over his mug.

"Later Peppi, later. We'll take a real run tonight."

Ruta 200 widened and rolled out smooth and easy before us at the intersection with Highway 17. Aníbal led our procession, keeping to a sedate pace. Farms, roadside businesses and traffic populated the area sufficiently to make an attack risky. Plus the forest thinned, limiting potential hiding places. Lura climbed in back and took a nap.

I used the driving time to ruminate on the case, comparing the new information from my interview with Aníbal at lunch to what I already knew. A picture formed. When Dex called later, I would add his information to mine and make a decision about what I would say in my weekly report to my client, due today. Giving up Lura would be a mistake, but so far I had no concrete reason to think she was in danger from her husband. A thought slipped into my mind. The green van and the unknown men could be Worthington's. The thought bothered me. Call it intuition, but I didn't think they were after me. That meant Polo had nothing to do with it. But Polo's men, Geraldo and Antonio, had shot at us from the grey pickup. How could that have anything to do with Worthington?

I kept a close eye on my mirrors to be on the safe side. We were on a straightaway, and most of the traffic passed us. Once a string of vehicles had gotten around us, I caught sight of a silver sedan about ten car lengths back, keeping pace with the combi.

"That's odd. We passed a silver sedan stopped on the road just after the attack," I said aloud. "And saw it again in Playa Azul as we were leaving." I slowed down to let the car get closer. "Aníbal. Aníbal. Are you there?" I called on the two-way.

"I'm here. What's up?"

"Slow down a little. I'm checking out a silver sedan behind us. If it has a red leaf-shaped deodorizer hanging from the rearview, we're being followed."

"I saw it on the side of the road. It's a Nissan. It looked empty. I assumed the driver was taking a piss."

"I can see the red dangle. Uh-oh, he's caught on. He's slowing down. Okay, who is this clown? He knows he's burned."

The Nissan dropped back. I wasn't able to make out the face, but I had caught a glimpse of him in Playa Azul. "Aníbal, speed up. Are there any turnoffs before Ixtapa? Let's see if we can get far enough ahead to lose him. I want to watch him pass."

"We're almost in Lagunillas. We can pull off there at a barbacoa joint I know. The tacos are great, and the stand is behind a market. He won't be able to see the cars. Anyway, I'm hungry. That lunch was awful."

We sped up and left our tail poking along in our dust. I followed the Beetle as it turned off the highway and putted around a small store. I parked behind Aníbal, grabbed my binoculars off the top of the cabinet and jumped out, swinging the door closed and almost hitting Pepper's nose.

"Stay boy," I shouted as we ran around the corner of the building into a covered area with a couple of turquoise vinyl-covered tables and a soft-drink dispenser. The steam coming off the barbacoa comal was rich, and my mouth watered. We settled in to wait.

I had a good view of the road for a block in each direction. The Nissan took four minutes to appear. I saw the driver's head move side to side. Searching for us? Luck smiled. A Coke delivery truck making a turn blocked the highway traffic, and the Nissan stopped almost directly in front of the barbacoa joint. Nissan man looked our way, and I got a gander through the field glasses. He appeared to be forty, possibly younger, a square-ish face, lips full, short medium brown hair. He wore mirrored aviator sunglasses and a white t-shirt. It was hard to tell what type of build he had, but I thought he might be somewhat stocky by the shape of his neck. One elbow rested on the window frame, supporting the hand holding his cigarette out the window. The size of his bicep said he was in great shape.

Aníbal snapped a digital shot of Nissan Man and then took one of the license plate as traffic started to move. The Nissan disappeared down the block.

"Did you recognize him?" I asked.

"No. But it wasn't a rental. The plate was a government plate from D.F., the capital. His coloring looked European, but that doesn't mean anything. He could be either a national or a gringo."

"Could he work for Polo?"

"Sure, anything's possible. Let's get some barbacoa and consume. Give that guy a chance to get to Ixtapa. Bet we'll catch up to him there."

CHAPTER TEN

What's Up with These Guns and Green Vehicles?

The Krystal jutted out of the sand at the north end of Palmar Beach, one of the last in a long string of highrise hotels hogging the beautiful view. I personally found Ixtapa too planned, without heart or soul.

It was four-thirty when we pulled into the parking lot outside twelve stories of white, v-shaped hotel surrounded by lush-looking gardens. I concentrated on finding a shaded parking spot.

Lura woke up and started rummaging around in the back.

"I can't go in there looking like this."

"Why not?"

"The Krystal is the hippest hotel in Ixtapa. We've got to look upscale, not like we've been in a street fight." She fished around in her tote bag. "Why don't you change into the outfit you were wearing last night? I can put my skirt back on."

Aníbal slid the camper door open. "Ani, we're changing. Close that door and make yourself presentable. What else do you have to wear?" She didn't give Aníbal an opportunity to

99

speak. He obeyed and returned to the Beetle. I thought he looked fine in his faded blue jeans and tight white tee. I pictured several ways to show my appreciation.

"C'mon, girlfriend. Get back here." Lura's voice pulled me out of my fantasy. She tugged out of her shorts and bathing suit and then fixed her lipstick and smoothed her hair. It looked like a mass of Shirley Temple ringlets after her swim in Playa Azul. One of the Keds she kicked off wacked me as I climbed in beside her to change.

"Ow, Lura."

"Sorry." She grinned. "Hand me my flip flops."

I had scouted the parking lot for the silver Nissan with its red leaf deodorizer as I walked around the combi. The man would know where we were going if he was any good at his job. I didn't see the car, but the hair rose on my neck, and I sensed someone watching us. Probably Aníbal, who came back with more bags, and handed one in to Lura so she could finish changing. I slipped into a blue and green batik sheath with spaghetti straps that had been stuffed into the mini-closet, exchanging my Nikes for a pair of low-heeled black suede sandals, and then combed my hair in the tiny mirror on the closet door. When Lura was finished, we got out so Aníbal could dress. He reappeared in the white pants from the day before and a red silk Hawaiian shirt he'd left open to flutter around his muscular chest. He was barefoot.

"God, you are such a slob, Ani. Button your shirt. You're in public. Where are your shoes?"

He started to laugh. "Gotcha!" He slipped on a pair of leather sandals and picked up the bags. "Let's go."

Lura headed the procession like Anne Boleyn to her coronation. Inside, she made a beeline to the fifth car at the bank of elevators in the lobby and inserted a keycard she'd pulled out of the Prada bag. The doors opened, and we stepped into Polo's private elevator to the top floor. I hadn't noticed much about the lobby except it was pleasantly decorated in earthy colors accented with dark blue and bright yellow. I would explore later.

The door opened to a vestibule. It resembled the Aguirre entry in Michoacán, only smaller and not as grand, but it contained fine art and another collection of the little copper figurines. Those Tarascans sure made a shitload of them. Every cool kid on the block collected them. I bet future anthropologists will say the same about troll dolls. The furniture was spare and hand hewn in the *rústica* style and, I expected, authentic originals not reproductions. Aguirre's typical three doors lined the foyer, but Lura led us straight ahead into a wide, brightly lit gallery.

We passed an elegant living room with its spectacular view of the ocean punctuated by a pair of small islands. On the other side of the gallery, I identified a kitchen by the sounds of pots and pans and the spicy smell of burning chilies. More closed doors led off the gallery. Only the public rooms stood open. A half-wall bounded the gallery on the ocean side, and low walls separated the entertaining rooms from each other, creating an airy expanse that I found both uplifting and soothing.

At the end of the gallery, Lura pushed through a set of double doors that led into a passageway accessing the living quarters. At the fourth door, she motioned Aníbal to toss in her portmanteau. I wondered where Aníbal slept. The burr of wings fluttered my gut.

"That's my room." Lura stated the obvious. "Ani's is next door, and let's see where you can sleep."

Aníbal's bag thumped into his room. I caught a glimpse of the spectacular view before the door closed.

"I don't need a room. I can go to Sally's. She's expecting me to show up about now." I needed to do some research on the Internet and preferred to do it in privacy, although I had no doubt this building was wired.

"No. You have to stay. We'll go to dinner at Bogart's and

do some dancing at Christine's Club. It's a disco. Polo will take us," Lura argued.

"Polo will take us where?" Polo snuck up behind us.

"Hi, Cuz." Lura threw her arms around his neck, giving him a noisy smooch on his cheek. "To Bogart's and Christine's tonight. You owe us a good time for what you did, you bad, bad boy."

"You can tell me about my appalling behavior later, Lura. First let me say hello to Aníbal and Miss Stone." He smiled at each of us. "I didn't expect to see my cousins so soon, but I hoped you would arrive for dinner tonight, Miss Stone. I trust you were well taken care of and your drive was pleasant."

I scrutinized Polo. His guileless expression gave no indication he was lying, and no irony when he mentioned the trip. Aguirre was not behind the attacks on our caravan.

"Senator." I smiled at him. "Everything was lovely, thank you. Your cousins and I had a wonderful cocktail hour overlooking the sunset last night. And the meals were wonderful. You've an excellent cook."

"Thank you. I will extend your praise to Goya when I return. Let me show you to the spare guest room. It is close to the outside elevator so you can bring your beast in and out without problems. The Krystal does not allow pets." He bent to pet the dog. "How did you get him in here?" He glared at Lura. "I'm certain the entire staff fears my cousin." He teased her as he led the way to the last bedroom in the corridor.

"Thank you, Senator. It's kind of you to include me with your family. Now, if you all will excuse me, I'll go downstairs and take Peppi out for a run." I dropped my purse on the dresser and rummaged for my keys. "By the way, how do I get back in?"

"Aníbal, will you make sure Miss Stone gets what she needs? I must return to the office. I have a conference call in ten minutes. Lura, when you are ready, please come to my office."

"Yeah. I need to talk to you, too. I'll be in as soon as you're done. Call me."

"I should come, too, Lura. I have a few things to say."

I raised my eyebrows, questioning Lura and Aníbal. "Senator, I have some things to say, also."

"Look, Cuz, we had an incident today. If your spies haven't already told you about it, you need to know. I agree. All four of us should meet," Lura informed Aguirre. "How 'bout you and I talk over our business, and the others can join us at seven-thirty? We can go to dinner when we're done. Make a reservation for nine-thirty at Bogart's when you get back to your desk, will you, Poli?" She patted him on the cheek in dismissal.

"*Pues*, I can see I am excused. *Entonces me voy*." He nodded to me. "I'll see you at seven-thirty."

"I'm going to take a shower and get that awful pool water off. And do something about my hair. Later, guys." Lura slipped into her room and slammed the door.

"I'll run with you, JadeAnne," Aníbal said.

He slid his finger lightly down my arm. The wings flapped and soared in my gut. "Okay. Give me five minutes first to freshen up."

"I'll get the keycards. See you in a few." He wandered back toward the main part of the penthouse.

I leaned against the closed door exhausted, using the doorjamb to hold myself up. I didn't really want company on my run with Pepper, even if my traitor emotions thought differently. I wanted to find a Delicado-smoking man driving a silver Nissan, not get myself into trouble with a younger guy when my boyfriend wasn't around. I was sure that the spy at the Aguirre farm was the same person following us. Perhaps the conversation with Aguirre would reveal some answers, but I doubted it. My intuition said the Aguirre clan knew Nissan Man, and Aguirre, at least, wanted to hide that fact.

I considered the possibilities while I washed up in the mosaic-tiled bathroom. The handmade sink swam with green-painted fish. Thick lime-green cotton terry towels crowded white ceramic bars, and the cotton shag bath rugs resembled turtles in darker shades of the tiles. I'd been thinking about upgrading my bathrooms on the Sarasvati, and maybe I'd steal some ideas from this one, especially the surround shower with the huge window facing the western sun, now casting a golden glow throughout the room. On the Sarasvati, the window would face Mt. Tam and the setting sun.

I'd washed my face and secured my hair in a high ponytail by the time Aníbal knocked. Pepper, ecstatic to be going out, dashed to the elevator.

"How'd he know where to go?" Aníbal asked as we stepped into the lift.

"Beats me. He's a smart dog."

The elevator thumped to a stop at a service patio. Cylinders of gas stacked along one side, garbage dumpsters overflowed with kitchen waste, and empty vegetable crates and cardboard boxes lay in a jumbled heap. I held my breath against the reek. The air hummed from some sort of turbine —air conditioning, perhaps. It did nothing to eliminate the stench. For such a grand hotel, you'd think they could arrange regular garbage collection.

A couple of local mutts sniffing around the garbage growled at us, but took off when they saw Pepper. Pepper grinned at me and strained against his lead, hoping for a little excitement, but we scurried off the patio and headed away from the dogs toward the combi. I quickly tossed my shorts back on and slipped into my running shoes. Aníbal tossed on a pair of baggy-style swim shorts and Merrill joggers while Pepper danced between vehicles, encouraging his people to hurry up.

We jogged north in the direction of the marina along Paseo de Ixtapa. The road was busy with cars, jitneys, taxis, and SUVs pulling boat trailers, forcing us to run on the sidewalk until we passed the Posada Real and Omni hotels. Luckily, few pedestrians used the sidewalk at this time of day. Most of the tourists were probably in their rooms getting ready for the evening's entertainment. A few locals waited for buses or walked to and from the marina.

We stopped at Marina Plaza to catch our breath. The last time I visited Ixtapa, the marina hadn't been built, and I was curious to see it.

"Did Polo's company build this?" I asked Aníbal.

"Polo's company built everything in Ixtapa. This is his little kingdom. When he doesn't have to be in Mexico City, since Maria and the kids died, he spends much more time here than at the farm. His group put in the Marina Ixtapa Golf Course only a couple of years ago." He gestured to the east.

"The one we passed on the road?"

"Yeah. The Marina went in eight or nine years ago. It has slips for two hundred boats, but the jetty entrance silts up, and the big sailboats can't always get in, so the fuel dock closed a few years ago. A couple of German women run the place. Both speak English. The clubhouse has showers and laundry, but since the cruisers can't get in and they can't get fuel, the money is going to Marina Puerto Mío in Zihua. I think Polo lost a bundle on the project. My guess is it's one of the reasons the group put in the golf course."

We were leaning over a railing looking across the canals to the moorings. "So why not dredge?" I asked.

"I don't know. I think it has something to do with environmental laws."

"Hmm, I didn't know anyone cared about the law here. What about the golf course? Make a profit?"

"I suppose. He built it to steal business away from Arturo Rodriguez, Polo's big competitor. His group holds most of Zihuatanejo, but other than another golf course, his holdings in Ixtapa are small. I think he put up one or two of the older hotels, but Polo has outbid him since. Rodriguez owns Marina Puerto Mío."

The evening gathered above the dark green mountains to the east and reflected blue-violet in the water. Puffy white clouds had built up over the peaks and were illuminated by the low western sun. I breathed in the familiar smells of salt, seaweed, marine oil, and paint, and had a sudden longing for home. I yearned for the Sarasvati, my familiar routine, and for Dex. Pepper leaned into my thigh and gazed up at me as though he, too, pined for home. I sniffed and wiped my eyes on the hem of my shirt.

"I was thinking of home. Did you know I live on a houseboat? I love the water," I explained. "Silly me. I suddenly felt like I would never see it again." My laugh sounded dispirited, even to me, and I felt heat rising through my face. Crying is really going to impress a guy. What an idiot!

Aníbal gazed into the distance. "I know what you mean… I know what you mean."

"Come on, let's run." I took off. Pepper loped at my side, and Aníbal shot after us.

We ran along the parking lot at the edge of the water to a beach access. I was running hard and beginning to pant. Aníbal had almost caught up with me, so I slowed and turned around. A movement behind Aníbal caught my eye. I saw a man step from between a silver car and a green Suburban and raise a rifle.

"Down!" I shouted, diving for the sand behind a rock planter.

I heard two sharp cracks. My heart raced. I lay flat in the warm sand, no longer pining for home. I had another more pressing worry.

"Pepper," I screamed and glanced around to see the dog combat-crawling toward me through the deep sand. The row of flowering bushes between the marina and the beach concealed him from view of the parking lot. I had forgotten the Semmerling in the combi. Apparently I needed it on the beach.

When I heard the sound of a vehicle starting up and squealing out of the parking lot, I sat up and poked my head around the planter. The tail end of the Suburban raced out of the marina.

"JadeAnne...pssst, JadeAnne. You two all right?" Aníbal's whisper came from a few feet away. I turned and saw him pulling himself along the sand in the same crawl the dog had used.

"Yeah, you?" I could see him now. One leg dragged, a red smear spread behind him like jam on bread.

"I'll live. Grazed my calf. He was shooting low. I felt the wind from the first slug. I think it was only a warning, JadeAnne."

"Warning? What, to keep the dog on a leash?" I snorted.

"Did you get a look at him?"

"No, dammit. I didn't see his face. I just saw the movement behind you when I looked to see where you were. Some sort of rifle. He was driving a green Suburban."

I looked back at the lot where the vehicle had been. The silver car was still in place. It was a late model sedan, and I looked for a red leaf dangling from the mirror. Nothing. Nissan Man probably removed it anyway.

"Seriously, Aníbal, who would be warning us? And of what?" I demanded. "Don't move. I need to look at that." I leaned in to inspect Aníbal's wound. Dark red blood oozed out of it, but he was right, it wasn't serious, at least if it was attended to right away. Infection is always a problem in the tropics.

"We've got to get back. Can you walk?" I pulled off my t-shirt and wiped the coagulating blood off Aníbal's leg with spit. Luckily the ooze was slowing.

"Help me up." He reached out his hand for support. I pulled him to his feet. "Hmm, yeah, I can walk. I'll call Polo."

"You have a phone? Call. You wouldn't happen to have a gun, would you?"

"In my bag in the penthouse."

"I don't understand how everyone is carrying a gun. How do you get them over the border? I mean, you flew, didn't you?"

"Hold on." Aníbal held up his palm while the phone connected. "Yeah, it's me. I need you to send someone to get us at the marina." He listened. "Uh-huh…yeah…uh-huh. No. You need to come now. Look, Lura, I don't want to alarm you, but I just got shot." I could hear Lura screeching over the cellular. "No, Lu, I'm fine, just a skin wound. Lemme speak to Polo. Now."

Aníbal gave Polo a quick rundown of the shooting and hung up. "Someone will be here in a couple of minutes. You can go back if you want."

"What? Are you out of your mind? There's no cover on the beach. I don't want to get shot."

"JadeAnne, it was a warning. They won't shoot you, whoever they are. It's bad for business. Get your exercise."

CHAPTER ELEVEN

Cartel Rivalry

Aguirre's man loaded Aníbal into his SUV after binding the gunshot wound with a strip of cloth, and Pepper and I piled in after him. The beach had lost its appeal, and anyway it was late, and I didn't want to make a bad impression by showing up after seven-thirty. We rode the short distance to the hotel in silence.

"I'm going to fill an overnight bag, Ani. Will you be okay?"

"Yeah, sure. I'll see you up there. Better hurry. It's seven." He held his smartphone up for me to see.

Pepper and I scooted to the VW and crammed some essentials and the dog food into a carry-on bag. Pepper was delighted to run to the service elevator once I'd locked up, although he looked disappointed the scavenging mutts were gone. I decided to skip the shower. Instead, I tossed the bag I packed for my stay at Aguirre's penthouse on my bed when we got to our room and gave Pepper some food and a fresh bowl of water then threw on a clean t-shirt after a swipe with a wet washcloth.

"I'll be back later, boy." I blew him a kiss.

Brilliant late sun lit the floor-to-ceiling windows and

blinded me as I entered Aguirre's office. When I could see again, I found the atmosphere thick with tension. Aníbal lay stretched out on a couch, still in his running clothes, a bulky bandage wrapped his thigh. Lura stood gazing out the window into the sunset, while Aguirre perched on the corner of his massive blond desk frowning at his folded hands.

"*Buenas tardes*, all. Aníbal, what did the doctor say?"

"Have to amputate." He managed a weak smile.

"At the neck," Lura added, turning to face us. Her smile was missing.

"Have you two briefed Polo yet?" I looked at Lura.

"No. We waited for you,"

"Let's have at it, then."

Aguirre raised his head, silently took measure of each of us, and shrugged. "I—"

"Polito, that wasn't funny. You could have killed us," Lura shrieked.

"What the fuck are you up to, Polo?" Aníbal shouted over Lura.

"Who is following us, Senator? No lies this time. Antonio and Geraldo were a red herring, weren't they?" I demanded.

"*¡Espérense!* Hold on. There were no jokes, Lura. I don't know what you are talking about. Let me address Miss Stone." He looked over at me. "I instructed Antonio to take the grey truck and follow you to Las Peñas. He was to make sure you left my estate safely. I know nothing about Geraldo, or red *peces*."

"I find it hard to believe, Polo. They were together, and they were shooting at us." Lura dropped her voice to a hoarse whisper.

"What?" Polo looked genuinely surprised.

Lura had turned around toward the sunset again. Her tone was flat. "I'm sorry, Cuz, I shot them. Your new truck crashed down the cliff." She spun around to face Polo. "I know you loved your truck."

Polo's expression went from stunned to angry. "Lura, you killed my men *y destruiste mi propiedad*? What *capricho es esto*?"

"So sue me. Better yet, take the bribe from Danny. You can buy a fleet of pickups," she shouted with a dismissive gesture and stomped to the couch, flinging herself next to Aníbal, a pout on her face.

"Ouch, Lura, be care—"

"Shut up Ani," she hissed. "Poli, do you think I like shooting people? You dumb ass. You thought we'd go down without a fight?"

"*Cálmate*," he snapped. "Get one thing straight, little cousin. I had no idea you were going to drag Aníbal here today. As I recall, I expressly forbade you to come to Ixtapa."

"So this was all to get rid of JadeAnne then," she said with a snide whine in her voice.

"Lura, *cállete*. Aníbal, tell me what happened," he ordered.

Aníbal described what he saw of the attack. I filled in the gaps. Aguirre leaned toward me when I described the green van and gestured for me to stop talking. I paused, feeling slightly affronted, but he made a call to his security, asking to have the wreck checked out as soon as it was light enough to get down the cliff and then turned back to me.

"I swear on the grave of my wife and children I did not order my men to harm you. I will have your combi repaired and will loan you a car while you are a guest in Zihuatanejo."

"That would be nice, Senator, but why fix the bullet holes in my bus if I'm not going to live long enough to appreciate it? I want to know who is following us. You claim not to know the green vehicle shooters. So who is driving the silver Nissan?"

Lura's lips tightened and she shot a sideways glance at Aníbal. "A silver Nissan? I didn't see any silver Nissan."

"No, you were too busy being an ass when he picked us up," countered Aníbal.

Lura sighed and turned away.

I went on, "Lura, he was pulled off the road just beyond the shootout. I saw the car again in Playa Azul, and we saw him outside of Lagunillas while you napped." I reported the details of the surveillance. "When I saw his face, I realized I'd seen him in the hotel by the pool while you were swimming. The man reclined on a lounge on the far side of the pool, smoking."

"Oh, yeah. Nice looking guy," Lura said.

"Yeah. And wearing the same boots he wore when he followed us to Sunset Point last night."

"What?" Aguirre exclaimed.

"We saw bootprints and Delicado butts. Fresh butts. It didn't register at the time, but the man in Playa Azul was wearing black boots and smoking. Odd for a sunbather, wouldn't you say?"

The room fell silent, and I observed the faces surrounding me. Lura's hand went to her brow, and she eyed Aguirre. Aníbal looked away. Aguirre looked guilty as hell.

"What's going on here?" I asked.

No one answered. The shadowed, mote-laced atmosphere sizzled. I had no doubt the Aguirres knew Nissan Man.

Aguirre paced in front of his desk while I talked, pushing his fist into his palm. Now he went to his chair and sat down heavily.

The sun dropped below the horizon and the shadows deepened in the corners. Ethereal layers of color glowed across the horizon outside the picture windows.

"I don't have a man driving a silver Nissan. What did he look like?"

With Aníbal's help, I described the man. Polo denied any involvement with Nissan Man, the men in green vehicles, or his own men. A pack of lies.

"But you think Danny is after me?" Lura said.

"Lura, we weren't going to talk about your personal problems outside of the family."

"Stuff it, Polo. My new friend has had her life threatened, my cousin has been shot, and I killed two men. I'm pissed off. Tell them what you told me."

Aguirre held his head in his hands again. He didn't speak right away. The silence in the dark room was relieved only by the muffled sound of the surf.

"This is a difficult time for me. *Presión* is being applied to sway my vote on the energy bill coming up. My colleagues are divided in opinion, and Daniel wants my vote. He has offered me shares in the consortium expected to bid for PEMEX if full privatization is passed. When I declined, he added a cash bonus, but I am already wealthy without selling my country into the hands of foreigners. When I still refused, he threatened to ruin me. They killed my Maria and the children." Aguirre's voice caught in his throat.

I gasped.

Aguirre sucked in his breath and continued in a low voice. "Worthington doesn't have the clout to disrupt my farm, although he can inconvenience certain of my banking arrangements. He can't kill me until after the vote, but he can take away the rest of my family." He looked at Lura.

"I'm his wife. Danny loves me."

"Your husband loves money and power, Lura, and you have influence with me, or so he imagines. Why will you not believe me?"

Aguirre was right on. I wondered if I ought to tell them Worthington had hired me. "Okay, Worthington knows the family history. So why did some guy shoot Aníbal?" I interrupted. "There's something else, isn't there?"

"You surprise me with your perception, Miss Stone." He glared at me for a moment, letting the irony in his tone sink in.

Had Aguirre found out who I was?

He continued. "Yes, there is something else. Purely business, not family. Arturo Rodriguez has had some setbacks over the last few years. Our president and the army, working with your DEA, has stopped production on many of his poppy farms. To compensate, he has diversified into new areas of commerce, but his business acumen is poor and he has made some bad investments. He is overextended."

"So?" I asked.

"So I have tried to assist him by buying up his bankrupt holdings, including some of his farms, mortgaged through Daniel's bank."

Was that a smirk on Aguirre's face?

"To date, I have added ten thousand hectares to the Aguirre estate along the Michoacán/Guerrero border."

"Rodriguez doesn't like you much, I guess."

"The Rodriguez family has controlled Zihuatanejo for sixty years. His father fancied himself a Spanish Don and didn't have the foresight to see that turismo and commerce were the futuro here. When Arturo took over, most of Zihuatanejo was built."

"I was telling JadeAnne about the marinas and the golf course," Aníbal added.

"Ah, yes. But there is more, Aníbal. Do you know that sixty percent of the opium poppies grown in Mexico are grown in Guerrero?"

Lura interrupted. "Poli. Are you telling me you've gone into heroin production?"

"No, cousin." Aguirre's voice sounded disgusted. "Aguirre Enterprises has converted poppy cultivation to tropical fruit production in the wetter regions and agave in the dryer mountains on the lands acquired from Rodriguez."

"Are you implying Rodriguez tried to hit us today?" I looked at Aníbal. "If you're being straight with us about everything, Senator, then maybe the green van this morning was Rodriguez's, not Worthington's. Maybe the Nissan is a Rodriguez tail. But why would he put a tail on your family— or me? Isn't kidnapping a popular form of coercion with the narcos?"

A light flashed on Aguirre's desk phone. He picked up the receiver, listened for a moment, and hung up. "You have a message waiting with the concierge in the lobby, Miss Stone."

"Thank you." I smiled. It must be eight o'clock. "I've been waiting for this call. May we adjourn this meeting until later?"

The shadows distorted Aguirre's expression. He forced a smile, which more resembled a grimace, and excused me. Did he suspect I was investigating his family? The feeling I'd been played gut-punched me.

Lura, sulking, said nothing, and Aníbal stood up as I started for the door.

"I'll go down with you."

We rode the private elevator to the lobby without speaking. I noticed a trend. Whenever I wanted to get away from the Aguirre clan, Aníbal went with me. Could he be watching my movements for Aguirre? Nothing Aguirre said answered my questions. I didn't believe he was telling the whole truth about any of it. And after their strange reactions to my Nissan Man story, I suspected Lura and Aníbal too. Not a lot of allies here. Who said, "Keep your friends close and your enemies closer"? I would be sad if Aníbal turned out to be an enemy.

The elevator doors opened, and I scanned the lobby as we stepped out. A stocky guest moving quickly caught my eye, and I swiveled toward the main entry in time to see a glimpse of the man from the Nissan slipping into the garden.

"Aníbal, would Rodriguez dare to send personnel into your brother's hotel?"

"No way. Polo has tight security here. All local boys—went to school together. Ixtapa/Zihuatanejo is small. If it was Rodriguez today, we'll know tomorrow. Why?"

"The Nissan man just walked out the door."

At the desk, I retrieved my message, a telephone number as promised. I asked for a pay phone and the attendant directed me to an alcove near the bar with a bank of telephones, some vending machines, and restrooms.

"I'm going to the bar," Aníbal announced. "Meet me when you're done. I'll buy you a drink before dinner."

I nodded, turned my back to the young man, picked up the receiver and inserted my calling card, then punched in the numbers on the slip of paper. The alcove was empty as I listened to rings, beeps, and clicks as the call switched from circuit to circuit.

"Yeah," said Dex.

"It's me."

"So, how's your Mexican vacation?"

"Just wonderful. I've been meeting some interesting people. The weather's been hot, though."

"How hot?"

I recounted the events of the last two days and described the man tailing us, giving information about the vehicles and license plate numbers I'd managed to memorize.

"And, Dex, check out the Aguirre clan, if you can. Lura's maiden name is Linda Aguirre. Aníbal may or may not be an Aguirre. He went to UCLA and graduated in 2000 or thereabouts. There's something fishy with these two. Lura is packing a Glock 29, and they have some sophisticated surveillance communication. Now, tell me your story."

Dex gave me a brief rundown of his Baja adventure.

They'd arrived just in time to see a tiny blonde woman toss her gear into the trunk of a car and roar off. Dex and Penn, thinking she was making off with their salvage, chased her to Puertocitos, where the woman left in a private plane. It was scuba gear in the trunk, but they saw she hadn't carried anything onto the plane.

"A vanload of Mexicans, obviously in a hurry, caught up to her at the airport and started firing."

"Wait a minute. Describe the men with the guns."

"JadeAnne, they were Mexicans with guns, and I got in the way. I didn't get much of a look at them. They screamed off when Penn and I started shooting. The woman was airborne by then."

"Their van? What kind? What color?"

"Um, let's see. A dark color. It was dark green, a dark green Ford. I didn't get a plate. I saw three guys jump in, so there were at least four counting the driver."

"Dex, a dark green van attacked us this morning. I thought it was Aguirre's, but it's pretty strange, don't you think?" I recounted the information I had gathered about Worthington and the coming Senate session. "Aguirre may not be lying."

"I don't see the connection, Jade. Some skank tried to get my salvage, and some armed dudes wanted to steal it."

"What did she look like?"

"I don't know. Short. Blonde."

"Like this?" I fiddled with my phone until I found my photo of Lura and sent it. Dex remained quiet for a few moments.

"Doesn't that beat hell. This is bad news. For whatever reason, Worthington is gunning for his wife." He paused. "I want you to come home."

"Fat chance. I'm going to Sally's tomorrow as planned, and I'm staying for the next two weeks. I'm on vacation, Bubba. I found my missing person and earned my salary.

Piña coladas and playas here I come."

Dex knew better than to argue, but he wasn't assuaged. "Okay, if you refuse to come home, I want you to watch these people without getting killed. Call the cell immediately if anyone goes anywhere. I'll arrive in two days. I'm going to do a bit of research."

"Where are you?"

"At an airport." The line went dead.

I slumped into the wall, weak, the fight knocked out of me. No "Hi, how are 'ya?" No "Gee I miss you." No "I love you." Not even a goodbye. I still held the receiver in my hand, confused and trying not to think about it as a wave of sadness washed through me. A woman passed by on the way to the ladies' room and passed by again a few minutes later going the opposite direction, giving me a disapproving glance. As I hung up the phone, I peripherally saw two groups arrive with luggage and approach the registration area. A couple walked toward the door with their bags. I needed to get a grip on myself and shook my head to clear it, sucking in a deep breath. As I refocused, Aníbal rushed across the lobby. Had Nissan Man come back? I clutched my purse and chased after him.

I ran out to the curb and scanned the street and the parking lot for his silhouette. A taxi was moving off toward the south end of Ixtapa Boulevard, but it was too far away to be carrying Aníbal. I turned back toward the entrance and noticed someone in the trees that shielded the grounds from the street. It was too dark to identify the shadow. I skulked after it just in case it turned out to be an enemy. Whoever the enemy was.

In the trees, the path turned. Tiki torches lit it every few feet, illuminating a small patch of cobbled stones and garden in their glow. I heard footsteps clattering on the stones ahead. It was not Aníbal, I was sure, because his running shoes would be almost silent on this pavement. The path forked. A signpost told me I could reach the waterfall if I took the branch, or would find the swimming pool if I continued on straight. I chose the waterfall path. It would probably be darker by the falls than around the pool, better cover for the bad guy. The runner in the hard-soled shoes would probably not want to be spotted by Aníbal who was presumably on his tail.

While I deliberated, the footsteps grew fainter and then silent. I sprinted around the next curves in the path, listening to the splashing of the water from the falls and slowed down, skirting the puddles of light. Around the next bend, the path dipped, and cobblestones gave way to packed sand lined in volcanic rock, marking the soft, damp edge of a pond.

I studied the ground under the first torch. A bootprint was distinctly visible. I decided to chance it, stepped into the light, and crouched to study the print. Up close, it was an exact match for the print at the promontory. How many people wear boots at a beach resort in the tropics?

I sprang up and ran as fast as I could through the garden, entering the pool area, which, as I expected, was brightly lit. A few people were swimming, and several groups sat at the palapa bar in the patio. Four pathways led away from the pool. I took off down the darkest, but ended up at one of the restaurants and returned to the pool. I'd lost the trail.

I went back to the hotel and let myself up the private elevator with the key card. I would tell Aníbal I looked for him. The penthouse was quiet but well-lit. I strolled down the gallery admiring the artwork. If I were rich, I'd invest in art, too. I would have a Queen Anne farmhouse on an oak-studded knoll overlooking the Petaluma River, with a huge organic herb garden surrounding it. In the back I would have a conservatory for my orchids, and the Sarasvati would be moored at my private dock on the river. I forgot to ask Dex if he'd checked on the flowers. I was going to miss the dendrochilum's pendulous spirals of crystalline white blooms this year.

I reached the guest wing and opened the hallway door. Loud music blared from Lura's closed door. No light showed under Aníbal's door, but my door stood open, and Pepper sat just inside. He jumped up and gave me a lick on my face when I came into the room. I tossed my purse on the bed and dropped down to give him a hug.

"Knock, knock." It was Aníbal.

"Hi. I looked for you, but you disappeared."

"You were right. The man from the Nissan was in the hotel."

"You chased him. I tried to follow you."

"Yeah, he ran into the garden. It was dark. I lost him."

"I'm certain Nissan Man was on Polo's estate. I found a bootprint on the path that matches the ones I found at the Point. He's got to be Polo's man."

"For whatever that's worth." Did I detect something in Aníbal's voice?

"Could he be following you, or better yet, Lura?"

"JadeAnne, why would my brother have us followed?" Aníbal asked.

I eyed the handsome young man. His expression was angelic, practiced, but his eyes were wary. "You tell me, Aníbal."

"What do you mean?"

I backed off. I'd do better if I didn't tip my hand too soon. "Well, Polo is a grower and smuggler, maybe he's being watched by the government. You said the license plate was government issue."

"Maybe. I doubt it, though. I go for the Rodriguez angle, personally."

"Then you're contradicting yourself. If he's Rodriguez's man, he wouldn't be in the hotel. And how do you account for the Mexico City license plate?"

"Okay, he's an outside man brought in from La Capital.

Who do you think he is?"

"Not Rodriguez's man. Hey, it's nine. I've got to get showered and dressed for dinner. Get outta here. We can talk later." A little current of electricity shot up my spine as I pushed him out of the room and closed the door.

As Polo's guests, the staff treated us like visiting dignitaries in elegant Bogart's. My whole *pompano mojo de ajo* was superbly cooked, lightly crisped outside and moist and flaky inside. The fish was served with a crisp green salad, fresh sautéed vegetables, and some sort of potato fritter. A California Fumé Blanc set off the delicate fish to perfection. For dessert, I tried the rich house *flan* with *cajeta crepes*. When we were finished, and I was sure I would never move again, let alone eat another meal, Aguirre suggested we stroll through the gardens before going to Christine's.

"Perhaps we can have a brandy by the pool and continue our discussion. I believe Miss Stone has asked some questions, which were not answered at our meeting this evening."

He was right. We'd talked little over dinner, and I wanted to get to some truth.

Aguirre guided me ahead and pointed out features of the grounds. He was proud of his natural-looking pool and the area for the kids. I didn't let on I'd seen any of this and complimented his designs and ideas, not hard to do as the grounds were lovely. We passed the footprint and I stopped.

"The garden has such magic at night. I so prefer the natural pathway to a more formal design, don't you, Aníbal?" I waved toward the footprint. Aníbal caught my hint and inspected the path in the direction I gestured. Aguirre led us on past his waterfall, and then seated us at a reserved table by the pool and ordered after-dinner drinks.

"Rodriguez isn't following you, Ms. Stone. My associates keep me informed of his movements, including the movements of his employees. Rodriguez is not involved in today's incidents. None of them. He would not hit me on my property. He would be crushed."

The waiter approached with our order, and Aguirre fell silent. When the drinks sat on the table and the chit had been signed, he continued. "As for our disagreements, our fight has been through the city councils and permitting offices so far. He controls Zihuatanejo's city council and sits on the Ixtapa design review board. His influence holds things back and costs a ransom in payoffs. His people are not loyal."

"Are yours, Cuz?" Lura received a menacing frown from Aguirre in response. "Let's drink to Polo's soldiers." She raised her glass.

"Shut-up, Lura. Let Polo finish."

"Thank you, Aníbal. I was saying that there has been little violence, and only among some of the low level personnel, until recently."

"Recently? What happened?" I asked.

"Rodriguez tried to bribe information out of two of my men. Both refused him and reported to me. Both are dead, but their deaths were recorded as accidents—one fishing and one on the highway. I do not take the killing of my men lightly, so I foreclosed on the mortgage of one of his farms. I own the local bank, you see." He paused, searching for the correct word. "I heard through the grape-news—"

"Grapevine," Lura corrected.

"I heard through the grapevine he is very angry and planning revenge. Grapevine. You Americans get information in odd ways." His eyes crinkled into a smile.

"I heearrd it through the grapevine, just how much longer would you beee mine," Lura sang loudly, and gazed off into the dark garden, a sly look on her face.

"Lura, we're having a discussion here," Aníbal

exclaimed. When he looked to see what she was staring at, however, he shot up out of his chair and dashed out of the well-lit pool area, into the shadows. I recognized the shape of one of the shadows and knew it was Nissan Man. Lura had seen him, too. And recognized him.

"You know who he is, don't you?" I confronted her.

"Who?" She turned toward me with an innocent smile. "I thought I saw something in the bushes. Ani," she called. "Ani, come back."

"My cousin is more stubborn than a *burro* and often just as stupid. Don't bother yourself, Miss Stone, she won't say any more. If she does, it will be a lie."

Aguirre frowned.

"Polo, you are such a jerk. I didn't see anyone. I don't know anyone here. I want to go to Christine's. Come on, Poli. Let's go." She tugged on his arm. She pouted and stood up. "You promised."

He let out an exasperated breath. "That I did." He excused himself from the table. The cousins walked off arm-in-arm toward the hotel. I watched them until they disappeared around a bend in the garden.

If Polo could be believed, Rodriguez was out to get him, but wasn't watching them or attacking on Polo's turf. I couldn't see any way Rodriguez could know about me, or Aníbal, for that matter. The shooter this afternoon knew one of us. He may have been a lousy shot, but he had aimed at Aníbal. Maybe it was time to have a little chat with my client. Everyone had left the table, so I thought I might as well put in a call to Worthington. My report was overdue.

I needed to organize my thoughts and wandered out to the beach to think while I walked. I found the usual lounges, another bar or a snack shop, thatched umbrellas, and sand chairs. Two people were talking nearby. Farther out, I saw lovers embracing.

The surf purred under the balmy sky. The night smelled

of damp greenery and the sea, laced with the faint odor of Malathion, which accounted for why I hadn't been bothered by mosquitoes. I walked along the beach until I was parallel with the doors into the hotel and sat down under an umbrella. The rising moon cast a shimmering reflection on the calm ocean. It had been a long day. I was tired. After I made the call, I could turn in. But I couldn't keep my mind on task. It spun with problems: the Aguirres, Dex, and most disturbingly, just how attractive I found Aníbal.

I gave up, heaved out of the sand chair, and headed to the phones.

CHAPTER TWELVE

Nissan Man

"Daniel Worthington? JadeAnne Stone here."

"Have you found her?" Worthington's tone sounded impatient.

"Let's not mince words, Mr. Worthington. You know where your wife is. She was never missing. She and Senator Aguirre are cousins. What other omissions did you make?"

"What are you implying?" His voice sounded hard. "My wife has not contacted me in a month. Her office still has no word of her."

"Her office said she's on vacation."

"Is she with Polo?"

"Why did you fail to mention Lura's background to me?"

"Senator Aguirre and I do not see eye-to-eye. I assumed my wife was keeping her distance from that bastard, just like I told her to."

"And you lied about the photo. You knew the Senator was under the—"

"Where is she?" he interrupted.

"If you want your wife, Mr. Worthington, you'll have to level with me."

"I paid you."

I ignored him. "First, do you have another investigator on this case?" Nissan Man might be Worthington's. If so, he already knew where Lura was.

"Why do you ask?"

He was evading the question.

"I'm being followed. The man comes out of Mexico City. Don't hand me any more lies." I shook my finger at the telephone. "By the way, I had to shoot your green van off the highway when your men attacked me. Oh, but you already know because your investigator would have reported by now."

Worthington shouted, "You did what? I had nothing to do with that."

"Is that so?" I answered.

Worthington was silent for a moment. I could almost hear his eye ticcing away.

"What did Aguirre say about me?"

"He told me all about your consortium and how you threatened him to make him vote for privatization. Why didn't you tell me about this?"

"No. Aguirre lied to you. He lied about Lura." Panic had replaced the impatience in his voice.

"Oh, Lura is not his cousin? I think you're lying." I'd knocked him off guard. "Why did you send me to him with the tip about the Krystal if you didn't want me to meet him?"

"I thought he might have her."

"Well, who else might have her?" Two can play this game. "I never got the list of your friends. In addition, Mr. Worthington, I want the names of your partners in the consortium and where I can reach them." As if that would happen. "And call off your dogs. I see another green van, I'm off the case, and you can kiss your fifty grand goodbye. By the way, you owe my firm five hundred forty-three dollars and twenty seven cents in out-of-pocket expenses."

I hung up and headed for the elevator; I didn't expect to get the information or the money, but I had called his bluff.

When I stepped out of the elevator, Pepper bounded to me yelping and wagging his tail wildly as though weeks not hours had passed.

I reached down to pet him. "Peppi. Hello boy. How's my good doggie?" The feel of his smooth fur and sturdy body reassured me, and the thought flickered through my mind: folks without dogs miss something deep, primal. My dog is my touchstone, my comfort I mused while I pulled on a pair of black spandex pants, a dusky purple-colored shirt, and my running shoes. A woman alone on the beach with a large dog may not be invisible, but I was sure going to try to fade into the shadows. I'd find out who this square-headed man was, and it wouldn't kill me. I remembered the Semmerling this time. Fastening the holster at my waist, I placed the little pistol so it rested in the small of my back under the oversized t-shirt. Pepper paced in front of the door, ready for action.

I patted my pockets: elevator key, phone, pesos. Water in my bottle. Leash. "Ready, Pepper? Let's go."

We rode down to the service patio and stepped into the night. I slinked around the building in the shadows with Pepper on a short leash until we hit the beach. I prayed the coast was clear but it was too dark to see anyone watching. I released the dog, and we jogged along the seashore. Pepper bounded off, picked up a hefty piece of driftwood, and pranced back. He danced, grinning with the stick in his mouth, enticing me to throw it.

After a while, my arm tired from the effort of heaving the waterlogged wood down the beach, and I settled onto a large snag half-buried in the sand. Pepper chased the waves as they tumbled in and rushed out.

Rejoining me at the snag, he leaned into my back, panting. I watched the waves in the moonlight, and Pepper watched the beach. It felt almost like a vacation, sitting in the cool sand by the quiet sea under the stars, except that I had an uncomfortable holster on and couldn't relax knowing there were killers lurking out there who might want me dead.

Pepper stiffened and sniffed the air. He stood up and growled. I dove for the sand behind the driftwood, pulling out my gun and softly whistling the dog into a crouch. I couldn't see anyone, but I wasn't taking chances. We waited for a few moments, both scanning the beach. Then my eyes caught movement along the shrubbery bordering the Krystal's gardens. A shadow edged toward us but kept close to the landscaping. When the shadow reached the fence separating the Krystal from the next hotel, it stepped away from the hedging and became silhouetted against the tiki torches.

The body looked square and short in the distance, and moved with surprising grace through the sand, avoiding the lights, sticking to the dark patches like a stalker. The figure reached the last of the lights and struck out across the beach, advancing close enough I could recognize it as a man—a man coming after me. I felt his intent like a weight pressing down on me, getting heavier as his bulk came closer. He was a black hole backlit by the lights of the distant hotel.

His head rotated, scanning the beach or listening for the muffled rhythm of footfalls on the packed sand. I guessed he didn't know my exact position, but he suddenly turned south and trudged along the layer of deep sand at the top of the beach until he was even with my driftwood snag seventy or eighty feet away. He stopped and reached under his cuff into his boot. A gleam of moonlight reflected in his hand as he straightened up and turned to face me. I cocked my gun.

I now knew why Nissan Man wore boots in the tropics. Pepper, on guard, crouched like a spring ready to release. The man moved closer, still faintly backlit by the landlocked lights, making him an easy target. What an idiot. An amateur.

He was ten yards away. I could shoot him and be done with it but wasn't sure I wanted to risk getting old in a Mexican jail. Anyway, I needed some answers: for instance, who the hell did he work for? Come on, sucker, another yard and I've got you.

Nissan Man advanced cautiously and swung toward me, arms flowing up into a shooting stance. "Police. Come—" he shouted in Spanish as Pepper leaped from behind the snag and knocked him over. He landed on his side with his arm pinned under his body in the sand, his gun lying useless in his immobilized hand. Pepper snarled in his face, and I scrambled from behind the snag and trained my gun on his forehead.

"Drop it," I demanded in English. Nissan Man let go of the gun.

"Push it away with your other hand."

He reached across his chest and inched the gun away, then rolled onto his back. I darted to the revolver and snatched it out of the sand.

"Okay, sit up." Pepper was still snarling. "Extend your legs in front of you and keep your hands over your head."

He complied, keeping silent.

"Why are you following me?" I demanded.

The man answered in English. "Control your dog and lower your gun. I'm AFI, Agencia Federal de Investigación, Señorita Stone. My credentials are in my pocket." He reached toward his back pocket. "May I?"

I whistled another tone and Pepper took the man's wrist gently and held it.

"I don't think so. Roll over. I'll get them."

He rolled enough for me to pull the badge out of his pocket. I stepped back to the snag, picked up Pepper's leash to unclip the mini flashlight, and quickly inspected the badge and ID card. "Esteban Eduardo Grijalves Nuñez." The photo matched the man in front of me. AFI. Grijalves? Where'd I hear that name before?

"Why are you following me, Grijalves?" And how do you know my name? I lowered the gun to a spot in front of his boots, realizing what a ridiculous question that was. Of course. There was a record of my crossing the border, and Grijalves was the name I heard Aguirre use on the telephone with Lura. They all knew him.

"Zocer. I go by Zocer. I am not investigating you, but I do know a number of things about you. I do not know, however, why you are consorting with known criminals. What are you doing with Aguirre?"

"You're investigating Aguirre? What for? It can't be drugs. Your division wouldn't be interested in that, would it?"

"¡*Ay!* Let me up. I will be happy to share my purpose with you once I have determined your purpose."

"Ah, the proverbial Mexican standoff. Yeah, get up." I retrained the gun on him. "March," I ordered and waved my hand toward the hotel.

I made Nissan Man stay in the deep sand, forcing us both to trudge along slowly until we were directly in front of the Krystal. Then I directed him to the bar in the patio where a combo played jazzy renditions of bubblegum pop. At the bar, I dumped the clip from the gun and handed it back to him.

"Put that back in your boot, Grijalves, and take that table over there." I waved to the empty places by the pool.

Once we sat down, I signaled for the waiter, who approached us, eyeing Pepper with obvious trepidation, and took our orders.

"You can pick this up on your expense account." I smiled sweetly at the agent.

The drinks arrived. "Now, Agent Grijalves, I ask you again, why are you following me?"

"What is your interest in the Aguirre family?"

"I don't have any interest in the Aguirre family. What's yours?"

"I don't believe you are a simple tourist come to enjoy our lovely beaches, Señorita Stone. You are armed and travel with a highly trained dog. You are carrying a weapon without a permit. I can arrest you for that."

I couldn't refute it. I'd pulled my gun and dog on him. Dex always said a partial truth was better than no truth at all so I said, "Aguirre kidnapped me off the highway," sidestepping exactly why I was in Mexico in the first place with a gun and a highly trained guard dog.

"I am not the only person to question your presence here. The Aguirre family has commented that you may not be the visitor you claim to be."

"Oh, and Lura and Aníbal are amateurs. Which one of them are you working with?" Oh, duh. How did I miss that?

"He's working with Lura."

Aníbal's voice startled me, and I whipped around to see him pull a chair over from the next table and sit down.

"JadeAnne's a P.I. out of California, Zocer. I traced it through her California gun permit." How'd he get that?

"So what are you doing here, JadeAnne?" His mouth turned down and his eyes moistened, as though he had been let down somehow.

"I was hoping to take a vacation until I got hijacked by your brother's henchmen. What's Lura doing?"

"She's Secret Service, FCD Financial Crimes Division. She's investigating corporate money laundering. Zocer has been following the money from a drug cartel, Beltrán-Leyva Organization. Their investigations intersected."

"And Aguirre is involved. Which cartel does he work for?"

"No. On the contrary, he got wind of the situation and tipped off AFI. It has long been known Americans launder illegal gains through Mexican banks. That's part of what

Lura does. She investigates banks and counterfeiting rings."

My jaw dropped. It was all about the money. What a cliché. "She's investigating her husband. The Senator wasn't lying, was he? The green van: Worthington. And I bet Lura's investigation led her to CalMex a month ago," I said more to myself than to the men.

The AFI agent nodded to Aníbal's glance. "She didn't have any proof. That's why FCD and AFI hooked up. Zocer has information and Lura has access."

"Worthington must have realized she was on to him. That's what he threatened your brother with Lura's death. But he has to get his hands on her first."

Aníbal grunted.

I continued, "But he can't because you're all protecting her. That's where I come in." I recounted the meetings and telephone calls with Worthington, including my conversation with him earlier. "I couldn't turn her over to him. I knew he was in the middle of something fishy."

"I'm going to believe you, JadeAnne. *Bienvenidos* to our team." Zocer's intense look bored into me. Not an engraved invitation.

I nodded.

"Lura thinks her husband is laundering profits from the illegal activities of a couple of energy and oil corporations to fund the takeover of PEMEX," Aníbal said. "We're all pretty sure he's laundering drug money."

"CalMex is subject to the same laws in or out of the country, but reporting enforcement is much harder offshore even though your government has agreements with mine," Zocer said.

"And CalMex has already been dinged a couple million in fines since the Money Laundering Control Act was passed back in the '80s." Aníbal took a pull off his beer the waiter had delivered.

He lowered his voice. "It's still sketchy how the deal

works, but money appears to be moving from the corporations in question through a shell corporation to Worthington's bank in Panama. The U.S. doesn't have any agreements with Panama, and the Panamanian government has tight banking secrecy."

"So how is CalMex involved? I don't get laundering," I asked.

"The money is coming back to CalMex in the form of loans and letters of credit. The really tricky part is funds from Mexican drug cartels, *especificáis* from the *heroína* here in Guerrero, are funneling into a Texas *empresa* and coming out clean. We suspect the conspiracy involves high-level government oficiales," Zocer answered.

"How high?"

Aníbal and Zocer exchanged a look. *"¡Quién sabe!"*

Lura wandered out from the disco and joined us, greeting Zocer warmly. She showed me her credentials and listened quietly while we briefed her on the evening's events. No longer a wild, petulant rich girl, she presented herself as a professional.

While Lura talked, I took the opportunity to observe Zocer. He was a handsome man with amber doe-eyes framed in long dark lashes. I thought he might be several years older, closer to forty than thirty.

He replied to something Lura said. Zocer's English was not perfect but his accent charmed me, and he was quite articulate. I riveted on his full, sensual lips. Kissable. Although stocky, his neck wasn't as thick as the shadows had implied, and his buff body exuded a calm strength. I noticed it on the beach, and I caught myself wondering what he might be like in more intimate surroundings. I forced my attention back to the conversation. I noticed Zocer watching me with a half-smile and a faraway look in his eye. Little prickles of excitement shot through me. Not wise to go there.

"Let's go over to Christine's." Aníbal looked at me. "I'd

like to shake the kinks out of my leg before bed. I'll run Pepper up to the penthouse and meet you there in five."

"Okay, Peppi, you go with Aníbal," I commanded. "Come on, Zocer, let's dance."

"In these shoes? I don't think I can." He looked at his boots.

Lura and I hooted. "Where are you from, Zocer?"

"Guadalajara, why?"

We laughed harder and broke into song. *"I once knew a man from Guadalajara..."* we sang, taking Zocer's hands and pulling him along the path toward the disco. *"In these shoes? Honey, you'd never survive."*

Sweating bodies packed Christine's dance floor, gyrating to the deafening music. Overhead, the lights swirled and blinked in a rainbow of colors. After Aníbal returned from the penthouse, Lura and I took turns dancing with each of the men. I found myself in Aníbal's muscular arms for a slow love ballad. He pulled me close. I could feel the heat of his body. He smelled earthy like a forest and I thought I would melt when he nibbled on my neck and nuzzled my ears. I ran my fingertips across the smoothness of his silk-shirted back. He tensed, then pressed harder into me, his heart beat a staccato against my chest. Familiar wings flapped through my stomach.

The mad whirl of the disco dropped away and transformed to a still, floating place. Electricity arced between us as we swayed in our embrace. I didn't realize the song had ended until the next song boomed out of the speakers and broke our spell.

Zocer sat alone. A new round of drinks covered the tiny table.

"Where's Lura?" I shouted over the music.

He shrugged, jumped up, and grabbed my hand,

dragging me onto the floor for an "oldie" from the radio, something about dancing and sweating. He was delicious to watch. His movements were graceful, like a big cat's. The music changed, and I was in Zocer's arms being led through the steps of a salsa. He twirled and walked me as though he owned my legs. I felt his muscles working under his clothes when he drew me into him. Then he tossed me out again and I wasn't sure my feet touched the floor. Again he pulled me tight and was holding me to him when the music slowed into a sad oldie popularized by Lucero, Mexico's pop diva.

"*Fue un privilegio tu amor*," Zocer crooned along with the singer. He held me tenderly, gazing into my eyes. I sighed and rested my cheek on his shoulder, feeling completely safe for the first time since crossing the border.

"Hey, girlfriend! My turn," Lura cut in.

Disappointed, I strolled back to the table, aware of Aníbal's eyes watching me. I gestured to dance, but he refused in a sulky-sounding voice. Jealous or just exhausted?

"Nah, I'm beat, Jade. My leg hurts. I'm going up to bed."

I was still running on adrenaline. It had been a very long day, and I should have been dead on my feet, but no, I wanted to keep dancing. I felt a little annoyed with Aníbal. He was to his feet when Lura and Zocer threw themselves into their chairs.

"Zocer, you can bunk upstairs with us. There's another room," Aníbal shouted over the hip-hop blaring out of the speakers. "I'm going up."

"Thanks, Aníbal. I could use a bed. I'll go with you. *Buenas noches*, ladies." Zocer started after Aníbal.

"Hey, wait for me, you guys. Don't leave me all alone." Lura took Zocer's hand and the three made their way toward the door.

Aníbal glanced back and beckoned, smiling. "Come on, JadeAnne." The birds fluttered.

Pepper herded us from the elevator to the guest wing. Zocer took the room between me and Aníbal. Now that we were all buddies, we hugged goodnight and closed our separate doors. I couldn't make up my mind which man I liked more. As if it makes much difference, what with Dex landing at the Zihua Airport the day after tomorrow, I thought with a twinge of guilt, but only a little one. After all, Dex hadn't said one personal thing to me on the phone tonight. It was pure business. Was this what I got for accepting the partnership offer?

I refused to spoil an exciting evening with depressing thoughts about Dex and Water Street Investigations. I'd think about the new men in my life. Which one would be for me? Aníbal was young, firm, energetic, and cute. Zocer was solid, calming, romantic, and handsome. Thinking about them aroused me. While I washed up, I fantasized having them both in bed with me, laughing at the unreality of two macho Mexicanos sharing. I made a mental bet. Zocer was probably in with Lura, if her flirting was any indication.

I settled under the sheet and turned off the light. Pepper jumped up and stretched out on the other side of the king bed. The feel of Aníbal in my arms, I fell asleep.

Panicked, I woke and cast my eyes around the room. The night gleamed black and starless outside the window. I must have been dreaming, I thought as the images flooded into my consciousness: Pepper and I were running through a forest. Something, or someone, was after us, but it wasn't clear. I heard shouts, and a cave appeared. We ran inside to hide. I saw a golden trough filled with shining silver coins at the end of the tunnel. I called Pepper's name and we ran toward the treasure but the passageway was thick with black oil. We became mired in the oil. I heard the echoes of the footsteps —pounding, pounding. If we could make it to the treasure, we'd be safe. Pepper foundered, struggling in a viscous puddle sucking at him like quicksand. I slipped on a slick patch and skidded down the passageway, landing on my butt in front of the trough. Faces surrounded me, appearing out of the darkness. The President's mother stepped forward and offered me a hand up. Standing, I was suddenly in the Round Room with the President, the Vice President, the Secretary of State, and the President's father. They had daggers raised and were closing in to strike me. The faces morphed into vampire faces. Blood ran from their teeth, turning black as it dripped from their mouths, soaking the ground with oil.

"JadeAnne, JadeAnne, JadeAnne," they chanted.

I sat up and gasped, shaking my head to dislodge the horrifying image from my mind. I was slick with sweat. As the images faded, I heard the pounding and chanting, "JadeAnne, JadeAnne." Pepper scratched at the door, wagging his tail.

"Huh? What?"

"JadeAnne, it's me, Aníbal. Let me in.!"

My eyes flew open and the dream webs cleared. Well, Well, Well. I grinned ear to ear when I opened the door. "Ani, what a surprise. What time is it?" I blocked his entry into the room with my body.

He drew me to him without a word, circling his arms around me and squeezing. He pushed me into the doorframe, and I felt his muscles ripple through the thin cotton of my nightshirt. He was only dressed in boxers, and I stroked his flawless skin. He bent down and found my lips with his, practically suffocating me with his deep kiss. When he let go, we both gulped for air.

"I forgot to say goodnight."

CHAPTER THIRTEEN

The Habit of Dex

July 30, 2007

"Good morning, Peppi," I whispered, blinking into the cool light filling the room. Pepper sighed and stretched, exposing his belly. Well-trained, I reached over to give him a pat. He thumped his tail against the bed and skooched onto his back for better exposure. I scratched him for a few minutes then swung out of the sheets and crossed the cold tile floor to the bathroom. Remembering my surprise visit from Aníbal, I smiled into the mirror, but the warm, fuzzy memory vanished, replaced with images from the dream: the faces with blood, which turned to oil, dripping from vampire teeth. But last night I woke up because I heard knocking on my door, not running feet. Ani had come to me, hadn't he?

I adjusted the shower temperature and stepped in, letting the hot water run down my body, soothe my sore muscles, and wash the ugly images out of my mind. Yesterday had been a long, stressful day. No wonder I was having nightmares.

I took a deep breath of the steamy air and exhaled. Today I would move to Sally's and start work on the investigation into Worthington. I wrested my attention from the evil dream to my to-do list. Constructive action usually put me right when I was feeling emotionally drained, and hopefully today wouldn't be any different.

First, I'd make an appointment with Lura when she surfaced. She could fill me in on plenty of details, including the list of Worthington's friends. They were hers, too, after all. I hoped she and Zocer had intelligence on the members of Worthington's consortium. I pictured the first family in my mind as I recalled last night's revelations: "...the conspiracy involves high level government officials." I grabbed a fluffy bath sheet and wrapped it around myself. The President conspiring to screw Mexico out of its oil? It was too farfetched, even for my left-leaning political sensibilities.

I glanced at my watch as I snapped it around my wrist. It read 10:00, and I recalled Mexico didn't observe daylight savings so my watch was an hour ahead. Or was it two hours? I'd forgotten if we were on Rocky Mountain or Central time, but either way, there was plenty of time for a run and a swim. Wasn't Aguirre's luncheon invitation for 12:30?

I donned my tiniest bikini and pulled a pair of stretchy yellow short-shorts and a tie-dyed camisole that said *Namaste* over it. My running pocket was already packed from the night before. I added some more pesos and a comb and slung it around my hips, laced up my running shoes, and grabbed a plastic bottle of water off the dresser. I'd dropped my Sigg bottle in the fracas on the beach. Darn. Today I would run by the snag and see if I could find it.

Pepper and I almost knocked Zocer over in the hallway when we burst out of our room.

"Good morning, JadeAnne. I hope you slept well."

"Good morning. I did, thanks. How about you?"

"Yes, I was very comfortable. I am looking for you."

"You found me. What's up? I'm on my way down to the beach to run the dog and take a swim. Want to come?" I glanced down at his feet and noticed that he had traded in the heavy leather boots for a sensible pair of huaraches.

He followed my gaze and laughed. "These are cooler, but not much better for running. I will wait to see you later. Will you be here for lunch?" His eyes gave me an all-over appraisal, and he smiled. *Gotta love those machos.*

"Yeah. I'll be starving by then—what time is it, anyway?" I touched his arm to see his watch, giving myself a little thrill. Again, I felt that sense of safety and well-being.

"It is twenty before ten. Senator Aguirre has loaned me an office with everything I need. I will be working on the investigation when you return. I will like to interview you."

"Okay, I better scoot. Oops, the leash. See ya then, Zocer." I dashed back into the room and found the leash under the bed. Pepper pawed the floor with impatience. "Okay, let's go."

I had forgotten my sunglasses and squinted until my eyes adjusted to the bright glare off the sea. We jogged north because it looked as though there were fewer people that direction. People have such strange reactions to the dog. In Mexico, I had observed, most were afraid of him, but that didn't bother me. I knew Pepper wouldn't harm anyone unless I told him to, whether or not he smelled their fear. Dex had seen to his impeccable training back in the days he'd cared about my safety.

Dex. I choked up and stumbled over a piece of driftwood. *What am I going to do?*

We ran along the packed sand. Dex's and my years together swirled around my mind. Fooling around with Aníbal was not good, I lectured myself. I accepted that things had changed between Dex and me. We weren't very close anymore, even though we lived and worked together. There was almost a generation's difference in our ages, and we'd always had separate interests. Our affair had cooled over the last several years. He was gone too much, and I sensed he had plenty of other women, but Dex was discreet, and I didn't pry. Yes, I love him, I argued with myself, but I didn't want to admit that it was mostly out of habit and fear of being alone.

The shoreline blurred and my feet dragged. I wiped the tears out of my eyes; I didn't want to face it, but if I admitted the truth, I'd lost my passion for Dex. I stopped running and gazed at the glossy waves, breaking and swishing onto shore, lost in thought. Dex had become a favorite old pair of sweats, familiar and comfortable, but shapeless and lacking style, perfect for coffee and the Sunday Chronicle on the deck of the Sarasvati. Aníbal...now he was a man to strut in public.

Pepper and I'd reached the entrance to the marina. Between my thoughts and the smells of salt water, oil, and seaweed conspiring together, I felt weighted down with melancholy again. Dex was another world I just didn't fit into. The run had worked the kinks out of my joints, but my eyes streamed, and my head pounded with all the thinking about Dex, or was that a hangover? I'd slammed back several tequilas in the disco. I felt like I couldn't breathe enough air.

Pepper charged a flock of seagulls quibbling over a dead fish left by the tide. They flew up in a complaining cloud. He looked after the scattering birds. If dogs could laugh... Then he stiff-armed around the fish carcass, snuffling, hackles up, tail swinging.

I sniffed and wiped my face on my t-shirt again. "Come on, joker."

We turned around and headed back toward the hotel, running at an easier pace. Maybe I should have said yes right then when Dex proposed in Piazza San Marco. That had been the turning point, or had it always been a temporary thing? Two years later, we still lived together, if you could call it that. Jeez, we'd only made love twice all year. But in retrospect, I thought, I was happy to be left alone. I'd remained faithful to Dex, but an image of Aníbal's skin, smooth as marble, unblemished by age, floated up into my mind.

Aníbal and Lura waved from lounge chairs back at the Krystal. I waved back and trotted over.

"Hi, kids. How are you today?"

"I'm great. Slept like the dead. Did you love Christine's? We had a blast last night, didn't we, Ani?" Lura's face shone under her lopsided grin.

"I knocked on your door this morning, but missed you. How far'd you run?" Aníbal's smile dissolved my bones, and I sagged onto the end of his lounge.

"To the marina and back. No suspicious green cars there today. I'm going to take a swim before lunch. Would either of you like to join me?"

"When?" Lura glanced toward the ocean with a slight sneer playing across her lips.

"When is lunch? Still twelve-thirty?"

"Polo hasn't said anything, but we'll need time to get ready."

"What time do you have?" I glanced at Aníbal's cellphone tossed on a towel.

He swiped it open. "Close to eleven. We have an hour. I'll race you." Aníbal jumped off his lounge and sprinted toward the ocean.

"Wait. Ani. I have to take my clothes off."

He stopped and turned around. "I'm watching you, babe. Oh, take it off," he called back lewdly.

Lura cracked up and hummed a few bars of the "The Stripper" while I hammed it up, pulling off my shorts and top. Aníbal whistled.

"You caught his attention in that suit, girlfriend. I think my baby cousin likes you."

"You think so?"

"Yep." Lura winked.

Aníbal and I chased each other across the hot sand to the water. Pepper barked and played with us.

At the edge of the surf, I stopped and coquettishly dipped my toe into the brine and made a kewpie doll face at Aníbal. He ran at me like a linebacker, scooped me up, and tossed me into a wave.

I jumped back to my feet and tackled him around the knees, causing both of us to fall into the water.

Dex's voice whispered into my ear, "Grow up, JadeAnne." I did my best to ignore him.

A larger wave rolled in and broke. I dove into it and came up on the other side.

Aníbal washed ashore, spluttered with a suit full of sand. I laughed at him from the top of the next swell. He dove under the incoming wave, emerging beside me beyond the surfline. He dove under again and started pulling my legs and poking me.

"Shark attack," he yelled when he popped up for air.

I giggled and dove down to fend him off. We came up in each other's arms and kissed long and deep as we bobbed in the warm, heavy water, buoyed up by salt and caressed by currents. I'd never experienced anything like this. We held each other, rising and falling with the glassy green swells. My eyes closed. I felt his heartbeat, the warmth of his skin, and I listened to the sigh of his breath. I drifted into weightless contentment. Peace.

"It's twelve," he whispered in my ear. "We better get upstairs and change. Polo requires diners to be properly dressed at table."

He kissed me once more, and we swam in.

Onshore, a happy dog met us. Aníbal took my hand and walked me back to the lounges where Lura waited.

"I knew it. My little cousin likes you, JadeAnne." She scrutinized me. My face burned. Sunburn, I hoped.

Lura wouldn't leave it alone. "Ani loves Jade-A-anne. Ani loves Jade-A-anne." She drew out my name to taunt Aníbal, who appeared nonplussed. "Ani, no snappy retort? Ah, well, let's get upstairs before Polo has a hissy fit. And I think it would be a bad plan to let Polo know you and JadeAnne are, well, whatever you are."

"Yeah, you're right, Lulu. Polo would pop an artery. Especially because he's had his eye on her."

"What? You've got to be kidding. The senator interested in me?"

"Not interested, per se. He's not interested in anyone. Let's just say you've caught his eye, like a piece of fine art, and when he admires a piece of art, he usually wants to possess it," Lura clarified. "Anyway, you guys, come on. Chop-chop." She clapped her hands together.

"I have to go up the service elevator with the dog."

"I'll go with you," Aníbal volunteered.

"Okay." I shot off like a bullet, my shorts a yellow flag flying in my hand. Aníbal didn't catch up until I rounded the corner of the building. "I won." I giggled.

"No, JadeAnne, I'm the winner. I've caught you."

CHAPTER FOURTEEN

Luncheon Meeting

"My guests will arrive at two-thirty and leave at ten. I do not want anyone near the elevator or in the business wing, especially the dog." Aguirre cast a disgusted look at Pepper, stretched out in the corner and snoring gently. "I hope this directive is clear." He rested his gaze on Lura.

"Why are you looking at me? You always pick on me, Polo." Her voice rose into a whine.

"Lura, it is always you who fails to comply with my wishes."

Lura opened her mouth to say something, but Aníbal shook his head. She grinned. "Pass the tortillas, please, Zocer."

The table made a collective sigh and relaxed. It seemed understood we would steer the conversation away from the troubles that had brought us together until after we ate. We chatted amicably about travel, books, films, and the weather.

I bantered with Zocer seated beside me. He didn't excite me like Aníbal, but my heart skipped a beat when he brushed my hand passing the limeade. What was up with that? I left California a faithful girlfriend and look at me now, about to cheat on Dex with a young guy, and flirting shamelessly with another one. I turned the sound down on my Dad's lecture about "tramps."

After the waiter served coffee, Polo dismissed the staff. Rarotonga's had catered an elegant lunch, and I felt sated and relaxed, ready for the discussion to come.

"I understand everyone here is properly acquainted." Aguirre gave us each a piercing glare. "We are all aware of the danger Lura faces from her husband. He is laundering money for a group of powerful men who presumably wish to take over the controlling interest in PEMEX. It appears Daniel became aware of Lura's investigation and has contracted for her death. We concur Daniel is responsible for the green van, correct?"

Everyone nodded and murmured in assent.

"During his surveillance, Agent Grijalves discovered Daniel had hired Miss Stone's firm in California to locate Lura. I couldn't allow you to turn my cousin over to her husband, so I ordered my captain, Enrique, to escort you to my house." He frowned directly at me. "Lura, unfortunately, arrived unexpectedly, and I was forced to detain you until I was able to verify your connection to Daniel." Aguirre bowed his head slightly in my direction. "And I deeply apologize, Señorita. You were never in danger. Agent Grijalves...."

Anger sliced through my gut. I didn't hear what he said, but I knew he'd played me big time. Zocer had followed me, reported on me. It was all I could do to keep my hands in my lap. I wanted to wring the senator's neck.

I gritted my teeth and waved off his apology. "Senator, I found Lura, thereby earning my fee. And I've made new friends." I smiled at Aníbal. "I'm planning to enjoy my vacation in Zihuatanejo as soon as this is over, but first we have to update my partner, Dexter Trouette. I briefed him. He's looking into the consortium now and will bring as much information as he can dig up. He arrives tomorrow."

"Ah, the telephone call," Aguirre remarked.

"Yes. And I spoke with Worthington."

"And?" Lura asked with interest.

"He corroborated my partner's account. The green van was after Lura. But we are still faced with the mystery of the green Suburban. I'm not sure I buy the senator's story about Rodriguez. I mean, wouldn't it be awfully risky to shoot your family in broad daylight on your own property?" I looked at Aguirre.

"A green Suburban? Did you see the shooter?" Lura asked.

"Not really. A man with a square head. Probably middle-aged. Had a paunch and a good tan, but he looked more gringo than local." I paused to think. "I saw his chin. He has a cleft."

Lura's eyes went wide.

"One of your friends?" I joked.

"Don't laugh. Danny's best friend drives a green Suburban, and he has a cleft."

"Medrick," Aníbal exclaimed. "That bozo? I don't think he's got enough balls to be involved with this."

Lura snickered.

I pictured the photo taken on the beach at Cuastecomate Daniel Worthington had given me and tried to overlay my hazy look at the shooter on the smiling face of Medrick Johnstone. Like that CSI fingerprint matching device on TV, I made a match in my mind, complete with circles and arrows.

"Lura, I asked your husband to fax me a list of your common friends, including the makes and models of their cars. I doubt he's sent it, but I haven't been to the desk to ask. Are any more of your friends going to shoot at me?"

Aguirre picked up his cell and dialed. "Aguirre here. Is there a fax waiting for Miss Stone? Thank you, Paco." He looked at me and slowly shook his head.

I went on, "I want to debrief you this afternoon, if you're agreeable. Zocer should come, too. Dex is still at the office and will investigate the list if he has enough time. He'll check out your friends' connections with the consortium. And what about the consortium? Does anyone actually know who is involved? I'm under the impression they're all *gringos*."

"I have my suspicions, and you're not going to like what I have to say. Look at this coin." Lura tossed a silver coin that resembled the Platinum Eagle Dex had been chasing onto the table. We passed it around.

"One like it made its way to the director of my agency in the months preceding George W. Bush's reelection. A team formed to investigate. They thought there had been a heist, but we soon realized that the coin was not an Eagle. More coins turned up about two years ago. A trail led to Mexico. I was already undercover here and was reassigned to the investigation. We think they're counterfeit. It took me about six months to trace the coins to a laundering scheme. That's how Zocer and I met."

Lura turned to me. "Banks in Mexico are notorious for laundering money. And guess what bank is smack in the middle?"

"Okay, so who's involved besides your husband?"

"We started tracing the wire transfers backwards and made it to Houston. We were stumped at first, but it turned out they went to a front for some pretty powerful hombres." Lura refilled her wine glass and took a sip.

"Lura, you may not have more wine. I need you sober," Aguirre said.

She pushed her glass away and made a face at her cousin.

"Thank you. Please continue."

"So eventually we traced a connection to three board members of Houston Energy Development. You'll be interested to know one of them heads up a U.S airlines known to be the CIA's front. A fourth name was implicated, too. How good at current events are you, JadeAnne?" She studied my face and grinned as I began to put two and two together. Texas boys.

"Yep, Little Willie, former CEO of HED and our current V.P." Lura squealed with obvious glee.

The rest of us sat in stunned silence. I pictured the oil-slicked altar and the bloody dirks from my dream, and my stomach took a sideways lurch.

"…links to Villahermosa where HED's Mexico operation is headquartered." Aguirre continued the story.

"These are heavy hitters. How did a pissant like Danny get involved?" Aníbal asked.

"Ani, this is my husband you're dissing. You have to keep in mind Danny's philosophy: it's not what you know but whom you know. He went to school with Powell's son. They were roomies. Danny does everything he can to keep in touch. Powell helped him get the job with CalMex." She laughed. "Small world, eh?"

"We haven't heard anything from Zocer," Aguirre said.

"Senator Aguirre got the investigation started in Mexico. The Agency assigned me to the case. The reality is, I am in charge of the case, but I like to get into the field now and then to keep my practice. I've gotten oxidized, as you Americans say in surveillance technique." I forced a chuckle at Zocer's joke.

"*Efectivo*, cash, is coming into Mexico *poco a poco*. I have operatives in customs at all ports of entry, and they say the money arrives packaged as toys, play money in a game. I thought it was interesting when I discovered this toy only arrived on flights from Texas and only on that airline. Bundles of money from the games are moved by *camiones*, to various *destinos*, primarily *bodegas, ay*, how do you say?"

"Warehouses," Lura said.

"*Sí,* warehouses throughout Central Mexico. Investigation into property ownership brought us to HED in Villahermosa and to CalMex *en la capital.* Some of the cash is shipped to Panama to Worthington's bank."

"Of course, there are no records of any funds transfers from CalMex," Lura added.

"So what are you doing about it?" I asked.

"We are going to stop them. I won't sit back and watch my country be raped by the United States," Polo said quietly.

"I mean, what are we five doing about it right now?"

"Building a case," answered Lura. "You're working for my husband. Continue looking for me and I'll provide the information you need to conduct your investigation exactly as if you hadn't gotten to me. Aníbal will partner with you. We'll see what we do with your Dex when he arrives. Perhaps it's best if he returns to the U.S. and works from there." Lura was clearly in command. Her eyes twinkled. She was enjoying every second of this.

"Zocer, you and I will continue our operations from this location until we have Danny. Polo has agreed to work with us and will lobby Congress for a no vote."

Zocer looked both pleased and frightened, and I felt relief. I guessed Lura was hot for him and wanted everyone out of the way. That solves my problem. Now all I have to do is figure out what I want from Dex.

"So, Lura, when will you have the list of Daniel's friends ready? I'd like to get it to Dex ASAP. Then I'm going to Sally's and get settled."

"I'll get it right away. Ani go with her. You can take the car."

I shot her a dissenting glance, but she argued, "It'll be easier to get around in than the combi. Polo, you have a spare car for me, don't you?"

"I'll find something, although I would rather you stayed in the penthouse until we have Daniel."

"Yeah, yeah." She made a face at him. "Okay, is there anything else? No? Then let's get busy people. Chop chop."

A clock outside the room chimed two. I went to gather my things, as did Aníbal. Lura and Zocer disappeared into the communications room, and Aguirre excused himself to his office. Pepper, refreshed by his luncheon nap, was ready to play on the beach. He pointed his snout at his leash draped over a chair.

"Not now, Peppi. We've got to pack up and go to Sally's." He let his eyes and tail droop, tossing himself to the floor with a great sigh. "Clown. You'll love it there. There's a great beach." Only the tip of his tail moved.

I ignored my dog and started to toss the few things I brought up from the combi into a bag. When I finished, I sat at the writing table and jotted down my contact information and directions to Sally's apartment on Madera Hill off the road to Playa La Ropa.

Sally Brown
Calle Eva Semano Lopez de Mateos
Postal #12
Colonia Madera, Zihuatanejo, Gro 40880
email: yogaladyinZihua@yahoo.com
tel: +52 (755) 554-9391

JadeAnne Stone
cell:415-335-0925
email: jade@waterstreetsalvage.com

I looked forward to Sally's comfortable casita and regretted she'd gone to visit her mom. I would've loved to see her. It had been several years since she and I practiced yoga together.

I met Sally when she opened an Iyengar Yoga studio in Sausalito in the Schoonmaker Building where I ran the secretarial service. I was one of the first students, and we became close friends. That was over a decade ago, before I met Dex and long before I went to work for Water Street Investigation and Marine Salvage.

When the Schoonmaker building sold, the new guy wanted to spruce the place up and pumped a few million into the property, jacking up rents and forcing out most of the artists and small businesses. Sally was one of them, but she'd been an astute investor and grew herself a tidy nest egg. She moved to Zihua, bought her casita, and started up yoga classes in the tropics. If not rich, she lived well and had everything she wanted, including satellite TV, internet service, and a phone line that couldn't be traced to me.

"JadeAnne? Are you in there, girlfriend?" Lura called from the hallway.

"Yes, come in."

Lura plopped down on the bed, her grin wider than ever. "Smooth work, huh? Zocer doesn't know what hit him. He's nervous about consorting with a colleague, and worried about offending his host, but I convinced him Polo had other things on his mind and would never notice. He's a marvelous lover." Her expression turned dreamy. "We went at it most of the night. My husband was such a wuss. It's good to be with a man again. What about you? Slick move sending Ani to help with the investigation, eh?"

"Frankly, Lura, I've got a big problem. Dex is my partner in the firm, yes, but he is also my lover. We've lived together for almost a decade. He's flying in tomorrow. I can hardly be carrying on with Aníbal, or even working with him."

"You're right. You can't fool around with your man there." She winked and made suggestive faces. "Not safely, anyway."

"Aníbal and I are not fooling around. We barely know each other." I tried to look innocent, but I doubted Lura bought it.

"It'll be a rush, sneaking around."

"Lura. Get real. We're almost engaged."

Lura thought for a moment. "I know. We'll pick him up at the airport, and I'll insist he come straight here for a briefing. I'll get him started on something, and then send him to Mexico City, or back to the U.S.—no. Panama City. He'll never go near Sally's, and Aníbal can stay out of sight so they never meet. If your man is any kind of investigator, he's going to figure it out, so it's better to keep them separated."

"No shit."

"Put it here, girl." She stuck out her hand, and I met her in a silly secret handshake we made up on the spot.

"You'd do that for me?"

"Sure. You didn't turn me over to Danny. I owe you, big time."

"Lura, you don't owe me anything. But, well, I want to see Dex. I miss him," I admitted. "He and I have to resolve some issues. Anyway, I couldn't turn you over. Your husband gave me the creeps. No offense. I only got involved because I got fifty grand and a vacation in Mexico."

"Only fifty grand? That cheap bastard."

We laughed. "No, no, Lura. It was fifty grand as a retainer. He said, and I quote," I pitched my voice an octave lower. "'Ms. Stone, money is no problem; I'll pay whatever it costs.' I thought he loved you. I was touched."

Lura shrieked and danced around the room mimicking Worthington's spiel. I was slumped against the bed on the floor where I'd landed, sputtering, tears rolling down my cheeks.

Aníbal arrived to help with my bag.

"What's going on, ladies? Is someone being murdered in here?" This set us to roaring. "Are you laughing at me?" He started to make strange noises while he hopped between us.

"Let's go, JadeAnne. We gotta get out of this place."

"If it's the last thing we ever do," Lura started to sing and tug at the brightly colored sarong that was slipping down her hips. I belted out the chorus, and Pepper started to howl. Aníbal howled with him.

"Lura Laylor, Aníbal Aguirre. Contain yourselves." The door banged open and Aguirre's angry face appeared. "Stop this noise now. My associates can hear you in the conference room. What, are you, five-year-olds? Get out of here, all of you."

"Okie dokie, Cuz. We're gone. Come on, you guys. Let's go have a drink before you leave."

Aguirre gave Lura a stern look. "Do not leave this hotel." He turned on his heel and left the room.

"I'll get my bag and toss it in the car. JadeAnne, is yours ready? Let me take it. Come on, Pepper. Meet you on the beach, girls." Aníbal grabbed the leash and my bag and ran for the door, still laughing.

"Hold on, Ani. Change in plans. We need you here."

He looked like Pepper when told to stay home. His eyes drooped and his head bowed. "Sure, okay. I'll take the dog and your bag to the combi, then."

When Aníbal was out of earshot Lura confided, "He's always been afraid of Polo. Poli snaps his fingers, and Ani is right there doing whatever he wants. He wants Polo's approval, God knows why, and he's a little suck-up to get it. Polo has never really accepted him the way my family has. He opposed Ani becoming a U.S. citizen. Good thing Poli adores me. Grab your purse, girlfriend. Let's get that drink."

The weather had turned muggy during lunch, and the wet heat smacked us like walking into a solid wall when we stepped out of the hotel's air conditioning. Afternoon showers loomed over the mountains. That was the part about the tropics I didn't like—it could be ninety degrees and ninety percent humidity. I missed the temperate Bay Area with its natural air conditioning—the fog. Not that I was complaining, though.

Lura led the way to Las Velas, the bar and restaurant on the beach. We found a coolish spot in the shade under a fan and ordered a round of cerveza Victoria.

"Here's to us. Now we're all cousins. Here's to cousins. We're cousins, identical cousins. We walk alike, we talk alike...." Lura sure loved to sing.

"We're not cousins yet, Lura. Bet Ani sees me as a vacation fling."

"How much? A hundred dollars?"

"You're on. A hundred dollars says Aníbal will dump me when he goes home, or sooner."

"Girlfriend, you don't know my cousin."

CHAPTER FIFTEEN

Sally's Place

With some effort, I convinced Lura to keep Aníbal in Ixtapa before he showed up at Las Velas Bar. I really didn't need any help moving my vehicle and suitcase to Sally's. I needed time to settle in, relax, and think about what I was doing.

Sally's low-slung cottage perched high on Madera Hill overlooked the village of Zihuatanejo and the brilliant-cut sapphire of La Bahia de Zihuatanejo and its municipal wharf. As I pulled up to the gated community, I found old Tomás checking cars in and out, clipboard in hand. A broad smile lit up his dark face when I pulled the *combi* up to his window at the guard kiosk and leaned out with my passport and driver's license.

"Señorita *Estone*! Welcome, welcome. I've been waiting for you."

"And here I am." I smiled, delighted to see my old friend again.

He stepped out of the guardhouse and pumped my hand up and down, his smiling eyes sinking into the creases of the weathered leather of his skin. Had Tomás turned ninety yet? He was already over eighty when I last visited. How many years had it been?

We exchanged pleasantries and news about his huge family until another car honked behind me. Tomás shrugged, wrote my license plate on his clipboard, and opened the barrier. I passed into the development and turned up the hill toward my destination with a wave, thinking how lucky Sally was to live in this safe, gated community. Tomás had instituted personal security and gated communities in Zihua. His son, Tomacito Ruiz, had taken over the security company when Tomás retired. Sally told me young Ruiz had expanded and gone high tech with the increasing problems of drug violence in the port. I'd be safe here, regardless of what the Aguirre clan might think.

Itching to get onto Sally's yoga patio and stretch out the kinks I'd developed in the last week, I stepped on the gas. The yoga would help me focus my mind on my dilemma. What was I going to do about Dex? Aníbal's handsome face popped into my mind, and I felt guilty. Reproaching myself yet again, I maneuvered the old bus up the twisting cobbled road.

"We're here." I set the brake and turned off the ignition. Pepper gurgled a reply of some sort, jumped off the backseat, and pressed his nose to the window. I grabbed my handbag, jumped out of the bus, and opened Pepper's door. He trotted toward the entry as it opened to a stout, dark-haired woman in her late twenties or early thirties. She held a baby wrapped in her shawl, and two identical toddlers clung to her skirt, thumbs in mouths, eyes wide. An older girl peeked shyly from behind the doorjamb.

"*Bienvenida*, señorita." The woman eyed Pepper. I dropped my bag and grabbed his collar. He sat immediately and offered his paw. The woman relaxed.

"Rosa?"

"*Si, soy yo*, señorita."

"Rosa. And these are yours?" I asked, indicating the children.

"*Sí, sí. Le presente a AnaRosa, las gemelas: Violeta y Daisi.*" She pointed to the twins attached to her skirt. "*Y mi chiquito papi, Tomasino Juan.*" She bent to kiss the baby.

"So, you and Juanito got married. Whatever happened to, what was her name? The *novia*? Wasn't she your cousin or something?"

Rosa laughed her throaty contralto. "Oh, you mean Lourdes? She ran off with a gringo sailor, dreaming of the rich life in America. The family went after her and married her off to an older man from the *Federación*. He died in a shootout with another cartel. She got her rich life."

"I bet Juanito was heartbroken. You must have been a great comfort to him."

Rosa laughed again. "He will want to see you, señorita. Come, let me help you with your things. How long will you be here?" Rosa grabbed a bag and led me into the house, trailed by the string of little kids.

"A couple of weeks," I said to her back, sniffing the rich smell of pozole flooding out of the kitchen as we paraded in and dropped my bags. "Rosa, you remembered." I lifted the lid off the simmering stew.

"*Sí.* Of course I remembered. It was the only dish I knew how to make then. *Y el señor*? Are you married?"

"No, Rosa, my luck hasn't been as good as yours. But we're still together." Because I'm afraid to leave, I wanted to add.

The afternoon faded as we visited and caught up on news over a cold beer and tostadas with fresh salsa. The children lost no time making friends with Pepper. Even shy AnaRosa giggled and climbed all over him with the little twins. They wailed when their mother pulled them toward the door after we said our goodbyes. I promised they could come back the next day to play.

With the family gone, Sally's home settled to serenity. Sally used the principles of feng shui, blending an eastern flavor with her collections of Mexican folk art. I pushed my suitcases into the guest room and wandered back to the kitchen to take stock. If I wanted something other than *pozole* in the morning, I'd need to go to the market soon, before all but the tourist trap tiendas closed. I polished off another bowl of Rosa's scrumptious stew and several tortillas while I made a list.

At the central market, ghosts of dead fish and rotting vegetables assaulted my nostrils, but the stalls had closed, and few people lingered, mostly vendors and their families sharing an early evening meal before cleaning up and going home. Skinny mongrels roamed the corridors, sniffed out discarded food, and skirmished over possession. Pepper trotted at my side with a scowl and a growl. His back hair stood up, and he pointed. I looked, catching a flash of bright yellow under a blue cap dashing around a corner.

"Let's get out of here, Peppi. This place gives me the creeps."

In the parking lot, I asked a matron packing her truck from the day's selling where I could find a supermarket. It turned out that Commercial Mexicana's Mega had come to Zihuatanejo, located near the turn up Madera Hill. When I'd last visited, there were no supermarkets. Now there were three, each the size of a Walmart Superstore. In fact, one was a Walmart Superstore, I learned later. I headed toward the Mega on Paseo La Boquita.

Shopping in a Mexican superstore was no different than shopping in an American superstore, except for the tortillaria stamping out hot fresh tortillas on one side and the panadaría with every form of pan dulce known to man arrayed on the other. I couldn't resist buying a selection of the warm, delectable sweet breads, including the super-sized sweet corn muffins and one each of the giant sugary cookies I remembered from my last trip. I stocked up on papaya and guavas, found a bottle of rum, and pushed my heavy cart through to checkout. I'd bought enough to feed an army. I envisioned several jolly parties with Dex and the Aguirre family. I wanted to be ready.

While I counted out the 867.23 pesos, I felt shivers run up my spine. Someone walking on my grave. I spun around and scanned the crowd. No faces in particular jumped out, but several yellow shirts caught my eye. One checked out at the next register, an American with a grotesque snake tattoo, but another disappeared down the escalator on the back of a large, tanned man wearing a boating cap.

"Señora, do you need help to your car? Señora?" A boy addressed me.

"I'm sorry, no, no thank you, but here's something for your trouble." I tipped him a couple of pesos and hoped he was the kid who had bagged the groceries.

Back home, I tried Dex on his cell. I wanted to hear his voice. I felt so conflicted about my attraction to Aníbal. If I loved Dex, how could I be attracted to another man? He didn't answer and I left a message then changed into my nightgown, prepared myself a little cup of hot chocolate, and broke out the pan dulce. A snack might help me figure it out, but probably wouldn't do too much for my figure. Oh, well.

CHAPTER SIXTEEN

Paranoia

July 31, 2007

Sally's grandfather clock bonged the quarter hour from the entry hall. I wondered how she kept that thing going here in the tropics. My mother's clock went on the fritz often enough, and she had trouble finding repair people in the Bay Area. I could imagine how hard it would be to find an English clock expert in a little Mexican fishing village. Pondering this, I managed to keep my mind off Dex for another couple of minutes.

I'd tossed and turned all night, waking from half-baked dreams, which vaporized before I could remember them. At least, there were no more bloody knives, but my poor sleep left me groggy and exhausted. Dex would land in several hours. Between his trip to Baja and my trip here, it had been almost a month since we'd seen each other, and I didn't want to greet him feeling like this.

I shuffled inside from the patio for another cup of cafe de olla, tripping over the doorjamb on the way.

"Walk much?" I asked myself. Pepper pricked up his ears, hearing his favorite word, and expectantly eyed me

161

from under the table where he napped.

"God, Pepper, I'm so tense."

Ever hopeful, he banged his tail on the tiles a few times, casting his eyes toward the gate, which opened onto the stairs to the beach.

"Yeah, yeah, we'll go to the beach in a while. I need more coffee first. Go back to sleep." Pepper's head flopped back onto the floor with that hangdog expression. "Sorry," I muttered to him as I slopped the rich brew all over the kitchen counter.

Pepper had the right idea, though. A run would help me relax. The strong, boiled coffee was just going to make me jittery and fog my brain even more. I feared looking in the mirror. I felt like crap, and I was certain to look like it, too. All the booze and rich food with Lura…how on earth does she stay so thin? And the complete disregard of my exercise routine for a week showed. I stirred an extra spoonful of the molasses-rich piloncillo sugar into my mug, took a gulp, and dribbled a mouthful down the front of my nightgown.

Dex's ring tone chirped from inside my purse, lying on the hall table.

I spilled more coffee as I banged the mug onto the counter and ran for the phone. "Hi, Dex."

"Jade, there you are. We just landed in Houston. My flight out was delayed on the runway, all this damn security crap. I've about had it with the Patriot Act."

"What do you mean?"

"You'd think people in San Francisco would be above mob mentality. Christ. A Stanford professor next to me on the plane. Middle eastern chap."

"What?"

"Homeland Security. Those fools, thought he was an Arab terrorist. Tried to arrest him."

"So what time should I pick you up?"

"I've got about thirty minutes to get off this damn plane

and hoof it to Terminal D where Aero Mexico parks, way beyond hell on the other side of the airport." He paused. "I may not make it."

"Dex, you have to."

"Jeez, Jade. I'll do my best. How's my bus, anyway? Wrecked it yet? Hey, line's moving, gotta go."

The connection went dead. Another lukewarm conversation, like my coffee. Somehow, I felt that this was going to define my day. Pepper followed me from the hall to the bedroom where I flung myself onto my bed and curled into a ball, hugging my pillow into my chest.

"He didn't say he missed me. He didn't even say goodbye." I hiccupped into my arms. "Peppi, Dex doesn't love me anymore."

He jumped up beside me, nuzzled his way to my face and licked me. I tried to push him away, but Pepper was insistent.

"Okay, okay. I'm getting up," I croaked.

Wagging his tail, he sprang off the bed and trotted into the open closet. In a moment, he was back on the bed, standing over me with one of my running shoes in his mouth. It's almost impossible to wallow in self-pity when you've got a huge, smartass dog poking and pawing at you to get up.

"I get it, Pepper." I sniffled, lurched off the bed, and crossed the room into the bathroom.

The mirror revealed a puffy-faced, red-eyed hag. A little current of anger surged through me. Here I was sobbing, maudlin over Dexter Trouette, and he hadn't had the courtesy to say goodbye. Why should I make myself look and feel awful for that? Maybe Lura should pick Dex up at the airport and send him home. That'd show him.

I tossed on my running clothes in a huff. Pepper waited by the gate with the leash in his mouth until I arrived and unlocked it. He dropped the leash at my feet and nosed the gate open wide enough to shoot through. I heard him thundering down the stairwell like a landslide and hoped no one was coming up. He'd bowl them over for sure. After carefully locking the gate behind me, I took off, too. Sally had impressed upon me the need to be security-minded, and I wouldn't want to be at fault for allowing her house to be ripped-off. Especially not that clock.

The uneven stone stairs switched down the steep mountainside between houses for about two blocks to the beach. High walls towered over my head, and thick sprays of honeysuckle, trumpet vine, and bougainvillea cascaded above them, entwined with the sounds of humanity and the smells of breakfast. Small trees burrowed into cracks in the walls, and tiny wildflowers bloomed everywhere they could take hold. The sun was warm, and the stones forming the narrow pathway radiated the heat. I sweated as profusely as the vines bloomed while I pounded after my dog.

A couple hundred feet from the beach, I heard a second pair of feet echoing off the stones. I slowed down and listened. The footsteps quieted. I hurried around a corner to see Pepper already bounding in the low surf at the water's edge. The feet came louder, faster down the stairwell. Not again. They weren't just footsteps, but footsteps coming after me.

"Paranoia strikes deep, into your heart it will creep," I hummed, winded and ready to rest, not run, but the lyric from that old Buffalo Springfield tune sounded an alarm in my head. My instincts took over. Paranoia or not, I had to get off that stairway, now.

A rush of adrenaline pushed me forward. I could see the beach and Pepper loping toward me. Only a few steps more. I launched myself into the air and skidded into the deep sand, losing precious seconds scrambling to my feet. The slap of rubber soles echoed loud and came fast. I heard them over my harsh breathing. Pepper flew past me up the stairs.

SET UP

There was nowhere for me to hide. Without looking back, I ran toward the only safety I could see—a family building sandcastles together. Pepper would hold my pursuer in check until I got away.

Beyond the picnickers, at the edge of the bay, I slowed and turned to look at the entrance to the stairway. Pepper sat one landing below a man wearing a bright yellow shirt. From that distance, I couldn't make out his features, but I could tell from the way he held his arms that he concealed a gun.

The size and shape of this man looked similar to that of the man in the marina the day before, but I couldn't be sure. I'd had too brief a glimpse of Medrick. If it were Medrick, I thought, as he disappeared back into the stairwell. I whistled to release Pepper.

Like Alice down the rabbit hole, this was getting "curiouser and curiouser." I wasn't carrying my cell phone or my gun, but I hoped I'd be safe on the beach in broad daylight, especially closer down by the wharf where there were plenty of people and a public phone, if it worked. I needed to call Lura. She was right again. I needed Aníbal to watch my back. No. Dex was coming. I needed Dex.

Pepper and I jogged down the beach at an easy pace. People stared as we passed. There was nothing particularly remarkable about a woman jogging on the beach, but Pepper's size always drew attention.

"Good," I huffed to myself, amused to see macho beach boys scooting out of Pepper's path.

I was still angry and hurt from this morning but, as advised by my dog, I felt two hundred percent better after jogging to the *muelle*, pier. We managed to get in a little swim, too, before calling the Krystal.

I reached the penthouse and reported to Zocer from a pay phone outside that old hamburger joint, La Sirena Gorda, The Fat Mermaid. He told me to take a taxi home and wait. He'd come as soon as possible.

Admiring the view as we drove up the hill toward Sally's, I thought about how Dex and I should rent a sailboat and visit one of those beautiful beaches I could see across the water. We hadn't had any fun together in ages. Maybe that would be the fix our relationship needed. Sailing together was how we started out, and the Zihuatanejo Bay looked idyllic.

At the *caseta*, Tomás waved us through, and we continued up to the house. I asked the driver to wait while I ran in for my purse. I heard him gunning the engine impatiently. As if my day hadn't been trying enough already, the *taxista* overcharged me for the ride and then charged more for the time it took me to un-alarm the house, check it, and get back with the cash, all of four minutes. Who would pay me for my wait? The wait for Zocer. The wait for Dex.

CHAPTER SEVENTEEN

Stalked

The hour for Dex's call came and went. Delayed in the air? Ignoring me? I'd stretched out on the yoga mat and was ready to do something. Zocer hadn't shown up yet, but he would. Probably with Lura and Aníbal. I didn't want to see either of them, and I sure as hell didn't want Aníbal around when Dex came.

I got into the shower, and the gentle stream of water on my skin made me think of how Dex ran his fingers over my body, giving me goose bumps. I relaxed and pictured how his deep blue eyes would light up when I met him at the gate. I let my imagination paint a loving reunion. I would run into his open arms, we'd kiss warmly, we'd pull apart delighted with each other and move off toward baggage claim, our arms around each other's waists. He'd tell me he was sorry. He was just so worried about me and stressed about the case. We'd kiss some more. Dex's hungry kisses, his probing tongue, softened into Aníbal's deep, soft lips and tongue devouring me.

The house phone rang, breaking into my daydream, and I jumped out of the shower, grabbing a towel as I ran to answer. I picked up on the sixth ring.

"JadeAnne. Zocer here."

"Hi Zocer, I was just in the shower." I hoped my voice didn't sound too disappointed. "Where are you?"

"I'm sorry. Did I disturb you? I can wait."

"No, it's okay. I'm done now. Are you here?" I mopped at the water I'd dripped on the tile floor with Sally's towel.

"Yes. I'm in the *caseta*."

"Can Tomás bring you up?" I heard a rapid conversation in Spanish then Zocer returned to the phone.

"I will be there *en un ratito*."

I left the towel on the floor and hurried into my room. I had no time to dress for my trip to the airport. It would have to wait until later. I tossed on shorts and a tank then ran a comb through my hair. I had barely finished brushing my teeth when the doorbell rang.

"Come on in, Zocer. Would you like iced tea or lemonade?" I asked as I led him through the entry hall into the living room. He checked his watch against the grandfather clock as we passed.

"*Una limonada, gracias*."

He sat down at my gesture and looked up at me with eyebrows raised as though he was waiting for something. I went to the kitchen and poured us each a cold drink. The house, with its southwest face, was heating up and becoming stuffy. Returning to the living room, I handed Zocer his lemonade and put my tea on the coffee table, then went to the windows and pulled the shutters closed. The afternoon sun filtered into the room in blinding shards of light, giving the room a fragmented, restive atmosphere.

We both started to talk at the same time.

"I was fol—"

"Tell me exactly wha—"

We laughed. "You first," I said.

"Okay. Tell me exactly what happened today." He was ready with a small notepad and a stub of a pencil.

"I think it was Medrick Johnstone. From the distance, I could see his square head, but not his face. He had on a very bright shirt—yellow. And I saw him, or the shirt, at Mega last night, too."

"You think it was Johnstone. Tell me what you know."

"It felt like the man was following me, and he held his arms like he had a gun." I gestured with my arms away from my body to show Zocer, feeling the color rising in my cheeks.

"JadeAnne, I know you are feeling jumping, but you cannot accuse anyone of following you because he had his arms away from his body or he wears a yellow shirt. Many men wear yellow shirts. They are very popular."

"Jumpy. The word is jumpy," I muttered under my breath. "You must have believed something I said, because here you are."

"Yes. Your *intuición* is good. You say the man's head was square?"

I nodded. "Zocer, how did they know where I was, or that I would use the stairs? I mean, I was sure no one followed me from the hotel."

"I am confident you were careful, but there is no way you could be certain you were not followed. And if you were followed, it is because you talked in public about coming here."

"What do you mean, I talked in public?"

"At the bar. At the table while waiters were in the room. You said you told your Dex on the telephone."

"It's impossible. You mean to say Polo's staff at the Krystal is connected to Worthington?"

"I mean to say a few pesos in Mexico can buy anything. We don't know if the man in the yellow shirt is Worthington's. There is still the problem of Rodriguez here in Zihuatanejo. I don't doubt you were followed. It is only a short time before they know what house you are in. You are not safe here."

The clock's two-thirty chime rent the silence. My head spun. Not safe at Sally's? Who was after me? Worthington was the only person interested in my movements. In my gut I knew yellow-shirt was Medrick, and Medrick was after me because of Lura.

I looked up from my contemplation of shadows and light playing over the tiled floor, "Zocer, you're right. I was followed, but this isn't about Polo's turf war. Think back to the bar. Think back to Christine's. Who can you see? Who took too much interest in us? Who didn't belong? Whose faces can you see?"

We lapsed into silence again. I played back the events of our encounter at the pool bar in my mind. Nothing. Christine's? No way to sort out the swirling images. The beach bar? I pictured Lura in her bird print sarong and the handsome, lithe bartender whose white g*uayabera* and trousers set off his deep tan. We had been sitting at the bar but turned to face one another. No one was sitting on the stools next to either of us, but someone sat alone two seats down from Lura. I hadn't paid attention to him, but had been aware of his presence. An old guy, sort of seedy, with a stringy ponytail and a grotesque tattoo of a striking rattlesnake. I registered his American accent when he ordered a beer. What else? It was the man's body language. Although his back was to us, he was leaning in, head cocked.

"I saw someone," I blurted into the still room and startling Zocer.

"Who?"

"I don't know, but he was at the Las Velas, sitting right by us at the bar before I left the Krystal. A gringo. He could have heard me tell Lura about Sally. This is Sally's house, you know."

"*Si*. JadeAnne, did you tell Lura where the house is?"

I hung my head. "Not exactly, but I told her what

development it's in when I described it, and I talked about the yoga. It wouldn't be hard to find Sally through the listings for yoga instruction. She holds private classes here. Stupid. Stupid. Stupid. How could I be so dumb?"

"What did this American look like?"

I concentrated for a moment. "You know, the soldier of fortune type. Wiry, scruffy-looking, graying three-day beard, reddish blond or silver moustach in need of a trim, and very pale skin like he hadn't been in the tropics long, or maybe he's a redhead." I stopped to think. "His arms had a lot of hair. And tattoos: snakes, creepy blue designs. He had on reflector aviator glasses and a scraggly grey ponytail hanging from under his cap. His cap, Zocer. It was the same kind of cap I saw disappearing down the escalator last night in Mega."

"Ponytail?"

"No, just the hat."

"Are you sure?"

"Yeah, he had a red and blue pin on it. I saw the colors on the cap last night. This proves he's another of Worthington's people. Zocer, he said money wasn't an issue. I said all along he hired someone to tail me. I just thought you were the tail."

Zocer and I stared at each other.

"Well it makes a lot of sense. He wants to kill Lura. He hires me to get her into the open and sends an assassin to follow me. But what doesn't make sense is why he's having Medrick follow me to the beach with a gun. They all know where Lura is. What would shooting me prove?"

"You are a witness."

"So is the recording I made of our conversation locked in the WIMS safe. So is the invoice and the retainer and everything I told Dex."

"Try to prove it."

"Yeah, well, better not to get shot. Okay, Zocer, we've

gotta find this creep."

Zocer closed his notebook and got to his feet. "We will. Do not go out without protection, JadeAnne. I'll send Aníbal right away."

"Zocer, I'm picking up Dex at the airport by myself and not Aníbal, Lura, or any of you will be at my house when I get home with him. So forget it."

Zocer opened his mouth to speak, but I jumped up, my palm raised. "I'm serious. I can handle myself, and Dex is a pro, former CIA. I'll be safe enough. Just go back to the Krystal and get the search started for the scruffy guy in a captain's cap, and Medrick Johnstone. He shouldn't be too hard to find. They're probably lurking on the stairs outside the wall right now." I was adamant. I needed to see Dex without a three-ring circus or a potential new lover in tow. Taking Zocer's arm, I propelled him toward the front door.

"I respect your wanting to see your *novio* alone, but you are in danger. I can't allow..."

"Enough. *Basta*. Just figure out who this fool is and catch him. I'll check in later." I shoved Zocer out the door and closed it.

The clock bonged three times, ringing out the hour and shoving the truth in my face: Dex was dissing me. He should have landed in Mexico City by now, and he hadn't called. What the hell was he up to? I wandered into the kitchen to see what there was to eat.

I made a ham and swiss sandwich on one of the *telera* rolls I'd bought at Mega. The Mexicans called it a *torta de jamón* and, although the light rye was missing, it was ham and cheese. I popped open a Victoria to go with it and stared dully out a window facing into the vine-covered stairwell. I was tired, crabby, and pissed-off at Dex. If his flight had been delayed, why hadn't he called me from the in-flight phone? If he was on time, what was he waiting for? He wasn't waiting for baggage. Dex never flew with more than an oversized briefcase. His idea was he could buy whatever he needed when he arrived wherever he was going. This meant that he showed up at home missing the clothes he'd ditched when they were dirty and new stuff that was usually totally inappropriate for our California lifestyle.

I was deep into my memories when I sensed more than saw, movement across the window. I focused my attention and saw the top of a tall man's head, and in Zihua most of the people weren't tall. I focused quickly enough to recognize a blue yachting cap before it vanished behind the bougainvillea. Zocer had emphasized the danger I might be in and he was right. Someone was on the stairs. And if he was on the stairs, he could be coming in the front door. Was it locked? I jumped off my stool and whistled for Pepper, disturbing his nap under the dining table. He opened one eye.

"Get up. Come." I whistled the alert command.

He lumbered up, stretched and sniffed the air. The hair on his back stood on end, and he growled softly as we trotted toward the door. I had locked it.

"Heel," I commanded.

We hurried around the house. I picked up my phone and gun from the bedside table and checked the windows. Most had graceful wrought iron cages protecting them. The bedroom windows had little balcony-like cages with window boxes overflowing with cascading pelargonium in shades of pink and purple. Only the French doors leading to the patio were unprotected, but the wall was sheer and topped with broken glass. A man could get over, but it would be difficult. This was the most insecure point, and there wasn't a lot I could do. I closed the patio doors, locked them, and went back through the kitchen to the service patio to check the security door into the carport. The clock chimed three-fifteen.

Locked into the house, I was punching Mexico's country code into my phone to call Tomás and report my suspicions when it finally chirped Dex's call.

"God, it's about time."

"I just landed, Jade. Calm down," he responded to the panic in my voice.

"Look, Dex, I'm being followed, stalked, you could say, and I just saw the guy outside the window. When are you getting here?"

"The Zihua flight takes off in thirty-five minutes. I'll see you in an hour and a half at baggage pickup. Who's following you?" His tone sounded patronizing.

"You checked a bag?"

"Just meet me there. I'll be waiting on the curb in front of Alaska Air." Impatience colored his voice. "JadeAnne, answer me."

I quickly recounted the events of the last few hours. "… and ten minutes ago, I was having a sandwich and spacing out at the window when I saw the top of the captain's cap hanging around on the stairs. Listening, I suppose, although there wasn't anything to listen to. Zocer and I talked quietly. When I got up to look, I heard his footsteps going down the stairs."

"Get out of there, Jade. Take the dog and go back to the Krystal. I'll meet you there."

"No. I'm picking you up at the airport. I need to see you."

Dex sighed, but remained silent. I couldn't guess what was going through his mind.

"Dex?" My voice sounded small, child-like.

"What do you want me to do, JadeAnne?" He sounded tired.

"I just miss you, Dex. This whole case is such a mess. I need to see you before we start the briefing with the others. I need some time with you alone." I tried to make my voice sound confident, positive, but I only got whiny and clinging.

"Don't, Jade," he said in that tone I knew was a warning. "Get out of that house. Do you have a gun?"

"Yes, of course."

"Then put it in your pocket. Put Pepper in the bus. And get out of there." He sounded like he was clenching his jaw. "I'll see you at the airport."

"Okay, Dex…" I was talking to a dead line.

CHAPTER EIGHTEEN

Lingerie and Fishheads

After a month apart, Dex's first look at me was going to be good. So good he wasn't going to keep his hands off me.

"Whadya think, Pepper?" I asked, twirling in front of the full-length mirror in the bedroom.

My white shorts and lacy tank set off my tan. Pepper, on guard, kept silent, but I knew I looked hot, except for my running shoes. High strappy sandals would look sexier, but risking running into bad guys when I couldn't run sounded stupid. Satisfied, I tossed on hoop earrings, an amber bracelet, and grabbed my purse. I'd already stowed the gun and phone in it.

"Come on, Peppi, let's go get Daddy."

The airport was about twenty minutes to the southeast. I stopped at the guard house and gave Tomás my itinerary. Someone needed to know where I was going and when I'd be back.

"If we're not back here by seven Tomás, please call this number and ask for Agent Esteban Grijalves. Give him the information I've written on the paper, okay?" I smiled my warmest and most innocent smile, the one I regularly used on Dex when I didn't want him to know what I was up to.

"Señorita, something is wrong, no? Perhaps you are in some danger?"

Obviously my smile didn't work on elderly Mexican security guards. "Tomás, I was followed by a gringo with a gun on the stairs this morning, and I think the house is being watched. I don't know who, or why, but it may be connected to a case." Honesty seemed the best policy here.

"Then I will send my grandson to guard Señorita Sally's house until your return."

"Thanks. It might be a good idea to tell Rosa to skip cleaning today until we get this sorted out. Dex will take care of everything when he gets here."

"*Sí señorita*, Tomacito and I will keep eagle eyes on the traffic coming in and out. They are *gringos*?"

"Tomás, just do what you usually do. We don't want them to know we suspect anything."

"*Pues*, drive carefully, Señorita Stone."

I pulled away from the *caseta* with a leaden feeling in my gut, eased the combi down the hill to La Boquita, and made a right. The late afternoon traffic was heavy, and I couldn't keep track of all the vehicles. A tail could be driving anything, but I suspected dark green vans and Suburbans. I turned right onto the coastal highway leading south out of town toward the airport. In a few minutes the traffic eased up, and I searched my mirrors for anything I could recognize. Nothing dark green.

"Peppi, I think we're safe."

The last time I'd visited the Zihua airport it was a one-horse affair. I got completely lost negotiating the turns and twists of lanes and wound up in front of international departures instead of domestic arrivals. There was still plenty of time before Dex's flight was scheduled to land, and I decided to find short-term parking rather than circling for half an hour. Anyway, I wanted to meet him at the baggage carousel. I smiled at the memory of my earlier daydream. Oh, boy. Dex was coming home. Or at least, vacation home. My stomach pirouetted with excitement as I set the parking brake.

"Pepper, you stay and watch the car. I'll be back with Daddy. Daddy's coming." He banged his tail against the seat with obvious enthusiasm. I hopped in back with him and gave him a hug, poured a bowl of water, popped the top, and turned on the fans. The Zihua airport didn't have covered parking, but before we left Marin County I'd installed a ventilation system in the bus to keep Pepper cool when I had to leave him. He'd be okay.

I picked my way through the vast parking lot toward the terminal with my head in the clouds. I had to remind myself to remain observant. The combi was in section CH-5. I'd written it down. I can't remember how many times I've lost my car in a parking lot. Not a good recommendation for a private investigator. As I closed in on the baggage claim area, the traffic became congested with taxis, buses, cars, people with luggage, porters, and police dancing through the jumble, blowing their whistles. And everywhere I looked, I saw a man in a yellow shirt or a captain's cap. Between the anticipation and dread, my stomach fluttered, my vision swam, and my bones felt like noodles. Maybe this hadn't been such a good idea, after all. I wasn't going to see danger until it kicked me in the shin.

The light at the crosswalk turned red, and I took several deep breaths while I waited for it to change. My watch said Dex was on the ground, probably walking toward me through the terminal. Still waiting for the light to change, I fidgeted and craned my neck to see into the baggage claim.

A movement caught my peripheral vision, and I turned to look. Parked at the curb in front of United baggage claim, a square-headed man wearing a bright yellow shirt sat at the wheel of a green Suburban. We locked eyes for less than a second and a searing chill rushed up my spine. Medrick.

The walk sign flashed and the accumulated crowd pushed me forward across the street and into the Alaska Airlines baggage area. I hurried over to a screen and found Dex's flight on the ground. The baggage was coming in on carousel three. I checked for men with guns then scurried through the throng to the carousel, my heart pounding. I positioned myself on the wall between the doors so I could monitor both the baggage pickup and anyone approaching me. I was taking a big risk, exposing myself like this in public. If Medrick had followed me to the airport, he probably wasn't above shooting me in plain view of scores of travelers. Or maybe he hoped I would lead him to Lura?

Boy, this puts a damper on my big reunion, I thought, as a man thrust a briefcase into my arms.

"Stay put. I've gotta pick up my bag," Dex commanded.

"Dex...." But he had already disappeared into the crowd milling around the carousel. So much for warm greetings.

"Ah, Miss Stone. Thank you for taking your time to meet my flight."

"What? Oh my God. Mr. Worthington." My chin hit my chest and bounced back, clattering my teeth together so hard my eyeballs shook. "I'm here to meet my partner," I said, recovering.

"You did not receive the message I left for you at the Krystal?" He cut me off.

"No. I'm not staying there. What are you doing here?"

"I've come to take my wife home."

Worthington grabbed my arm and yanked me away from the wall. Something hard rammed into my kidney. The normally muffled acoustics of the baggage area amplified into a roar around me and no one turned toward my groaning.

"Medrick. Good to see you, old boy." Worthington's

voice sounded downright jovial. "Miss Stone, I don't think you have been properly introduced to my friend, Medrick Johnstone," he went on while he pulled me toward the door.

"We've run into each other a couple of times, Danny. It's nice to finally meet you, JadeAnne. By the way, where's that monster dog of yours?"

He gave me another jab with what I assumed was a gun. Pain shot through my back, but I planted my feet and opened my mouth to scream bloody murder as Dexter appeared.

"Trouette—" Dex pushed his hand at Worthington. "Dexter Trouette, Senior Partner, Water Street Investigations."

Worthington dropped my arm and glowered at me before turning to Dex. "Good to meet you, Trouette." He nodded toward Medrick. "My associate, Medrick Johnstone."

I wrenched away from the men, but not until another jab of Medrick's gun sent pain shooting up my spinal column.

"Howdy, Dexter," Medrick drawled, his grin as open as his hand. "Welcome to Mexico. I was just meeting your little lady here." He smirked at me. Had Dex seen the gun?

"Miss Stone is my business partner, Mr. Johnstone." His voice was cold. "Where will you boys be staying? Can I get you a cab?"

"No thanks, Trouette, Medrick has a car. Perhaps we can drop you off. We can talk on the way to the Krystal. I'm worried about my wife. I don't know what she's said, but I'm sure we can get it settled." He glanced at me with that same odd look I'd noticed in my office, complete with the tic.

"We have a car, thanks. I'm afraid I don't know anything about your wife. Is she still missing?" Dex asked.

When Worthington remained silent, Dex continued, "No? Then I'll call over to the hotel in the morning. Perhaps we can meet. You are staying at the Krystal?"

I had to hand it to him, Dex was smooth. He took the

briefcase from my hand and guided me toward the exit. "Where are you parked?"

I smiled at my lover. "Somewhere near Acapulco, I think. Ready for a hike?"

"Let's go." He smiled back at me as he guided us through the door. "Gee, Jade, you really know how to greet a guy."

"I didn't plan to meet Worthington at the airport, Dex. But I can tell you with one hundred percent certainty that Medrick Johnstone was the shooter at the marina. He followed me on the stairs this morning and—would you believe it?—he's the guy I saw in Mega last night. The idiot has on the same shirt. What a pig." I backed out of the parking space and headed toward the exit.

"He obviously doesn't know much about tailing people. That shirt is loud. You could pick him out from two blocks."

"Yeah, maybe it's why he hasn't shot me. But I don't know why he's after me anyway. Just because they're friends…. Get some pesos out of my purse, would you, hon? Three or four."

I pulled up to the parking cashier and handed him my ticket. I saw Medrick's vehicle turning into the exit behind me.

"I don't trust those guys, Dex. I bet they waited for us."

"*Tres pesos*," the attendant said.

I handed over three coins, "*Gracias. Un recibo, por favor*."

The attendant gave me a receipt and I pulled away as Worthington and Medrick pulled in to pay.

"Where's your gun?" Dex demanded.

"In the hidey-hole. You better get it. Medrick is a lunatic. I'm sure he was the one shooting at me in the mercado. Jeesh, what did I get into?"

Dexter fished my gun out of the compartment, checked and cocked it.

"Domestic problems are always a bitch. I wouldn't have taken the case, Jade, but you already knew it. Why did you?" he asked, derision sounding in his voice.

"Be careful, Dex," I warned. "Look, you were running around in Baja. I wanted a trip, too. Anyway, he's paying Water Street a lot of money." It sounded lame, even to me.

We turned back on Ruta 200 and headed north to Zihua. Medrick had caught up to us and was keeping a close tail, but not trying to overtake us or run us off the road.

No cliffs, I thought. Pepper stood on the back seat where he'd been since Dex got into the combi, crooning and madly swinging his tail into the back of his seat.

"Greet the dog, Dex. He's missed you."

Dex swiveled over the seat. "Hello, boy."

Pepper barked and jumped onto the floor, then lunged up to be petted, placing his paws onto the cabinet behind Dex's seat.

Dex scratched his ears, "Good dog. I've missed you, too. You've taken good care of JadeAnne. Good job, Pepper."

I maintained the speed limit, and soon a long line of traffic backed up behind Medrick and Worthington. Witnesses. They wouldn't start shooting at us unless they wanted to shoot out their own windshield. Frankly, I wouldn't have put that past Medrick.

Horns blared.

Dex shot me an evil grin. "Slow down. That'll really piss off the traffic, and they'll start passing."

I laughed and let my foot up on the accelerator. As the combi slowed, Medrick dropped back. I gunned it and drew ahead before he knew what I was up to. A delivery truck shot around the green suburban. I continued to accelerate. The truck crowded bumper.

"I can't see Medrick. Can you?" I asked Dex.

He leaned out the window and looked back then pulled into the cab, chuckling.

"Not much of a driver. Three more vehicles have passed him. Ditch the asshole, Jade."

"Why? He knows where we're staying. Let's just fuck with him."

"No. Ditch him and go to the Krystal. I want to be there when Worthington walks through the door. It's time to have a little tête a tête with Worthington and his wife. I want the cousin there, too. I don't get this family dynamic."

I pulled over behind an auto repair shop, and we waited. Medrick really was a poor driver. He'd let a third-class bus get in front of him and was riding its tail through clouds of black exhaust. Once he and several more vehicles passed, I pulled back onto the highway.

"Dex, wouldn't you like to settle in before we meet at the Krystal?" I smiled my most seductive smile and winked at him. He didn't answer.

"I want to spend some time with you. We haven't seen each other for a month."

Dex shifted in his seat. Something about his posture gave me a sick feeling.

"Dex, I've missed you. What's the matter with you? Say something."

"Look, JadeAnne, I'm tired. We've got a case going bad. Give it a rest."

"Give what a rest, Dex. What are you saying?"

"I don't want to talk about it now."

"About what?" I demanded.

"Christ, you're like a pit bull. Once your teeth are in, you shake it until it's dead."

The dread sinking down into my stomach left me speechless, my jaw flapping without any sound. Hot tears pricked my eyes, and I turned toward my side mirror. I didn't want Dex to see how he'd hurt me.

"It's great to see you too, Dex," I muttered under my breath.

The turnoff to Ixtapa was about 20 minutes north. We made the trip in silence. I thought for a moment that Dex was napping, but realized that he was pretending to sleep. My mind was racing and dark. I felt like I was driving over an icy abyss, and no amount of pressure on the brakes was going to make the bus stop. What was happening here? Dex had never been too tired or preoccupied for me before. I couldn't understand the signs. I wouldn't understand the signs.

I gave myself over to driving, concentrating only on the road and the operation of my vehicle. Well, Dex's vehicle, if I told the truth. My mind stilled, but I was in shock. Looking back, I couldn't remember any of that trip except the Krystal emerging from a great darkness as I turned into the parking lot.

"Do you want to be briefed before we go in?" I asked.

"No. You've told me enough. I want you to call that Judicial—what's his name?"

"Zocer Grijalves. He's a Fed not a Judicial."

"Whatever. Just get him to the lobby. And Lura Laylor. I have some questions for her."

I turned off the ignition, took my phone out of my purse, and dialed Zocer's code.

"Zoce, it's me. Dex and I are here and want you and Lura to come down for a briefing. Some shit's goin' on." I paused, listening. "At the Krystal... Okay then, we'll see you when you get back. Meet us in the bar. Yes. Send Lura down." I hung up and turned to Dex. "Zocer is at the cop shop with Aníbal."

"Who?"

I didn't answer for a moment, then spun in my seat. "Is Lura going to recognize you from Baja?"

"I doubt it." Dex slammed the combi's door shut.

"Did she see you?" I slipped my arm through his as we walked.

"Sort of, I guess. I don't know, Jade. Why does it matter?" Dex was looking away from me, checking out the hotel.

"I'll just be embarrassed if she knows my boyfriend has been chasing her around a foreign country."

"I'm not—oh forget it, JadeAnne. Who cares?" He pulled away from me.

"You're not what?" Not interested in Lura Laylor or not my boyfriend?

Dex disappeared into the men's room while I ordered us each a Victoria. What was he saying to me? I felt nauseated as my mind tossed in the wake of his half-said declaration. I'm not...I'm not...not in love with you anymore? I wanted to run outside and bury my head in the beach sand.

"JadeAnne, what's going on? Danny is here?" Lura shrieked at my ear.

I barely glanced up, "He came in on the same flight as Dex. Medrick picked him up. I'm certain that Medrick is the marina shooter and the asshole on the stairs this morning. You heard about that, right?"

"Of course. So what does my husband want? Did he ask about me?" Lura's voice oozed sarcasm. She sat down. "He must miss me." She changed her voice to syrup and signaled for the waiter.

"He's come to take you home," I retorted and shifted in my chair. The carved back was digging into the bruise Medrick left with his gun.

Dex joined us, and I made introductions.

"You. You were tailing me in Baja. You and that bald guy. Thanks for holding off the bandidos while I got away. But why were you following me?" Lura bestowed her most charming smile on Dex.

Dex tried to appear nonplussed, but I could see that he was embarrassed.

He clenched his jaw and growled, "What were you doing

diving our wreck?"

"Yours?" She dismissed him with a wave of her hand. "I'll tell you that story later. What information have you got regarding the consortium?" Lura was all business now.

"Wait a minute." I interrupted. "Shouldn't Zocer be here for this?"

"He's briefing the local police," Lura explained. "You didn't notice the uniform outside the door?"

"Yeah, I did," Dex cut in. "What's that about?"

"Zocer doesn't have jurisdiction. Shooting tourists in the marina isn't a federal offense, you know. Aníbal is with him, swearing out a complaint against Medrick for yesterday. He'll be popped as soon as he shows up."

"Arrested? Why didn't they do this yesterday?" I asked.

"We weren't sure it was Medrick, remember?"

"Can you actually prove he was involved in any of this?" Dex quizzed Lura.

"He's carrying a gun, right JadeAnne?" She looked at me, and I was reminded of my bruised back again. I nodded.

"That's illegal," Lura continued, "and he'll be held long enough to bust Danny's scam wide open. I can't believe I married the guy. What was I thinking?" There was a silence at the table. What could we say?

We sipped our beers while the silence grew uncomfortable. Happy tourists toasted and chatted around us in the tropical elegance of the bar, but Lura looked very sad. Dex shifted his weight on the caned seat of his chair, and I fought back tears. What a mess. Two of us were losing our men, but at least Dex wasn't gunning for me.

"Look, guys," Lura suddenly spoke. "Let's go upstairs to HQ and wrap this caper up." I heard the false bravado in her voice. I imagined Lura's world felt like it was caving in around her.

"Yes," Dex agreed as he tossed some pesos on the table and pushed his chair back. "Come on, Jade." Always a gentleman, he helped Lura with her chair then helped me.

"Thank you, Dex. Polo is waiting to meet you. C'mon."

We heard a scuffle in the lobby as we left the bar. Three uniformed cops had Medrick on the floor, an arm held in a hammerlock behind his back, and it looked like that god-awful yellow shirt was ripped. The blue cap lay on the floor, but I didn't see the pin. A crowd closed in as we scurried into Aguirre's private elevator. Just before the elevator door shut, I saw Daniel Worthington slip out the main entrance with a tall, black-haired man.

"Did you see him?" Lura's voice cracked.

"Uh-huh. Recognize the other man?" I asked.

"Maybe. He might have been one of the goons who chased me around Baja, although I don't remember any of them being so good-looking." She slid a glance at Dex. "Not you, the ones shooting at me."

"Well, I should think not. I rarely find a man pointing a gun at me to be all that sexy, do you, Lura?" I joked, hoping to cheer her.

She ignored me, but her face looked drawn, pale.

She spoke to Dex. "I thought it was you and your buddy who were after me. Then those green vehicles kept turning up. You know," she said, brightening, "CalMex has a corporate fleet of green vehicles. I can't believe I didn't think of that before."

The elevator arrived, and we strolled through the gallery on the way to Aguirre's conference room. Dex gawked at the splendid view, the rich appointments, and Aguirre's art collection.

"Is this real?" He stopped to inspect a jade and mother-of-pearl skull mask displayed on a shelf.

"It's Mayan from Caracol in Belize. Eighth century," Lura replied. "It's one of my favorites. I get kind of tired of the Tarascan coppers."

"How did he get it? Isn't it ill—"

"Diplomatic pouch. My cousin is a senator, don't you know?"

"Of, course. Don't ask, don't tell."

Lura opened the door. "Something like that." She smiled.

Dex and Aguirre hit it off instantly. I was a little miffed that my boyfriend accepted Aguirre's apology for kidnapping me so readily, but considering the bigger problems we were facing, I held my tongue. After his apology "the boys" chatted about sports, hunting—boy things—until the conversation turned to fishing in Baja.

"So how did my little cousin land in your net?"

Dex chuckled and launched into his shipwreck spiel until he was interrupted by the arrival of Zocer and Aníbal. Ani smiled warmly at me, and my heart flip-flopped. Dex stood up as Polo introduced them. The men shook hands, and everyone sat down. I felt my face burning and turned to search the bag at my feet for a pad and pencil, until the wave of attraction and guilt subsided. Had Dex noticed?

Dex finished the story about his buddy, Penn Guinn, and the salvage operations. Lura summarized her investigation with additions from Zocer. Aguirre gave his opinions on the PEMEX privatization vote, and Aníbal and Zocer reported on the arrest of Medrick Johnstone.

"I had my office do some research into Worthington and the consortium. It's an incorporated holding of PetroGlobal S.A. out of Panama." Dex paused, looking meaningfully around the room.

"PetroGlobal is actually a holding of a Texas company, which I believe you are already aware of," he said.

"Panamanian?" Lura interjected.

"Yes, ma'am. And surprise of surprises, the shell corporation is owned by—"

"Banco PanAmericano," Lura and Aguirre chimed in.

"Exactly. Daniel Worthington has quite a stake in the

future of Mexico's oil."

"Okay, so all this confirms Danny is up to his ass in alligators, but who are the others?" questioned Lura. "There are rumors, of course, but frankly, we don't know for sure. What have you uncovered, Dex?"

Lura didn't tip her hand. Didn't she trust Dex?

"You mean the president? I can't confirm that, but named officers of PetroGlobal include cronies of his. The consortium's board has a couple of key names too. Not just U.S., but Salinas de Gotari's cousin is on that board. This is big, people. And these boys play mean."

Lura swung around to face Aguirre. "Cuz, they'll kill you if you vote against it. What are we going to do?"

"*Cálmate*, Lulu, this is why we are here," soothed Zocer. "We'll—"

"For starters," Dex interrupted. "Aguirre, order your own security to guard your elevator. Is there any other way to get in here?"

Zocer leaned forward to address Dex. "Senator Aguirre has security in place in the lobby, on both stairwells, and at the service entrance to the penthouse. If Worthington enters the hotel, he will be detained and we will be notified. Both the senator and Mrs. Worthington are secure."

Zocer didn't look too pleased about Dex showing up and taking charge. Dex glared at him but remained silent.

"The police are cooperating with our investigation and are setting up a dragnet for Worthington. We'll handle communications and coordinate the search from here. He can't get too far in Johnstone's Suburban, which we assume he is driving, although it's not in the parking lot. JadeAnne, did he say where he was going to stay?" Zocer smiled, and I felt Dex stiffen in his seat next to me. Ah, so that was it. Dex was jealous. Good. And he picked up on the wrong guy.

"He said he was coming here. Nothing else."

"Here? What nerve. God. How did I ever fall for that

guy?" groaned Lura. "Well, it's divorce court now." She winked at Zocer.

I felt Dex relax.

"So what shall Dex and I do if you guys are operating from here?"

"We need more information on the consortium and Worthington. We need enough for a warrant. So far, we can't prove Worthington's done anything illegal."

"My office is on it. They'll call when they have something."

"Then we wait. Go to the beach. You're safe on my beach, Trouette. Now, if you will excuse me, I've got work to do." Aguirre stood up, signaling the end of the meeting, and left the room.

"Okay, Cuz. See ya later," Lura called after him. "Come on, Ani, Zocer, you guys. Let's all go down to the bar. I need a drink."

"What, are you crazy, Lura? You can't go down there. Anyway, we're leaving. Dex is tired."

"JadeAnne—" Dex's tone was short, which I ignored. I'd be damned if I was going to sit in a cozy group at the beach bar with my long-term boyfriend and my new infatuation. Aníbal, although silent, gave off vibes that he, too, opposed Lura's plan. Pangs of guilt struck me again. Aníbal looked crushed.

"We need to go back to Sally's," I said firmly. "Come on, Dex. Zocer, don't let her out of this penthouse. Aníbal either."

"I hadn't planned on it." Turning to Dex, Zocer held out his hand. "Trouette, I'm glad to meet you. You've provided some valuable information for my case, thank you. We'll be in touch later."

"Grijálves." Dex inclined his head coolly as they shook hands.

I wanted to shout, "Stupid macho rivalry isn't going to

get us anywhere."

Pepper had everything in the combi under control as I slid into the driver's seat and turned over the engine. We hadn't spoken on the way down. The cold tension between us was beginning to air condition the bus.

"I'm going to lie down in back." Dex moved to the back, sliding the side door shut.

I turned west toward the bluffs. I sure hoped the police were stopping green vans. I didn't relish the thought of being pushed over any cliffs into Zihua Bay. Where did Worthington go, anyway? I bet he'd dumped the Suburban. Probably changed to whatever vehicle the dark-haired man was driving. Was this man with Medrick on the stairs earlier? If so, Worthington might be lurking outside Sally's house at this moment. I doubted Worthington was as much of a screw-up as his buddy. Lura would never let him wear such an ugly shirt.

The road climbed, and I downshifted. I had to concentrate. Narrow roads and tracks intersected the highway, appearing out of dense growth. Just like the coastal road, there were many places to hide a vehicle. I probably should have taken the *autopista*, but I had wanted to show Dex the fabulous scenery, a romantic interlude, and wow him with that first view of the bay as it spread out below us.

The sun hung low over the ocean, and the bay, a deep sparkling sapphire ringed with emeralds, was dotted with brightly colored boats. Silhouetted against the sun, one of the many cruise ships that put in at Zihuatanejo's wharf glided through the narrow mouth into the Pacific, but Dex and Pepper snored in two-part harmony, missing the spectacular view.

"We're back, Tomás. Did anything happen while I was gone?"

"No, señorita. Just the usual traffic in and out."

"Did you send your grandsons to the house?"

"*Sí. Jorge y Juanito*. I'll call and let them know you are coming."

Dex's head popped between the seats. "Well, for goodness sake, is that you Tomás? Still on the job. I'll be."

"Señor Dex, *bienvenido*. Yes, I'm still here. Sometimes I hear the angels calling, but a good job is nothing to waste."

"I know what you mean, *viejo*, I know what you mean. By the way, Tomás, your boys any good? They armed?"

"*Claro que si*. They're the best. I trained them myself."

"I could use some men. Where's your son these days?"

"He's in charge."

"Good. I'd like to talk with him. Will you send him over later?"

"You think there's going to be trouble?"

"Nothing your boys and I can't handle, Tomás." Dex reached over me and patted the gnarled old hand resting on the combi's window frame. "Let's go, Jade."

"*Nos vemos*." I waved and pulled away from the *caseta*. "What are you planning, Dex?" I shouted over the roar of the little engine as it strained to push the bus up the hill. It was slower with the extra load of Dexter Trouette's 190 pounds inside.

"I don't have a plan, but I'm going to have an army."

"I thought you and I could spend some time together."

"Don't start, Jade."

"Dex, we've got to talk. And now's the time. You're being awful to me."

"Drop it, JadeAnne. At least until we get in the house and secure it."

"Well, here we are, so get yourself secure," I snapped.

A young man who looked remarkably like Rosa, but

with a scraggly moustach, stepped into the carport from the service patio. He had a double bore rifle cradled in his elbow and moved with the taut grace of a jungle cat. He waited for us to get out of the combi and leash Pepper, then stepped forward.

"Señor Trouette, permit me to introduce myself. I'm Jorge Ruiz, Tomás Ruiz's grandson. My brother-in-law, Juanito, is on the patio waiting for us."

"Thanks for coming, Jorge. Let's go in."

I unlocked the door, thinking Rosa must have let her husband onto the patio, and let Pepper lead the way. He was alert and tense as he sniffed the air. I followed him as he trotted around the house, looking into every corner and sniffing under every piece of furniture. He lingered in my bedroom, snuffling at the bed, and finally whined in front of the dresser. Nothing looked out of place or disturbed, but it smelled fishy to me. Literally. I must have stepped on a dead fish while running on the beach, I thought. I'd wash my shoes later.

"Shush, Pepper. Let's go get your dinner, boy."

He gurgled and moved the tip of his tail but didn't leave the dresser. His whining put me on edge. I reached for his collar to lead him out of the room but he pawed at the air and batted at my hand with his snout, pushing it toward the top drawer.

"What is it Peppi? What do you want?" I shivered, although the evening was warm and balmy. The dog wanted me to open the drawer.

Slowly, I reached for the drawer pull and I began to open it. An awful stench poured out, and Pepper's ears shot up. He left off whining and started to sniff, crowding the opening drawer, "Move," I shouted. He still crowded in, his head dipping into the opening. Then he sprang back. I looked into the drawer.

"Dex. Dex," I shrieked. "Come here."

The men's sandaled feet clattered across the tile floors to my room. I stood by the bed pointing. "Look! Look what they've done."

Jorge reached into my lingerie and pulled out a stinking, dead-eyed shark's head. Its mouth frozen ajar displayed rows of sharp, red-stained, foul teeth. The work of severing the head from the body had been poorly done. The cut was ragged and turning putrid. I was going to have to burn all my underwear, that is, when I stopped shaking.

"It's just a little shark, JadeAnne, relax." Dex was so reassuring.

"Someone is warning you," Juanito said. "This is what the narcos do. These warnings, they're common here."

"What do you mean? *Narcotraficantes*?" Dex turned on the boy. He had circled his arm around me and I leaned into him, my shivers calming.

Jorge continued, "The *heroína* and marijuana growers are always fighting. Whoever has the port has the business."

"We understand, but why would drug pushers threaten tourists?"

"This Worthington, does he know how it is here?"

"He lives in D.F. His wife's cousin is a bigwig in Ixtapa. He's a senator, in fact, from Michoacán."

"Aguirre. He's in the middle of the *heroína* wars. He wants the port. Everybody knows that."

"But Aguirre is against Worthington." I burrowed deeper into Dex's arms. I wanted all of this to end and leave us alone. I surreptitiously caressed my lover's butt. He pressed closer to me.

"I don't think we're going to sort this out now. Get that fish out of here, and go eat your dinners. We'll meet back here at nine-thirty with Tomacito and the rest of the men."

"Okay, boss." Jorge left with the shark's head, Juanito close on his heels.

CHAPTER NINETEEN

Dumped

Dex groaned. I raised my face to his. "Kiss me, Dex." I felt his blood pulsing and pressed closer to him. He stepped back and sank onto the bed, pulling me down onto his chest and squeezing me tightly. I squirmed against him, feeling his body with mine. I kissed him long and slow. "I've missed you so much." My voice sounded breathless.

Dex's heart pounded. We kissed hungrily, devouring each other. He was rock hard, every muscle tight, and breathing in fast, ragged breaths. I tugged at his t-shirt and yanked it over his head. He let go of me long enough to toss the shirt away and unbuckle his belt before falling back on top of me, his knee pushing between my legs. I kneaded his back, tracing the ripples of his muscles and losing myself in his full lips. I couldn't remember why we had stopped doing this. My legs entwined around his, and I dragged at his jeans with my feet. Dex groaned again and rolled off me. I sprang up, dropped my shorts to the floor and pulled his jeans around his ankles. He kicked them off and yanked me against him, pressed his lips to mine, and flipped us over.

His hands squeezed me, caressed me. I gasped, pulling away from his lips to kiss his neck, lick his shoulders. The sound of our beating hearts was deafening in my ears. He held me tighter and ground into me, panting even more heavily. I gasped for breath and pushed him to the side so I could breathe.

He rolled onto his back. "Come'ere," he whispered, and guided my hand to his erection. "Jade. I've missed you, too."

I forgot about our troubles. Everything was perfect. We were together and in love. I slid down his chest, kissing and licking him until I reached his thigh. His skin felt almost hot to the touch. I took him in my mouth. A sound of pure pleasure escaped him. He reached for me and began to prepare me.

"Come on Jade, come here. Now, Jade."

I reared up and flung myself over him. We fit together smoothly and sailed the tempest as one. I ground my hips into him and rode the peaks and valleys of the storm, not knowing where I left off and Dex began. The shadowy room lit suddenly with a shower of brilliant meteors falling around us.

"I love you, Dex." Sated, I fell into slumber in his arms.

I woke up alone. Voices came from the living room so it must have been after nine-thirty and the meeting had started with the Ruiz men. My stomach growled, annoying me. Besides, Dex hadn't awakened me for the meeting. I knew more about what was going on than he did. I should brief the Ruiz clan, I thought, annoyed. I whistled for Pepper, wondering if Dex had fed him, and stepped into the bathroom to clean up.

Pepper waited by the door when I finished my "Navy" shower a couple of minutes later. I jumped into some fresh clothes, but avoided opening the fishy underwear drawer. My old skivvies would have to do. I wandered into the kitchen.

SET UP

"*Buenas noches*," I called to the men. "Dex, did you feed the dog?"

"No. Hey open some beers, would you?"

I got a cold six-pack and a half a dozen glasses and put them on a tray. I noticed a jar of spiced Spanish peanuts and dumped them into a couple of bowls and added them to the tray. I couldn't believe it. Here I was, a partner in the firm, and Dex expected me to don a waitress apron. Why hadn't he gotten refreshments when the men arrived? The rosy afterglow of our lovemaking faded, darkening with the speed of the tropical sunset.

I carried the tray to the coffee table and set it down. The men remained silent while I was in the room, not even a "thank you." Obviously, I wasn't invited to this get-together. I went back to the kitchen to feed Pepper, and the men started talking. What was Dex's problem? He made passionate love to me then he acted like I was a servant. I wasn't putting up with it. I sat down at the counter to listen. I knew it would be futile to try and crash their little party. They'd never say anything in front of me. How did they think it was different when I was only feet away in a kitchen open to the living room? Machos could be really irritating.

"…on the street is Rodriguez is planning a move on Aguirre."

The name Aguirre caught my attention, pulling me from my snit. Tomacito Ruiz, Tomás' son, was talking about the heroin grower, the man who owned most of Zihua.

"Where? The Krystal? Aguirre never goes out, I heard." Dex looked in my direction.

"He won't hit him at the hotel or at his estate. He won't attack Aguirre at all. Rodriguez will go after the family. He has a history of leveling the competition through eliminating the competition's family. Emotional blackmail, of a sort," Tomacito continued.

"A couple of his guys bragged about offing Aguirre's

197

wife on the highway several years ago. I didn't believe it then. Now I'm not so sure," Jorge added.

"No. Worthington claims to be behind it. Aguirre told me," I called across the room.

"What do you mean Jade?"

"Part of the blackmail to get Aguirre to vote for the privatization. Worthington claims to have arranged the crash. He threatened to have the family killed one by one until the senator complies."

"Why would Rodriguez's men claim credit then? Unless Worthington has some tie to Rodriguez. Is this possible, Tomacito?" Dex asked.

"I don't know. There's talk Rodriguez has affiliated with the Beltran-Leyva Organization. I'll see what I can find out. We think Aguirre is affiliated with the Sinaloans."

"But what does this have to do with Worthington?" Dex asked.

"Look, gentlemen, let's assume Worthington is connected to Rodriguez. Worthington showed up today in Zihua on Dex's flight. In fact, the police arrested his buddy in the Krystal, but I saw Worthington slip out with another man. The police haven't found him yet. Someone must be helping him. It all makes sense," I was thinking aloud as I came into the living room and sat down. I had everyone's attention now.

"Worthington is up to his eyeballs in this scam. His wife is going to arrest him for money laundering, so he hires me to flush her into the open. He plans to kill her. He's had a small army of thugs following her around the country, but they keep missing. Where'd he get the *matones*, the bullies? Right here in Zihuatenejo." I grabbed a beer off the tray.

"I don't know, Jade, this sounds too easy. Why would Rodriguez let his men work for Worthington?"

"Not only the men, Dex, but the green vans. Tomacito, what do Rodriguez's people drive?"

"He's got a Mercedes."

"No corporate fleet?" I asked.

"*Claro*, Papi, his guys always drive around in green pickups and vans. They have signs on them, Familia Rodriguez, S.A., Zihuatanejo and the logo: a crest with a marlin." Jorge spoke to his father. "You've seen them."

"Coincidence. The green vans I saw didn't have any corporate logos," Dex declared. "Did you see a logo, JadeAnne?"

"They're magnetic. They come right off. I've seen guys do it in town." Juanito spoke for the first time.

Jorge nodded sagely. "*Simón.*"

"Not so coincidental anymore, is it?" I heard a tinge of sarcasm in my voice and hoped the Mexicans hadn't noticed. Professionalism was the only way I was going to gain their respect, but they probably couldn't distinguish the nuances of the language since I spoke in English. Dex spoke awful Spanish.

"No, but I still don't understand what motivation Rodriguez would have to help Worthington. What do you think, Tomacito?"

"I have no doubt it is money. And his hatred for Aguirre. It is common knowledge Aguirre has bested Rodriguez in several business deals in Ixtapa over the years."

"Why does he need money? Doesn't he control the heroin in this area?"

"There have been some obstacles preventing the smooth flow of *heroína* from his estates through the port here. He has lost money, people say," continued Tomacito. "His *mercancía* must be transported to Acapulco, controlled by the BLO, to ship. But the BLO and the Sinaloans have gone to war. They've brought the violence to the tourist area. Acapulco has turned into gangland."

"I'm not familiar with the problems down here."

Tomacito swallowed the remainder of his beer. "The

Beltran-Leyva brothers splintered their people from Chapo's Federación. They're Chapo's cousins and felt they should get a bigger piece of the pie. Now you have the Sinaloans fighting to regain the plaza. Not much is getting through. Rodriguez is sitting on tons of *heroina.* "

"So what obstacles keep him from moving the drugs through Zihuatenejo? Legal problems?" Dex would have made a great Inquisitor.

"When you're a narco you've always got legal problems, expensive ones. I heard he's had increases in his payoffs," Jorge affirmed through a mouthful of peanuts.

"Aguirre told me he recently foreclosed on the mortgage for some property of Rodriguez's heroin production in the mountains." I smiled at Jorge. "Aguirre tore out the poppies and planted agave."

He grinned back at me. The young men snickered.

Dex took a long pull on his Modelo Negra and swallowed. "So the truth is Aguirre has made a horse's ass out of Rodriguez."

He was beginning to get the picture.

I continued the speculation. "Then Worthington shows up and offers him money, lots of it, I bet—he owns a bank in Panama. And a way for Rodriguez to save some face. I'd wager Worthington was up on local news and gossip when he approached Rodriguez."

"Well, I'll be." Dex had such a way with words. "It isn't so farfetched to find fish in your undies then, is it, Jade?"

I grimaced, picturing the shark's head.

"Tomacito, how did Rodriguez's people get into this house? Your boys were watching it." He'd switched to his halting Spanish.

The older man glowered at his son.

"Papi, no one entered this house while Juanito and I stood watch. *Te lo juro*. We were here within thirty minutes of Abuelito's call, and everything looked fine in the house, but we didn't open the Señora's *buro*."

A thirty-minute window? No one was that good unless he was really close. Medrick was at the airport jabbing a gun in my spine, so it wasn't him. Could we trust the Ruiz clan?

"Tomás said no one unusual came in or out. Is it possible a usual person did?" I asked Jorge.

Dex thumped his beer bottle onto the coffee table. "I don't follow you, Jade."

"Where do Rodriguez's people live? Where does Rodriguez live?"

The room silenced, but practically crackled with the energy of five boy-brains hard at work.

"Who lives in the neighborhood?" I asked.

"Santiago Tafoya." Jorge slapped himself on the forehead. "Papi, you know him. Across the street several doors down. He's in transportation, shipping."

"How's he connected to Rodriguez?" Dex asked.

Jorge's eyes cast downward. "Papi, last summer? Maria Elena Cruz's wedding? She married Holmon Arango, Rodriguez's nephew."

"She's Tafoya's wife's daughter. I went to school with her," Juanito finished.

Dex looked at me quizzically. "So Tafoya is in Rodriguez's pocket?"

"Maria Elena isn't much of a prize," Jorge mumbled.

"So this Holmon, what's he look like?" Dex asked.

He described the tall, black-haired man I saw leaving the Krystal with Worthington this afternoon. Did this mean Worthington might be across the street?

"Did you boys sweep for bugs?" Dex demanded.

My heart missed a beat. I could picture Worthington laughing at us while he and his army prepared their attack. They wouldn't even have to leave the living room.

I got up and excused myself. I had to call Zocer, but if the house was bugged, there was nowhere I could talk except away from here. I went into the bathroom, looked everywhere I could think of to plant a bug, turned on the water, and dialed Zocer's cell phone. If they were listening, neither Spanish nor English would be secret. Lura probably spoke Pig Latin, but so could Worthington. What American kid couldn't? I tried to come up with a plan while the phone connected. Where was he, anyway?

On the eighth ring, Lura answered.

"Sorry, Lura, were you sleeping?"

"Nooo, but this better be good. What's all that noise? Are you standing by a waterfall?"

"Your husband left a severed shark's head in my underwear tonight."

"Say what?"

"He's hooked up with Rodriguez. I'm in the bathroom with the water running."

"The house is bugged?"

"We don't know, but I think I know where he is: right across the street. Dex and I need to get out of here, but I can't bring him to the Krystal. You saw Aníbal's face today."

"Yeah, my little cousin is pretty down, you heartbreaker. You owe me a sawbuck."

"Don't make me feel worse than I do, Lura."

"Hey, a bet's a bet, girlfriend. Have you guys eaten? Polo wants to go eat fish stew at Mare e Pesce on the pier. We've got a reservation for eleven. Why don't you come?"

"You folks are supposed to be staying put. Talk about into the mouth of the lion, or in this case, onto the sword of the marlin. That's Rodriguez's territory."

"So? We've got a little army coming with us. And we're armed. That old codger? He'll be in beddy-bye. You've got to tell me about the shark."

"Later. Since when can you take guns to restaurants?"

"It's a Mexican right. Like drinking beer while you drive."

"Lura."

"I'll call and add you to the reservation. See you in an hour."

I flipped off my phone. Lura was crazy. How did she convince Aguirre to this mad plan? I was hungry, though, and I loved Italian food, but I didn't think I'd have the stomach for fish.

I went back to the living room and picked up the tray to get more beer. Tomacito stood up and headed for the bathroom.

"Dex, I spoke with Lura just now. They want us to join them for dinner on the pier. An Italian place."

"Mare e Pesce? Best restaurant in town," Jorge commented.

"¡Simón! Very expensive," Juanito added.

Dex's expression was hard. "Didn't you just tell me the pier is Rodriguez territory?"

"A buddy of Aguirre's owns the restaurant. A little joke on Rodriguez." Juanito chuckled.

"Forget it, Jade."

"I said we'd come. I'm starving."

"There's never been trouble. You'll enjoy it, and we'll be posted outside," Jorge reassured Dex.

"Tío, Señor Trouette and la señorita are going to Mare e Pesce for dinner," Juanito informed his father-in-law who had returned to the room.

"I don't know, Tomacito." Dex appealed to the security man. "It sounds dangerous, but I do have questions for Aguirre. You should be there, too. Can I buy you dinner? You can ride with us."

"Gracias. But please, let me drive. My vehicle is armored. What time are we meeting the senator?"

Tomacito scared me, and I wasn't pleased about adding

him to our party, but we would be safer. "At eleven. Dex, what if they're listening?"

"Let them."

We'd thrown down the gauntlet. Was this war?

Tomacito checked his watch. "Forty-five minutes. I will organize some additional men to meet us at the pier. My boys will be armed and will escort us to the restaurant. Juanito, get moving. Bring the Escalade. Jorge round up the men. Leave Flaco here with the dog."

The Ruiz men stood up and started toward the door. Tomacito walked toward the carport with them, giving his son more instructions in a low voice. All I wanted was dinner with my boyfriend, not a major production. It was tough enough having to share Dex with the Aguirre clan. My stomach fluttered. Would Aníbal come?

"Dex, you should clean up," I suggested.

He grunted, but got to his feet.

I added, "What am I going to put on? I don't have any clean underwear."

We were laughing when Tomacito rejoined us. "It is arranged. My men will be in place. Now, if I may trouble you, señorita, for that beer?"

Tomacito settled down with his Modelo Negra to wait while Dex and I dressed for dinner.

"Dex, we need to talk," I said as soon as we closed our bedroom door.

"Christ, JadeAnne, you were the one who wanted to go out. I've got to clean up."

He pushed past me and slammed the bathroom door.

Thirty minutes later, Juanito arrived, driving the Escalade, and we were ready to go. I had tossed on a black dress and my sexy sandals. Dex still wore his jeans and running shoes, but he had changed into a silk shirt and linen jacket, which brought out the midnight blue of his eyes. Almost fifty, and he's still hot. I loved the way his dark hair, now shot through with threads of silver, curled onto his collar. The grey made him look distinguished, a man to take seriously. I grabbed my bag and my honey's arm, and we climbed in ahead of Tomacito and settled onto the luxurious suede seat. Two identical Escalades waited along the curb. As we backed out of the carport, the first pulled ahead of us. I didn't see who was driving.

Our vehicle had tinted windows, a privacy screen, roll-bars, a DVD player, a mini-bar, and had been sprayed with eau de nouveau automobile. I assumed the others were the same. We formed a mini-flotilla of pimp-mobiles, or in Mexico, narco-mobiles.

The Escalade rode smooth and silent. The driver pointed out several landmarks, but it was hard to see through the smoked glass in the dark. No one else said anything, and he soon stopped talking. My stomach growled again. The peanuts and beer hadn't cut it. I tried to hold Dex's hand, but he pulled away from me and, confused, I pushed my nose to the glass and let the lights of the city and a nagging sense of dread trail along behind us.

Inside the cabin of the Escalade, the silence became oppressive. Was everyone holding his breath? The cabin air felt cool but stuffy, and I cracked my window. Odors of propane seeped into my nostrils with the warm rush of city air from the street. The tires wooshed on the asphalt and echoed off stucco walls as we sped along Avenida Juan Alvarez toward the parking lot at the anchor end of the *muelle*. My sense of dread mounted with the arrhythmic beat of my heart. Static played in a staccato over the two-way radio and everyone flinched. I wasn't alone, then, in my anxiety. Even Dex, I thought. No other vehicles drove on the street, and it worried me. The radio crackled again, but I couldn't hear what was said over the wind rushing through my window.

Jorge turned and announced, "The parking lot is secure."

Like a balloon with a sudden tiny rent, the pressure dropped perceptibly in the Escalade as we all exhaled.

"The restaurant?" Tomacito Ruiz asked Juanito.

"No sign of Rodriguez's people in the area. It's quiet."

"What about Senator Aguirre? Has he arrived yet?" Dex sounded like he was looking forward to seeing him. I wondered again if Aníbal would come. Half of me quivered in trepidation while the other half thrilled in anticipation. What was I going to do about Dex?

We turned left into the parking lot and rolled toward the pier. A limo blocked the entrance. I assumed it was Aguirre's. Juanito pulled up behind it and parked. Our escort dropped back and I could see armed men positioned in the lot and along the pier.

"The senator's people," Tomacito explained as he and Dex slid out of the SUV. Dex nodded and said something as the door slammed.

Juanito opened my door and helped me out of the Escalade. The air hit me like a wet sponge. We were feet from Zihuatenejo Bay, and the balmy night was drenched in humidity as black clouds stacked up on the mountains and blotted out the stars. It was probably going to rain. Breathing deeply, I savored the familiarity of the waterfront, sea-salt laced with the effluvium of marine oil, and yearned for the Sarasvati and Sausalito with a sharp stab to my gut. I needed to hug my dog, but Pepper was back at Sally's on guard duty. I looked around for Dex.

Tomacito stopped to talk to one of the men. Dex strode down the pier ahead of me. I hustled to catch up.

"Dex, wait for me."

He slowed down but didn't stop or face me. His expression was half hidden in shadow as I reached him, but I linked my arm through his and smiled.

"You must be starved, love, you didn't even wait for me."

He jerked away, spinning to face me. "Let me go."

"Oh, you are hungry."

"No, JadeAnne. There's no nice way to put this, so I'll just say it. We're through."

It was as though I'd been slugged in the solar plexus. Every nerve ending tingled and pulsed with a burning pain. The night felt suddenly black and suffocating.

"I've already moved my things off the Sarasvati. I'll be living on my sailboat, for now."

"Wh—what?" I stammered. I couldn't think. I couldn't think.

Dex's voice was flat. "I'm sorry Jade. We just don't have anything in common anymore."

"But, Dex.…"

"Don't make me say it," he interrupted with that warning tone.

My world blew apart around me, and I whirled away from him. It was true. Dex didn't love me anymore. I didn't belong. Blindsided, I ran. My sandals thunked deafeningly on the wood planks. I should have worn my tennies. I caught my right heel between the planks and sailed out of the shoe and started to fall. Who cares? It was over. We're over. The railing loomed up, I was going to hit it and plunge into the black water below. Picturing the shark's toothy grin in my drawer, I snapped back into reality and rebalanced myself as a shadow darted in front of me.

I slammed into a bulletproof vest with a sickening thud. The wind rushed out of me, and I collapsed. Aguirre's guard eased me down to the pier, and I wheezed wet gulps of air into my flattened lungs. Slowly, I got my breath back and opened my eyes. I was looking between the slats at the shifting blackness under the pier. A flashing red light arced in the darkness, barely illuminating the yellow-painted prow of a *panga* floating between the pilings.

Footsteps echoed off the splintered timbers and hands pulled me to my feet. "Dex?"

"What happened, señorita? You shouldn't run like that." It was Jorge Ruiz. "Let me help you to the *restaurante*. Here's your shoe."

He held my elbow to steady me as I slipped the sandal back onto my foot. I didn't seem hurt, but my heart felt like a lead weight in my chest.

"Thanks, Jorge. Let's go."

As it turned out, the restaurant was right there. I just hadn't seen the sign. Jorge walked me to the door and held it open. I saw Dex across the room with Aguirre, Jorge, and Tomacito Ruiz, sitting together at one end of the table with Aguirre at the head. Lura sat in the middle across from an empty chair with Zocer to her right. Aníbal was across from Zocer, next to Jorge.

Lura hopped out of her seat and waved. "Over here, girlfriend." Then she wobbled toward me on spike-heeled sandals.

"I see I'm not the only one in unsensible shoes, Lura." It was all I could think of to say.

Winking conspiratorially, Lura gave me a hug. "I don't know what's up, but here's your chance." She nodded toward Aníbal.

I let her lead me to the table. "Look, Cuz, here's JadeAnne," she sang out.

Aníbal and Zocer stood up. Aníbal pulled the end chair out for me, his face a blank mask. I sat down. Zocer seated Lura. The men at the other end of the table didn't pay any attention to us.

CHAPTER TWENTY

Dinner was a Blast

"*Bienvenidos a Ristorante Mare e Pesce. Soy Antonio y seré su servidor esta noche,*" a middle-aged waiter said and handed out the menus.

"Waiter, bring us three pitchers of margaritas and glasses for everyone," Lura shouted. "And can't you liven up the music?"

I was enjoying the melancholy strain of accordions, what I call "gondola" music. It suited my mood, but Lura was ramping up to what I was sure would be an uncomfortable and embarrassing situation for everyone. Judging from the looks on Aguirre's and Zocer's faces, they shared my assessment of the situation. She'd already had too much to drink. Her regular behavior.

"Waiter, bring the lady a margarita, shaken without salt." Aguirre looked at her. "Cousin, it might be better not to have too many of those tonight, at least until your husband has been taken into custody."

"You stinker, you would have to mention him and spoil the party," she retorted, a coy pout on her lips. "Poli, I'm not worried. Your little army out there will protect us, won't they?"

"Lulu, we're taking a risk just being outside of the penthouse, and you know it. I'm not drinking anything, well, maybe a glass of Chianti with my spezzatino di cinghiale." Aníbal read off the menu. "And a Bellini if it's made with fresh peach juice. You make Bellinis? Fresh?" he asked the waiter.

"Of course, sir."

I looked at Aníbal and smiled. "I'll join you. *Due, per favore.*" I wagged two fingers at the waiter.

Dex and Aguirre drank grappa. So much for Aguirre's little speech. The other men ordered bottled water. Zocer frowned and slumped in his chair. He didn't touch the beer in front of him. He looked like I felt: dejected. Lura certainly wasn't paying any attention to Zocer as she discussed their case with Dex. I could plainly hear Dex pontificate on the consortium from the other end of the table.

"They would be protecting the president, but you can be sure he and his family are involved."

"Oh, do you really think so, Dex?" Lura batted her eyelashes then lowered her voice to murmur some nonsense from behind her dorky grin.

He angled toward her and said something I missed when Zocer asked me to pass the bread, but it was clear Lura hung on his every word. I didn't know if this was for my and Aníbal's benefit, but I could tell Dex was flattered. I wanted to laugh out loud, but I wouldn't give him the satisfaction of knowing I was watching. Aguirre, Tomacito, and Jorge had their heads together, making a plan of some sort, but Lura and Dex resumed their loud conversation, and it was hard to hear anyone else.

The Bellini tasted sweet and strong, but didn't dispel my glum feelings. I picked at a breadstick and wondered how Dex could sit down there and laugh and carry on in front of me after what he'd done. Bastard. Tears burned my eyes, and I turned away from the table.

SET UP

I hadn't really noticed the restaurant when I came in. It was appointed in gleaming dark woods, burgundy and hunter green brocades, copies of Italian Renaissance portraits, tapestries, and paintings of hilltop castles, outdoor markets, and fishermen. I particularly liked one painting, hanging near our table, depicting a Venetian fishmonger's stall with a low tub of sea snails escaping, I hoped, to the sliver of muddy canal in the background.

Booths lined the seaward wall, the tables set with white linen and illuminated by Murano-style glass pendants. The interior lights reflected in the windows, lighting the dark bay and night-black hills beyond as though hung with mini-Christmas lights. Dex and I had talked about getting married in Venice. I saw myself wearing a white linen cocktail suit like the Austrian bride we met in Harry's Bar, and I wanted to carry a white Burano lace parasol. Several rounds with the happy couple, and Dex had proposed. It was a crazy idea. I said no. And he'd been paying me back ever since. Asshole.

My tears stopped, but I felt shaky and tense. Forget Dexter Trouette. My mother was right, a low class libertine. I'm so stupid, wasting almost a decade of my life on a slime bucket. I clenched my fists, wishing I had that Burano parasol. I saw myself beating Dex over the head with it.

"What's wrong, JadeAnne?" Aníbal asked me, his face a study in concern.

He caught me off guard, and I stammered, "I, uh, I-I'm worried about Rodriguez. What if—?"

"We'll be fine. The men outside have our backs. Don't worry." He slid his open palm across the table to me.

"I've got to use the ladies' room." I hoped the grimace I made looked like a smile. He frowned in disappointment, but I had to leave the table. Get away from Dex and Lura and the stupid mess with Aníbal. He didn't deserve what I had to offer, which amounted to not much. I concentrated on my surroundings, passing among the mostly empty tables. There were few diners at this time of night. Oddly, neither Aguirre nor Tomacito had posted anyone inside the restaurant. Only couples and families dined, and I couldn't imagine them to be armed. No one sat at the polished bar, well stocked with wine, and taking up most of the back wall. Well, if the bad guys show up, maybe they'll shoot Dex. I slipped through the door marked *Damas*.

The old world bathroom charmed me. Its tiles might have been Italian and were set like Byzantine mosaic. I latched the door, plunked down on the lidded toilet, and took several deep breaths to calm my tense body and clear the hateful thoughts from my mind. What was I moping around for? A very attractive man itched to get to know me better. If Dex were so stupid to give me up, then I'd show him. I liked Aníbal. Why not flirt with him? A plan.

I washed my face. In the mirror, I grinned back at myself. I'd make Dex squirm with jealousy. The plan was already working.

The music had changed to an opera by the time I returned to the table, and my caprese salad waited at my place. I smiled at Aníbal and dug in wondering what to say to him. I was suddenly ravenous, and I practically inhaled the succulent tomatoes with basil and fresh mozzarella cheese. I hadn't given much thought to the execution part of my plan. The noise of conversation at our table rose a decibel or so, punctuated by the sounds of forks and knives clinking on china. A smell of fresh-baked bread and garlic wafted on the air, and it seemed to me the table had relaxed and become friendlier with the arrival of food. I stole a glance at Dex.

"JadeAnne, what were you telling me on the phone? About a shark's head?" Lura boomed.

I looked up from my tomatoes. Everyone's eyes turned

to me, and my neck and face flushed.

"A shark's head?" Zocer's brow furrowed. Slowly, his expression changed to recognition and alarm. "Where?"

"Pepper smelled it in my underwear drawer," I choked. How embarrassing.

"Your underwear? Did you hear that, Poli? JadeAnne has dead fish in her undies," she announced. "Well, the whole thing sounds fishy to me, girlfriend." Lura's laugh escalated out of control, and I wished she'd shut up.

Thank God the pasta arrived. I played footsie with Aníbal under the table, my face hot again, but I winked at him, and he replaced his sad look with a grin. Mouthfuls of exquisite fresh ricotta-stuffed ravioli tossed in sage butter muffled our conversation. The machos at the other end of the table continued talking about the dead shark.

"A couple of clients reported discovering dead fish. A lawyer, Lopez, Papi—" Jorge reminded Tomasino, "—hired us after the family dog had been beheaded and tossed into the swimming pool. His kids found it. He was trying Rodriguez's cousin for murder. Packed up the family and left town."

"Jorge, what's your take on this?" Aníbal asked, joining the conversation. "JadeAnne isn't investigating the cartels."

"No, but we think Worthington has teamed up with Rodriguez against the senator." He repeated the theory we'd developed back at Sally's.

Aníbal glared at Aguirre. "So this was a warning to Polo?"

Obviously, the irony wasn't wasted on Aníbal, or anyone else at the table, except Lura who hadn't been listening anyway. Aguirre squirmed under the scrutiny of the assembled party. I watched his senatorial immunity leaking into a puddle around his feet. The law enforcement personnel didn't give a crap about his office. Aguirre was right in the middle of a war over control of the port.

"A toast to Polo, the best cousin a girl could have and the best senator in all of Mexico." Lura sloshed wine onto the tablecloth.

Once again, the waiter saved us from major embarrassment by arriving with our steaming-hot main courses. The locals in our party ordered the fresh fish I guessed Mare e Pesce was renowned for. Aníbal ordered some sort of meat in a heavy sauce.

"Ani, what's that?" I asked, stealing Lura's trick and fluttering my lashes at him. No time like the present to carry out my little "jealousy" plan.

"Wild boar. Well, here, it's actually feral pig, but what's the difference, really?"

"Is it good? May I taste?"

He held his laden fork toward me and fed me the bite he was going to take. I locked eyes with him and sucked the food from the fork like Mrs. Waters in Tom Jones, or so I hoped.

"Mmmm. That's delicious. A bit gamey tasting, but really different. Not like pork at all."

"Want another bite?" he asked me, with a sensual gleam in his eyes.

"Sure." I darted a sidelong glance at Dex then smiled and opened my mouth. Dex was watching.

"Mhhhm," I groaned and ran my tongue over my lips slowly, still smiling at Aníbal. I felt his toes caress my leg.

"I always get this here. It's the best in the world. At least, outside Tuscany."

I swallowed my bite and opened my mouth to speak but closed it, distracted by a commotion at the entry to the restaurant. I heard a series of rapid popping noises coming from the direction of the shore and whipped around in my chair. Were those gunshots?

Juanito raced toward our table, gun drawn. "*Suegro, suegro.*" He called his father-in-law. "*Ven, ven. Rápido.*"

The heavy carved chairs grated on the floor as Tomacito and Jorge pushed away from the table in unison and pounded toward the door. Their boots thudded hollowly on the tile. Aníbal took off toward the kitchen, drawing his gun and shouting in rapid Spanish as he rocketed through the swinging door.

"Get down. Get down. Under the tables," Zocer bellowed at the diners as he launched himself from his chair and tackled our waiter, pushing him back toward the kitchen. "Is there another way out?" I heard him ask. He turned back to the table. "Protect the senator." He disappeared into the kitchen.

Was he talking to me?

Then I couldn't mistake the rapid fire of automatic weapons. Whose? Ours? Theirs? Pandemonium erupted. I watched, momentarily transfixed. The racket of several dozen feet running higgity-piggity for exits, along with the screaming, the clatter of tipped-over chairs and dishware crashing to the floor made a mad cacophony.

"Jade. JadeAnne. JadeAnne." The urgency in Dexter's voice brought me to my senses. He was pushing Aguirre through the double doors leading to the terrace on the far side of the building.

I grabbed my purse off the floor and felt for my little gun, slung the purse strap across my body with the Semmerling in my fist. Lura had her Glock in her hand and leapt across the room after Zocer. She was like a ballerina in high-heeled sandals instead of toe shoes.

The sounds of the battle outside raged. I started after Lura. She slammed open the kitchen door to a deafening blast. Outlined against a blinding flash, her body hung in the air, legs doing the splits in a grand jeté. The force of the thunder blew me back into my chair. I fell to the floor, numbed by the shock of the tremendous impact, and inched under the table, protecting my head with my arms. Pieces of the restaurant rained around me in silence, and I felt the pier shudder as the kitchen collapsed. I held my nose against the stench of burning tar and dust.

Nothing moved in the dark restaurant except several candles, which had survived the concussion, flickering ghoulishly in their glass holders atop the debris-laden dining tables. From my position under our table, I could see several crumpled forms near where the kitchen and bathrooms had been. I pinched my eyes closed. Lura had been caught in the blast. I discovered I could pull myself onto my knees, but I ached all over, like I'd been beaten. Did Dex get away? Gingerly, I crawled out from under the table, watching for shards of glass and metal, and stood up on shaking legs.

Lura's gun lay discarded a few feet away. I picked it up. Where was she? I hoped against hope she'd gotten away. I called her name, but I could only hear a high-pitched keening in my ears. I stood in the middle of the room and scanned until I found her. She lay on her back in a tangle of limbs, tablecloth, and chair. The evening breeze flowing through the blown-out windows had dissipated the smoke from the room, but I smelled Lura's burned flesh. There was nothing I could do for her. I covered my mouth and nose with my hand to filter the stink, but it was no good. I heaved what I'd eaten of my fried jumbo shrimp with grossly colorful vegetable confetti onto the floor and coughed and heaved until my throat rasped and my nose bled. My mouth tasted like rusty baling wire when I put my head back to stop the nosebleed.

I realized I hadn't heard the sound of guns since the blast. The keening in my ears mellowed into a dull roar, and I wondered if I would hear a gunfight. Regardless, I had to get out of there, the entire place could collapse at any moment, or the gas cylinders could blow up, or...

There was no point in imagining what could happen. Best to find survivors and help them to safety. But where?

On shore? I circled the room, tripping over rubble, furniture and ruined dinners. Most of the diners had gotten out. I found the hostess and a chef badly burned, and two waiters who must have been crushed by the concussion. All were dead. In the corner, a movement caught my attention. I ran toward it. A young couple cowered under a table.

"Are you all right?" I called out as I approached. My voice sounded strange, like I'd inhaled helium. The couple didn't seem to hear me, and I called out again, waving my hands.

They shrank further under the table, fear playing across their faces. I almost heard the girl's scream. I still had the Glock in my hand. I must look like an insane killer.

"No, no. I'll help you." I shoved the gun into the purse I still clutched to my chest and held out my hand, palm up. Scraped and cut from the glass and debris I'd crawled through, my hand was bloody. I looked at the other one and rubbed them both across my skirt, smearing blood and filth onto the cloth. I tried to smile. I couldn't feel anything, but I didn't have time to worry about it.

Eyeing me nervously, the *novias* mouthed to each other, coming to a soundless agreement. They were barely more than children. I helped them up and guided them to the hole in the wall where the glass terrace door had been. I didn't see anyone outside. Was that good news? What happened to Dex and Aguirre?

"I don't know what to tell you to do. Hide. Far away from the restaurant." I pantomimed hiding actions. I wanted to tell them to wait for the police, but in Mexico, the police might be the bad guys. I knew it didn't really matter. They wouldn't hear me anyway.

As the young diners faded into the darkness, I crept back inside to the smoldering remains of the kitchen. I peered over the edge of the collapsed floor and saw two pilings had been destroyed, and the pier was on fire. The flames lit the surface of the bay, and it looked like a couple of bodies were submersed just under the inky surface. Carefully, I made my way to the entry. The roof had collapsed too, blocking my exit. I would have to go back through the outside terrace. The way Dex had gone.

I felt glass and crockery crunch underfoot as I navigated the room. I looked down and saw the blood and vegetable confetti spattered on my sexy sandaled feet. God I needed my dog. And I sure as hell needed a shower.

Outside, I edged around the corner of Mare e Pesce and looked down the pier toward the parking lot. Black smoke billowed from the kitchen, obscuring my view. The pier felt solid, and I decided I had to chance whatever was on the other side of the smokescreen. I crossed to the leeward side, closed my eyes, and ducked into the smoke, holding my breath and the safety rail for guidance. I hadn't seen flames on this side, but I also didn't know if the explosion had severed the structure, and if it was still passable. I inched along, sliding one foot and then the other, slowly, shifting my weight only when I was sure there was solid wood underneath. My chest constricted, and the urge to breathe wracked me until I sucked in a lungful of greasy smoke. Coughing violently, I pulled myself along the rail for what felt like a century. God, don't let me die here of smoke inhalation.

My eyes stung and teared up. I gasped, gulping in huge swallows of fresh salt air. I opened them and saw the parking lot, but no one was in sight. The Escalade remained where we had left it, but Aguirre's limo was no longer parked at the head of the dock. Did Dex get him away? Why didn't he take me? Behind me, the restaurant was in flames. I felt the heat and ran on my toes to keep my heels out of the cracks between the planks. I kept my head down below the railing. I didn't want to be picked off like a wooden duck in a shooting gallery. Hopefully, it was too dark for anyone to see me.

I sprinted the hundred-yard dash toward the Escalade until my smoke-damaged lungs hurt so much I had to stop and catch my breath. I squatted down behind an overturned rowboat chained to the dock and panted. I was almost there, only a few more yards.

My hearing was returning. I heard my own ragged breathing and suddenly the familiar popping noise. I dove to the deck as a shower of splinters sprayed from the spot where my head had just been resting. Someone was shooting at me.

There was a tiny space between the guardrail and the boat. I wriggled my way into it. It wouldn't take the killer long to figure it out and come after me, though. I pulled Lura's Glock out of my bag. More popping noises came from the parking lot. I saw muzzle flashes through a break between buildings, but I couldn't see the entrance to the pier.

The prow of the rowboat fragmented into a thousand splinters above me and I felt the vibrations of footsteps on the rough wooden planks getting stronger as someone approached me. I grasped the Glock with both hands, steadying it. Whoever my stalker was, he was a goner.

"Lura. Lura, darling…." A tender voice called Lura. I knew instantly it was Worthington. That bastard thinks I'm Lura.

"Come out now, Lura. Don't make this harder for both of us."

I could hear him more clearly. He was almost to the rowboat. I held my breath.

"Why did you have to stick your pretty nose into my business, Lura? I tried to head off your investigation. You wouldn't listen to me." His voice at first was plaintive, then shifted to resignation. "You've forced me to kill you."

I heard him sob.

"Lura, Lura, I love you so much. But I can't let you ruin everything. I can't go to jail. I can't."

One more step and I've got you, you slimeball.

"Hold it right there Danny. Drop the gun." Aníbal's voice carried from a distance.

"Ani, don't come any closer. I'll kill her. Toss your gun into the water and get down on the dock," Worthington shouted.

By the sound of his voice, I could tell he'd turned away from me. I peeked over the keel to see Worthington's back. He was about ten feet away, pointing an assault rifle down the dock. I couldn't see Aníbal.

Several bursts of gunfire rang out in the parking lot, and Worthington fired. I heard shouts, screams, then engines starting, and the squeal of tires as cars roared out of the lot. A set of headlights illuminated Worthington. I swung the Glock up to position, but banged the hull with the barrel in the tight space. He spun around, the rifle aimed at my head. I squeezed the trigger once, twice, three times. My shots went wild.

"You stupid bitch. I've got you."

Worthington's chest exploded a fraction of a second after I saw the flash. The sound of the report followed, but he was already flying toward me in a cloud of his own blood and guts. I heard myself scream, and the night went black.

CHAPTER TWENTY-ONE

Sibling Rivalry

August 1, 2007

Purring, a sleek jaguar curled around me and rocked gently. Its musky-sweet scent swirled on the heat rising from its muscular body. Enveloped in warmth, protected and content, I dozed in the big cat's lair. Maybe I was a jaguar, too. I couldn't see myself, couldn't quite open my eyes. But something, something signaled from way back in my memory. Some memory wanted to get out. I snuggled closer to the jaguar. It snarled, disturbed, and showed its dagger-like claws. I spun away, my eyes flying open. He wasn't a cat. He was a man without a face leaning in, leaning in, his black blade poised for the thrust into my heart.

"JadeAnne," a voice called in the distance. The dagger man disappeared, and I was adrift in blackness with only the voice. It sounded kind.

"JadeAnne Stone. Miss Stone, JadeAnne." The voice called out, a sharp prod. Someone shook me. A mean boy had picked me up and was shaking me so my head flopped over and back. *Make him stop.*

"JadeAnne, it's me, Aníbal. Shhhh. Shush. It's okay. I've

got you."

I felt the movement of the vehicle, heard the hum of the Escalade's engine and opened my eyes. Aníbal's arms encircled me, holding me close against him.

"It's over, JadeAnne," he said softly. "Worthington is dead. Rodriguez's men retreated, and we're on our way home."

Where was Dex?

Recollection swept over me like a brush fire out of control. Dex's words. The deafening blast. Lura. The smoke, the fire, and the fear. Memory came on too strong to shut out. I shook as tremors wracked my body.

"Lura," I croaked.

"Don't talk, Jahdey. You've inhaled a lot of smoke." He handed me a bottle of water. "Have a drink. We'll debrief later."

Jahdey. He pronounced my name in almost a Spanish accent. Soft. Like a little endearment. "Thanks, Ani," I whispered, grasping the water with a trembling hand.

The next thing I remember was pulling into Sally's carport. I groaned as I heaved myself to a sitting position with Aníbal's help. My head pounded, and my ears were still ringing when the Escalade's engine died. Tomacito was driving. He beeped the horn once, and the boy-guard burst out the door with a large, frantic dog, howling on his heels.

"Peppi." I was out the car door in an instant. Dropping to the garage floor, I flung my arms around my dog and buried my face in his ruff.

Pepper let me know he was overjoyed to see me, crowing between sloppy kisses and dancing steps.

"Come into the house, señorita," urged Tomacito, trying to pull me up by my elbow. "We aren't safe out here."

Pepper had caught a scent on me, smoke probably, and sniffed me all over. He whined as I allowed the security man to guide me to my feet. My dog looked toward the Escalade and back at me and ran between the men, sniffing at each, frantic, looking at the vehicle doors for Dex.

"He's not coming, Peppi." I lunged for his collar to guide him back inside the house. "He's not coming home to us, boy."

Aníbal clattered into to the kitchen and rummaged around in the cabinets. The others clomped into the living room, the sounds of their boots incongruous when I should hear clacking and slapping of sandals. In the hallway, Tomacito talked to the boy, I'd forgotten his name, if I'd ever learned it. Our meeting seemed so long ago, before the world spun off its axis.

I followed after Aníbal. "What're you doing?"

"Making a snack." He picked up the pineapple I'd bought at Mega and prepared it for slicing. "Did you know bromelain, the enzyme in pineapples, alleviates inflammation in the bronchial tubes? I'll make some salad, too. Chlorophyll also helps inflamed lungs. I'm sure the burned tar and creosote we were breathing can't be good for us."

The tea kettle whistled, and Aníbal went on as he poured the hot water over a tea strainer he'd placed in a mug, "Your friend has this tea. I think it will help your lungs, too. Why don't you go clean up, Jahdey. I'll finish this and talk with Tomacito. When you're comfortable, we'll debrief."

I looked down at my arms and legs. I was soot-covered, torn and bloody. My clothes were tattered and stained with vomit and blood from abrasions and gashes in my skin. Horrified, I fled from the room.

Under the bright lights in Sally's bathroom, I discovered most of the cuts and scrapes were superficial. A gash on my left knee might need some attention, and as I washed away the caked blood and dirt from my body, I uncovered several splinters embedded in my hands and arms, which would have to be removed. Not masked by the delicate scent of tea rose soap, the stench of me rising in the steam was disgusting. The smell of hell.

I scrubbed myself again with the loofa and lathered my hair for the third time. Images flashed through my mind: Lura suspended against the blinding light of the blast. Daniel Worthington, grisly with spouting blood as though he were a victim from a slasher film. Dark, puffy zombies submerged in a watery grave. Dex's face looming in upon me, fangs bared and bloody. The black oil-dripping knives of my dream several nights before. I shook my head violently, willing the visions away. Who else died tonight?

The taste of burned flesh coated my mouth, and I gulped in a mouthful of hot water, swished it around my tongue and teeth, and spat it into the drain. I wanted to sit down in the tub under the stream and let the hot water soothe me as it slid down my body and washed away all memory. I wanted to curl into a ball and disappear. I wanted to drip down the drain and rush out to sea. The weight of my heart in my chest was so heavy I was bent low, and my legs ached from the toil of holding me up. I wanted to go home.

"JadeAnne, are you okay?"

Startled, I hadn't heard Aníbal come in to the bathroom.

"Yeah. Yeah, I'm fine."

"I knocked. You didn't answer. I'm sorry to barge in on you."

"It's all right. I should get out. The water's cold."

"We need to talk about what happened."

"I don't want to. I can't take any more. I need my dog. And sleep. I'm exhausted." I felt panic clutching at my lungs.

"I know, Jahdey," he soothed, "Pepper's right here waiting for you. I'll close my eyes and hold your towel for you. Come on now, get out. I won't peek."

Did he think he was cute? I cranked off the water valves, reached my hand through the gap between the shower curtain and the wall, and said in his same smooth tone, "Just hand me my towel, Ani, would you? And leave? I can't...."

He interrupted, his voice firm, "You know we have to talk, JadeAnne. Tomacito is waiting. He lost several of his men tonight. People are missing—Lura—"

My head jerked up. *Aníbal doesn't know Lura is dead.*

"I don't care. I can't talk about it. Leave me alone." How could I tell him?

"I understand, Jahdey, really I do. I had a first time, too. But it will be worse if we don't debrief." His voice remained quiet.

"Get out of here," I shrieked. I had wrapped myself in the towel he'd handed me. I flung the curtain aside and hurled the shampoo at him. "Leave me alone, I say. Get out. Get out!" Water flowed down my face, hot and salty.

He picked up the shampoo bottle. It had bounced harmlessly against the door and dropped to the floor. "I can't do that, JadeAnne. Come on. Come get dressed."

"Aguirre, isn't that woman dressed yet?" boomed Tomacito from the doorway. "Get dressed or come in the towel. I haven't got time to put up with this."

"Get out of my bathroom, you, you...who do you think you are?" Panic gripped my lungs spread into my stomach. I felt sick, and suddenly my muscles turned to jelly. Why wouldn't these people let me be?

"¡Cállate, mujer!" Tomacito snapped, raising his hand and stepping into the bathroom menacingly. Was the bastard going to hit me?

"Get dressed."

Pepper growled behind him. He knew I was afraid of Tomacito. But Tomacito would sooner shoot Pepper as not. I was certain ice ran through his veins. How could he be sweet old Tomás's son?

"Okay, okay, I'm getting dressed," I whined. "Just get out of here. Please." I thought of the "magic word." God, I hated myself for being so submissive, but I was in a towel.

He grunted and stalked out of the bathroom, leaving the door open and kicking at my dog. He missed, but Pepper snapped at his leg.

Good dog, I mouthed.

All my warm steam escaped. Aníbal gave me a hard look and said, "Don't push him, JadeAnne." His voice sounded more fearful than commanding. He slid out of the bathroom, gently closing the door behind him. So Aníbal was afraid, too.

I toweled off and tossed on a muumuu I found hanging on the bathroom door. The face that looked back at me from the mirror belonged to someone I didn't recognize. I ran the comb through my hair and decided to skip my makeup. It wouldn't improve my looks much, and I didn't have the energy to care.

Barefoot, I shambled into the living room, Pepper at my side, and tossed myself into a chair. Pepper plunked down between Tomacito and me, a snarl curling his lips. Good dog, good boy. Aníbal handed me a cup of lukewarm tea.

I stared at Tomacito. "So what do you want?"

"I understand it's difficult, but I need to know what happened. Where is the senator?" His voice was hard and impatient.

"Aguirre? How would I know? He's with my ex-boyfriend. Maybe they're dead, too. Didn't you call him?"

"Too? Who else is dead? JadeAnne, where's Lura? Polo took her, right?" Aníbal's eyes pleaded with me.

Maybe I'd imagined it. Maybe she was back at the Krystal with Polo and Dex, dancing at the disco.

I looked at Tomacito. "You tell me what happened. We heard gunfire. You and your boys ran out of the restaurant. Aníbal, you followed through the kitchen. Lura went after you." I tried to smile at him.

"Where was the senator during the explosion?"

"What difference does it make, Señor Ruiz? You, our security, left us unprotected at the table. Your father would never have done that," I goaded him.

Tomacito's dark face reddened and he glared. "Answer my question."

I couldn't answer him. If I did, I'd have to tell Aníbal Lura was dead. I just couldn't do it. I glared back at the man.

"Call him. His limo was gone. I bet he's locked in his penthouse sleeping right now."

Aníbal dialed Aguirre. We waited.

"Polo. You're okay? Yes, we're back at JadeAnne's. She's fine—shook up… Yeah, me, too. Polo. I gotta talk to Lura. I shot Danny dead. Polo, he was going to kill JadeAnne. I had no choice. Put 'er on, would you?"

Aníbal's eyes went round, wide. His handsome young face turned ashen then sagged like a defeated old man's. An animal cry bubbled up his throat and escaped his lips; high and soft, the sound built into an anguished roar. He jumped to his feet and threw the cell phone onto the tiled floor, smashing it into several pieces, startling Pepper who sat up and snarled.

"No. Noo. Nooo," he wailed, holding himself as though to keep from flying apart. Tears streamed down his face.

Tomacito's phone rang. He stood up and walked into the hallway toward the front door before answering. A look of pure disgust painted his face as he left the room.

I got up too, and caught Aníbal in my arms. "Ani, I'm so sorry. I'm so sorry," I whispered. "I'm here, lean on me."

"Lu-Lu-Lura is dead."

"I know dear, I know." I was crying too. I dropped my arms and took his hand, "Let me put you to bed. There's nothing we can do tonight. We'll both be better after sleeping."

"H-how did it ha-happen?" he hiccupped.

"Shh. Not tonight, Ani."

He stopped. He was shaking, tears flowing in a sheet across his cheeks, but the sadness wouldn't wash from his eyes. "She followed me? Through the k-kitchen?"

"Yes. You and Zocer." I pushed him gently toward my room.

At my door, he looked down at me, "Zocer? I never saw him."

I led him to the bed and turned back the covers. "Get in, Ani." He sank down onto Sally's comfortable guest bed, and I pulled off his shoes. He rolled into the ball I had wanted to become and moaned. I had no idea what to do for him. I curled around him and sank into blessed sleep.

I awoke to the sound of Aníbal's voice shouting from the living room.

"Put him on now. Now, I say." He went silent, then continued shouting louder, anger and frustration laminating his words into hard pellets. "You *pinche burro pendejo*. I don't care if he's with the Pope. Put my fucking half-brother on the line, now."

I buried my head under my pillow. I wasn't ready to remember. I wanted to snuggle back into the peaceful ignorance of sleep.

"No I won't leave a message." I heard him from under my pillow, followed by the thunk of the receiver hitting the cradle, or maybe the wall. My eyes opened, although I willed them shut again. No good. I was fully awake. Dex had left me. Lura had died. A maniac Aguirre went ballistic in the front room, and a malevolent black blob oozed from my brain into my chest. Time to get up and deal with it.

"Get up, JadeAnne. We've got to go to the Krystal." Aníbal slapped down the hall toward my room in what I assumed were Dex's flip-flops. "Polo is refusing to talk to me." His tone sounded angry and terse as he poked his head around the door.

"So I heard. Who were you talking to?" What happened to the Jahdey?

"One of his flunkies. I don't know. He blames me for Lura's—" he whispered hoarsely, choking on the last word. "Oh, God, Lura is dead."

He sat down on the edge of the bed and hung his head, sitting statue-still, barely breathing. I sat up, slid my arms around his waist and leaned my head into his back. His clothes smelled faintly of gun blast. We sat like that for several minutes. I couldn't think of anything to say.

His voice jabbed the still air. "It's his fault."

"It's whose fault?" I asked.

"My brother's."

He said it like he had a bad taste in his mouth, and I suddenly understood just how much Aníbal hated Polo. If Ani hated Polo so much, why is he visiting him? Strange thoughts took shape. I swept them aside. I didn't have the leisure to contemplate the dysfunctionality of the Aguirre clan right now. There were more pressing issues at hand, like collecting Dex's things to leave at the penthouse. I guessed that's where he'd gone.

"Was Polo there?"

"He wouldn't pick up the phone. He was in a meeting." Ani sneered.

"Did Dex make it off the wharf okay?" My voice quavered as my chest loosened and the black blob slipped toward my belly.

"See for yourself. We're going there now. Get dressed," he ordered in a flat voice.

The emotional weight of Dex's bag was almost too much for me. I half lugged, half dragged it out to the combi and shoved it in the side door. Pepper whined, and his eyes questioned me. I reached out to pet him, but he leaned away, tucked his tail between his legs, and rolled his eyes toward Aníbal who was fidgeting in the front seat. I backed out of the bus and slammed the door, then went around to the driver's side and climbed in. I noticed Ani still had on Dex's sandals as I buckled myself into the seat.

We rode in silence. I cut through town and onto the highway, rather than over the scenic but potentially deadly cliffs. Who knew what dangers lurked? I was pretty sure Rodriguez's boys were going to be cruising in force, hoping to catch any of us "Aguirre Cartel" folk unprepared. My combi was a dead giveaway. Lura's Glock lay in my lap like a coiled snake ready to strike. Ani wore his holster strapped under a blue Hawaiian shirt. Something else of Dex's.

"I'm going to kill him."

Aníbal's calculated words burned my skin like ice. He meant Polo. I was certain of it.

"I'll take him down and see him rot in hell."

I glanced sideways at him. His face was twisted, ugly. I felt little pin pricks of fear up my spine. He was serious. The strange thoughts crept up into my consciousness.

"Why are you here, Ani? Why in Mexico at this particular time?" I asked.

He concentrated on something in the distance. I downshifted into second with the traffic on Ruta 200 and looked directly at him. His mouth drew into a thin line, tight, as though he was fighting to keep his words in his mouth.

"Why, Ani? It's no coincidence. What are you?"

"What do you mean? I'm vacationing with my cousin." His voice dropped to a whisper, "Or I was."

"Lura wasn't on vacation. She was on a case. What are you really here for, Aníbal Aguirre?"

The traffic sped up, and I shifted into third and then back to fourth. A sedan passed, honking at the on-coming vehicles. Crazy asshole. Aníbal seemed to shrink into the seat, but I was sure it wasn't from shame or fear. He had no reason to fear me. I was no match for his strength. The thought fluttered into my mind: should I fear him? It alighted on one of the strange images and rested, slowly fanning its flame-patterned wings.

"You're here to kill Polo. It wasn't about Lura at all."

Aníbal's head spun around and a sick grin spread across his face. "No, not to kill him, JadeAnne. Not at all. I want to see him suffer. Killing him is too good, too fast. A pretty boy like Polo? Let him be some gangbanger's bitch. Let him see what it is to take it in the ass, lose everything. He's going down, I tell you."

I slowed for the exit to Ixtapa. We'd arrive in five minutes. What did he mean, "going down"? Could I trust Aníbal not to blow away his half-brother when we walked into the penthouse? And then, to have to see Dex—well, Dex might keep Aníbal in check. But I dreaded seeing him. What would I say?

"Are you going to be okay, Ani?" The whine in my voice embarrassed me, but he didn't seem to hear it.

"Am I going to blow him away, do you mean?"

"Yes. That's exactly what I mean. Are you? I won't go in if that's what you're doing. I'll just go back to Sally's, collect my stuff, and drive home through the interior. You crazy Aguirres won't be able to run me off any cliffs." The whine had turned to mild hysteria. Tears burned behind my lids, and Pepper crowded the seatbacks, growling.

"Calm down, Jade. Watch the road," he yelped as I came millimeters from sideswiping a parked car, but his voice sounded cool. "I'm not going to shoot him."

The Pacific sparkled sapphires and diamonds under the midday sun behind hotel row as we chugged down the slope from the highway. A breeze pushed the coruscating water into gleaming whitecaps and swayed the palms in a tropical beat around the luminous hotels. The view was breathtaking, and I momentarily forgot about Dex, about Lura, and admired the brilliant day.

We neared the Krystal, named, I was certain, on a day just like today, crystal clear and brilliant. Everything looked so clean. If only our lives were equally as clean. I dreaded my interview with Dex. What could I say? The tension, which had lifted for that second of beauty, crashed back. My stomach eddied in anxiety. I almost sent Aníbal through the windshield when I parked in the Krystal's lot. He glared at me, but mercifully remained silent.

The wind was gusting off the sea and through the gardens around the hotel, carrying a strong scent of salt laced with plumeria and tuberose. The palms clacked their fronds in wild applause over the roar of the breakers. My door was blown shut, and I had to hang on tightly to the combi, or I might have sailed away. Aníbal came around with Pepper on a leash and took my arm, marching me toward the service patio on the north side of the building. He wasn't letting the hotel staff call ahead of our arrival. I supposed that was a wise plan. I didn't think Aguirre would receive us with aperitifs and a luncheon today.

"Do you have a key to the elevator?" I broke the silence.

"I have a key to everything."

"That's surprising."

"What? That I have keys to my brother's locks? He gave them to Lura, and I copied them."

"Figures. What is it between you two? Why do you hate him so much?" I snatched Pepper's leash out of his hand.

Aníbal was silent while the elevator descended to ground level. We stepped inside. He punched the up button, the door closed, and the elevator silently moved upward in its shaft. "Hate Polo? Why would you ask?" His tone sounded contemptuous. "He destroyed my mother."

"Your mother? Well, he loves Lura. He dotes on her."

"Yeah, and he looks at me like I'm a bastard servant.

Lower than a bastard servant."

"I think you're wrong, Ani. He's only been kind to you in my presence. He was genuinely worried about you after the marina incident—"

"Because of Lura. He's always nice when she's around." He hung his head, softly moaning, "Now she's gone, she's gone. Lura."

The elevator came to a smooth stop and the door slid open. Aníbal stiffened, stood straight and patted the small of his back. I swung around to face him.

"You're carrying a gun? You liar. Give it to me." I held out my hand.

"Shut up, JadeAnne. I'm not going to do anything, just talk."

"You're not killing a man in cold blood in front of me. I won't stand for it. Who do you think you are?" I felt my cheeks redden in anger and my heart thud in my chest. Aguirre was a drug dealer and a sad sick excuse for a human being, but he didn't deserve to be gunned down by his resentful little brother. Rather, he deserved to be apprehended by the authorities and sent to prison for a long, long time.

"I'm not going to shoot him, JadeAnne. If you'd shut up, I'd tell you who I am." He growled as he stepped into the rich foyer and turned toward his brother's offices.

CHAPTER TWENTY-TWO

There's Always a Choice

Dex and two of Aguirre's security men stepped into the hall in front of us, blocking our path. Pepper crowed and wagged his tail furiously, straining on the leash, pulling me toward Dex.

"Dex." I dropped the leash, and Pepper and I rushed to him. I momentarily shut out the painful breakup on the wharf the night before.

"Hello, JadeAnne. How are you?" he said in a bland tone, his eyes veiled as he held out his hand as though to shake. He ignored Pepper.

Oh, so that's how it is. Stepping back, I replied in an equally bland tone, "I'm fine, thank you." I told him I had his things downstairs. "Dexter, I wish to speak with you privately."

He nodded toward Aníbal. "Good to see you made it off the pier."

He took my elbow and guided me away. Pepper pushed between us and leaned into my leg. I softly whistled.

"Don't command the dog to do anything we'll both regret," Dex said quietly.

I was beginning to wish Ani would shoot someone,

Dexter Trouette in particular.

We headed through the gallery with security flanking Aníbal, who had taken the lead. Dex, Pepper, and I brought up the rear. We marched toward Aguirre's office. Our footsteps echoed off the cold tile. Tension lay in the atmosphere like a smothering blanket.

One of the guards knocked on Aguirre's closed door with two crisp raps. A voice I didn't recognize instructed us to enter as the door swung open. Aníbal and the guards went in. I pulled away from Dex and followed Ani, but an armed man filled the doorway and prevented me from entering. Pepper growled and tensed. I screamed and threw myself over my dog as three weapons came up.

Pepper howled, and Aguirre shouted, "Shut that dog up."

"Aguirre, you ass, call your men off," Dexter roared over the commotion.

"Stand down. Stand down," someone shouted.

I peeked into the room from the doorway. The three guards lowered their guns, but Aníbal glowered at his brother who looked small behind the hand cannon he pointed at Pepper and me. Dex pushed past me into the room.

"Put that gun away before I kill you, Aguirre," Dex said evenly. More harshly, "JadeAnne, control your dog."

"You'd kill me over a cur and a bitch? Americans have such misplaced loyalties," Aguirre mocked, but lowered his gun. "I hold Miss Stone responsible for the death of my cousin."

"What?" Aníbal, Dex, and I exclaimed in unison.

"*Cállate hermanito*," he snapped at Aníbal. "Yes, had your woman not shown up looking for my cousin, Señor Trouette, Lura would be alive."

"You kidnapped me," I shouted, hoisting myself off the floor. Pepper bounded up and shook himself.

"You knew Lura would be at my farm. Worthington led you there. He hired you to find her."

"You knew all along I'd been hired by Worthington. You meant to kill me. What stopped you?" Fear, shame, and deep loathing for Aguirre undulated through my veins with my quickened pulse.

"You were part of his plan."

Aníbal spoke for the first time. "Polo, of course she was part of his plan. She was his plan, but when we figured out what Danny really was up to, she did everything to protect Lura. You can't really think JadeAnne had anything to do with Lura's death."

Dex took over. "Lura was blown up by your enemy. If it's blame you're looking for, Aguirre, look to yourself. Your Lura was a casualty of your heroin war with Rodriguez. Worthington would never have gotten Rodriguez's boys behind him if it weren't for you. I should have left you on the pier. Come on, Jade."

Aguirre's face turned purple, his ears smoking as we left the room. I trailed behind Dex who stomped along the gallery to the main elevator. The doors opened, we stepped in, and we rode in silence to the lobby.

"Bar," Dex seethed and stalked to a quiet table in the back of the lounge.

The waiter hurried over, eyeing Pepper, who was making himself comfortable under the table.

"Jack Daniels. Neat," Dex ordered before the waiter could say anything about the dog.

This didn't look promising. Dex never drank before noon or, in his words, "before the sun was over the yardarm."

"And for the señorita?"

"*Un café con crema, gracias*," I replied, trying to smile.

"*Para sirvirle*," he said and hurried away.

I sat quietly, avoiding Dex's gaze. I felt him staring at me, but was afraid to get him talking. I was afraid he would hurt me again. I hurt enough already.

The drinks arrived, and Dex downed his in a gulp. "Another," he demanded before the waiter could set mine in front of me.

I knew better than to criticize him, but I didn't think another drink would improve his humor. I shouldn't have come here. What did I think I was going to accomplish? Aníbal could have given him the suitcase. On top of everything, I looked terrible. My clothes were rumpled, my hair a disaster. My skin was bruised and scraped, and, even after ten hours of sleep, I had dark circles under my eyes. Looking at me now, Dex would avow his decision to leave me. My shoulders sank, and I felt the familiar pinpricks of hot tears welling up behind my eyelids. I shifted in my chair and busied myself stirring my coffee, hoping he wouldn't notice. I'd be damned if I'd give the bastard the satisfaction of knowing he was breaking my heart.

His second drink arrived, and Dex downed it as he had the first. "Coffee, please," he said and cleared his throat. After a long pause he said, "Look, Jade, I'm sorry for last night. I-I didn't know how to say it. I wasn't kind."

"No, you weren't."

"We've grown apart. I don't know what to do about it."

"Obviously, you do. You're dumping me," I replied, my voice salted with resentment.

"I didn't mean for it to sound like that, Jade. I meant, I meant…" He trailed off.

"Yeah, what did you mean, Dex? 'It's over' is pretty clear." I tensed up, my voice rose in anger.

"I meant I think we should take a break from each other. See where we are. Maybe get some counseling." He mumbled this last bit.

"A break? What've we been doing for the last six months? You've been gone most of the time. It would be a break to spend some time together."

"I mean, some time apart so we can decide what we

want."

"I know what you want, to get away from me."

"No, JadeAnne. Just time to figure it out. What do you want with me? Can you answer that?"

The waiter came back with Dex's coffee and refilled my cup from the carafe he carried. I looked hard at the man I'd loved for so many years. I knew he was right. What did I want with him?

"I love you, Jade," he continued when the waiter left. "But I'm not sure where we're going, not since you refused to marry me." He smiled at me sadly. "I want you to stay here in Mexico. Take the vacation you planned. You earned it. Stay at Sally's, swim, run on the beach with Pepper. Spend some time on the yoga patio. Think about it, us. We'll talk when you get home."

"I don't know, Dex. With all that's happened—"

"That's part of it, love. You've been through a lot. You've lost a friend. You need to sort it out, grieve, and come to terms with the violence and death. No one can do it for you."

"How can I be safe here? Rodriguez will come after me."

"No he won't. Aguirre and I have taken care of everything. With Worthington dead, no one has any interest in you, and if they did, they'd have me to reckon with."

I sneered, "Right, Dex. A lot of protection you'll provide from California."

"Aguirre has contracted with the Ruiz clan to see to your protection. What a loser that guy is. How did he ever get voted into the senate?"

"Lura and Aníbal hinted he bought his way in. You know what he is, don't you?"

"A drug cartel boss."

"And you trust him? After pissing him off like you did? I don't think so. Anyway, he blames me."

Dex looked thoughtful for a few moments. The lounge was filling, and the smells of food, the murmur of voices and clatter of dishes as guests ordered lunch broke the quiet. My stomach growled. I hadn't consumed anything except coffee since the day before.

"I trust Tomacito Ruiz."

"No. He hates me. He almost hit me last night, Dex." I was whining now.

"Then what do you want to do?" A thin veneer of exasperation covered his words.

"Drive me home."

"I can't do that, Jade."

"Then I'll leave your bus here and fly," I snapped.

"They want you to stay for Lura's funeral. Aguirre doesn't blame you, not really."

"Then why did he say he did?"

"He's torn apart. Acting out. He just lost his cousin, for Chrissakes. Please, Jade, please stay for the funeral, get some rest, decide what you want, and come home when you're ready."

"I don't have much money. I didn't bring a lot of cash with me. I didn't put any into my own account. Worthington owed the firm for expenses."

"All you wanted was a Mexican holiday. Well, now you have it. You're doing everything you can to get out of it. I don't get you, woman. You've got $50,000. Spend it. Have fun." He tossed some pesos down, pushed back from the table, and got to his feet.

"Wait. Where are you going?" I called after him as he started toward the door.

"C'mon. I have a plane to catch," Dex said over his shoulder. "Let's get my suitcase."

Pepper and I scrambled from the table and hurried after him, catching up in the lobby.

"Stay with us, Dex. We'll work out our problems here." I

took his hand and stepped into pace with his stride. He squeezed my hand and kissed my knuckles.

"Can't do that, Jade. Someone has to run the office. My flight leaves at three-twenty." He dropped my hand.

I slowed down and looked at my watch. It was twelve-forty-seven.

"I'll drive you."

"No need. I ordered a taxi for one o'clock. I'll just take my bag and say goodbye here."

We had reached the combi. Dex opened the side door with his key. Pepper jumped in and looked at him expectantly.

"Sorry old boy, gotta go," he said to the dog and gave him a stroke. "You take good care of your mommy for me." He grabbed his suitcase and turned to me.

"I'll miss you, JadeAnne. Take care of yourself."

And he was gone, loping across the parking lot toward a waiting taxi. He turned back toward me and waved as he opened the door to get in. "And take care of my bus."

I felt oh so tired. I was a stranger in a foreign country. My boyfriend had dumped me. I was beat up and sore, and some really bad, bad people were pissed off at me. But I'd found my missing person and kept my firm's doors open for another couple of months. I should be proud of that.

I closed the side door, walked around the bus, and climbed in. This must be how a zombie feels. I sat in the driver's seat for a long time, my mind numb, before I turned the key in the ignition. The feeling of being an outsider, alone, long corralled, burst its fences and galloped over me. But I had a choice. There was always a choice. Dex had made his and good riddance. In my heart I knew I didn't love him anymore. I could let him go.

I took a peso from the ashtray in the dashboard and

flipped it into the air. North or south? I caught it, slapped it into my palm. Quetzacoatl whispered to me in Lura's voice, "Go south, girlfriend. Relax. Get a tan. You haven't lost that bet yet."

ANA MANWARING

COMING MAY 18, 2022
THE HYDRA EFFECT

CHAPTER ONE

Lura's Funeral

Wednesday, August 8, 2007"

Chills ran down my spine; someone was watching me. I scanned the wide plaza bordered by the church and a low, ornate, red-painted building, but I couldn't see anything that looked out of place for Coyoacan. No *malos hombres* behind the well-pruned park trees nor the black clad phantasmal shooters I imagined flitting in and out of my peripheral vision, sighting their sniper rifles from the rooftops along Calle Felipe Carrillo. As if I'd actually see my assassin. I hurried across Plaza Hidalgo toward La Iglesia de San Juan Bautista.

I couldn't shake Senator Polo Aguirre's hateful outburst after my friend's death last week: "I hold JadeAnne Stone responsible for the death of my cousin." Aguirre was a dangerous man—a criminal involved with marijuana and heroin cartels—Hell, he headed up a drug cartel, didn't he? Wealthy and powerful, he had the backing of Mexico's ruling class. I had my dog and a prayer.

This whole thing had started because Aguirre was the swing vote on the coming Senate decision on the Privatization of PEMEX. But *ni importa la culpa*, if the senator wanted to retaliate against me because his kingpin rival in Ixtapa, Arturo Rodriguez, blew up his cousin Lura on the pier in Zihuatanejo, then he had the means to do it.

I hurried on.

Parking in the Coyoacán district of Mexico City was a joke on a good day, and I was afraid I'd be late to Lura's funeral. I'd driven the *cuota*, toll road, Mexico 95, from Acapulco that morning after a lousy night's sleep in a rent-by-the hour motel, recommended by the waiter at my resort hotel in Papanoa. Located near the highway on the pimply backside of the posh Acapulco hotel district, the motel was filthy with trash, both on the ground and on two legs. But it was late and I was too exhausted to search for something better. I was wrong.

Revelers appeared to be coming or going from the disco next door, which had cranked up the volume of the music so loud that the shock of the bass almost felt like the bomb blast I'd survived in Zihua—the one that killed Lura. I'd peeked out my door a couple of times when the thumping and screaming got particularly obnoxious and was reminded that most hookers don't look like Julia Roberts in Pretty Woman. God what an ugly lot—and they're screamers. "*Ay Papi! Cójeme Papito, eres mi rey.*" Well, if I ever need to "do it" in Spanish, I'll know how.

The plaza was filled with vendors. I noticed a couple of kids selling hippie paraphernalia—Mayan braided wristlets, peace sign earrings and pendants, Balinese batik shifts, tie-dye headbands, Rasta-colored t-shirts—the usual stuff found on any street vendor's table in Berkeley. The pollution that afternoon stank and hung yellow and gritty around the vendors and their customers. I could barely breathe, and scurrying across the plaza had me gasping so heavily that I slowed down, forced to catch my breath. A clown proffered me a bouquet of helium balloons while a white-clad man pushed an ice cream cart by, his bell jangling. I salivated. A scoop of coconut ice cream would have been a balm for my smog-irritated throat, but I swallowed hard and hurried on.

"Lay-dee, señora. Tengo tu futuro."

I glanced toward the throaty voice. A gypsy-like *bruja* sat at a folding table and laid out Tarot cards on a black velvet cloth. Seeing my interest, she pulled a card from the deck in her palm and displayed the Knight of Swords. I slowed down.

"Venga, lay-dee. Así es el futuro." She swept the displayed layout to the side and placed the card in the middle of her cloth. "A *príncipe* looks for you señorita," she paused and extracted the King of Hearts from within her deck and placed it over the first card with a meaningful look. I started to move on, but she flicked a third card out of the pack and crossed it over the King. A man lay dead with a forest of swords sticking out of his back.

"¡Ay! ¡Dios mío!" The witch crossed herself and gathered up the cards, her wrinkled, bony hands moving like the wings of a hummingbird.

My heart dropped into my gut and shivers ran up my spine. Someone walking on my grave. I hurried the last couple hundred feet to the church. Well-heeled mourners in small groups filed between the massive, scarred wooden doors leading into the dim interior. Most of the women appeared to have stepped from the pages of Vogue magazine, and I saw a lot of important jewelry sparkling on fingers and ears and around necks and wrists. I stood back to calm down, admiring the lovely relief sculpture on the façade, and checked out the attendees as they arrived, hoping to see someone I knew—Anibal.

I glanced at my watch. Last minute mourners in

limousines and chauffeur-driven SUVs drew up to the curb opposite the main doors. Uniformed drivers helped rich urbanites, *chilangos*, out of the vehicles and onto the sidewalk. It was obvious by the unusual lumps under jackets that some of these drivers were really bodyguards. Drug Mafia, I supposed. I mean, do senators need bodyguards? I wouldn't know. I realized, too, that there were way more armed police in the area than should be normal for the funeral of an American. Again, my skin rippled with the thought of being sighted in somebody's crosshairs. I shuddered and pushed through the crowd into the church.

After the bright haze in the plaza, it took my eyes several seconds to see in the shadowy interior. I heard the sounds of clothes rustling and jewelry jingling, coughing, the thump as someone's butt landed too hard on the pew, and what may have been muted sobs floating in the pious atmosphere. It struck me that there was no music, no conversation, no babies crying; there lacked life at this celebration of death.

Lura would be pissed off. She'd have wanted a wild Irish wake—"Let's all get drunk and dance and tell funny stories," she'd have said. Maybe that would come later. The phone message I'd received from Anibal two days before had only said where and when the funeral would take place.

I made my way up the center aisle toward the altar looking for a place to sit. and made out the Aguirre family in the front pew—Senator Polo Aguirre sitting ramrod straight, eyes forward, and absolutely still; a thin, bent woman perched to his right, swaddled in black—black dress, floppy-brimmed black hat draped in a black veil, black gloves. The matriarch.

To his left, a grey-haired man and a small woman with short blonde hair leaned into each other. The woman appeared bird-like, her movements quick and restless. She reminded me of Lura in a way. Next to the blonde sat another woman, whose hair shone dark and glossy. She leaned in to speak to the man next to her and I could see she was wearing dark glasses. I'd noticed other people wearing dark glasses inside and thought it must be a disguise for the drug people, but the woman had to be Lura's sister Alejandra, or Alex, as Lura had called her, and I bet she wore them to hide swollen eyes. I assumed the man next to her was her husband, Jason.

And then I saw Anibal. He was straining around in his seat to view the crowd. Looking for someone?

Our eyes locked for a heart-stopping moment then he started out of his pew. I wanted to see him, and I wanted to run away and hide. What if he blamed me, like his half-brother, the senator, did? My stomach clenched and my skin prickled. I backed up the aisle and fled into a rear pew. The hard looks of a pair of burly, neck-less gorillas with suspicious bulges discouraged me and I stumbled back into the aisle.

Anibal had made it halfway up the aisle, a hint of a smile on his lips. Butterflies danced in my heart—no mistaking it. I'd flirted with him before the explosion. Before Dex left. A smothering blackness drifted down from the nave's ribbed vault and settled around me. My muscles went weak, and I staggered forward, jostled by the crowd now rushing for seats.

Oh, God, I can't! I can't. It was too soon. Lura was dead, my client was dead, drug cartel people were mad at me, my boyfriend had dumped me, and the Aguirre family blamed me for everything. How could I get involved with one of them? I simply needed to pay my respects and head out of Dodge.

I felt as exposed here in the church as I had outside, and my neck hairs were damp again. I needed to sit down and blend in. Ahead of me in the aisle, I saw a pew with only three mourners, and one sported a familiar square head. It couldn't be. Zocer was dead, wasn't he? Didn't I see him killed in the blast trying to save Lura?

Elated, I rushed toward him and collided with Anibal.

"JadeAnne! Where've you been? Why haven't you answered my messages? I've—we've—been so worried about you—Polo too. And the whole family. We've got a seat for you. C'mon."

He took my hand and pulled me toward the family pew. This was certainly a change from the hateful outburst a week earlier. To give the guy credit, though, he did stand up for me against Aguirre when that maniac tried to scapegoat me.

"Ani, no. No! I can't sit with your family. That's reserved for the…well, the family."

"We're expecting you, Jade. Besides, what about that night at the Krystal? I thought—"

Anibal went silent. We'd reached the family's pew and all Aguirre eyes turned on us. The men stood up and waited until I sat. I packed in next to Jason and we all sat down as Lura's coffin was lugged in by several gorilla-guys and placed on the waiting stand. The priest in purple robes appeared with his incense and smudged the high altar. I guess he was afraid this crowd would bring in some bad juju. Judging from what I'd seen of the Aguirre family, the Padre was right-on.

When the incense disbursed, the prayers began. The service was held in Latin, not a language I'd studied. I hadn't been raised in the Catholic Church and had only experienced Mass a few times in childhood after a Saturday night sleepover with a Catholic girlfriend. Most of the congregation knew the words, when to stand, when to kneel, and when to sit back down. I followed Anibal's lead and, thirty minutes later, found myself kneeling at the communion railing with my mouth wide to receive a small wafer and a slurp of some pretty awful tasting wine from the same chalice everyone else had sipped.

We took communion in the first group since we were

sitting in the first row. I dreaded the hours it was going to take to move what I estimated to be three or four hundred mourners through communion. But I was wrong, it took all of fifteen minutes. That priest knew how to manage a crowd.

After Christ's body and blood fortified the congregation, the family, sans Anibal, clustered at the closed coffin. I squeezed my eyes shut against the memory of Lura's burned body suspended in the doorway of Ristorante Mare e Pece's exploding kitchen.

"Is she going to be buried here?" I whispered to Anibal, hoping to switch my thought train.

"No, Uncle Beto is taking her home to L.A.," he whispered in reply. "They'll have a memorial there and a burial service. My aunt and uncle are pretty broken up."

"Those are Lura's parents?" I asked, gesturing to the grey-haired man and his tiny blonde wife.

"Yeah, and that's Alex, my cousin and her husband." He gestured with his chin, eyes red and full.

The group stood at Lura's coffin, holding hands, crying.

"Who's the lady in black?"

He sniffed, and blew his nose into a pressed white handkerchief that had materialized out of nowhere. "Aunt Lidia, Polo's mother. She arranged the service—all these people are her friends, Polo's colleagues, and government VIPs."

"Lidia has some dangerous-looking friends. Do you know many of them?"

"No. I was never part of this group. Aunt Lidia doesn't completely embrace me as family—just like Polo."

"That reminds me, I thought I saw Zocer back there." I swiveled around toward the pew with the square-headed man, but he was no longer there.

"Impossible. He's dead. His funeral was yesterday."

"You went?"

"No, private family funeral."

I lapsed into silence as the family filed back into our pew. No testimonials to Lura?

The organist began to play something from Beethoven. Mourners streamed up to the coffin, left flowers, mementos, candles, stuffed animals and dolls on the lid. Or they just touched it. Some knelt and prayed. The bodyguards escorted their charges and stood back, scowling at the congregation while the mourners said their "goodbyes." The procession went on and on and on.

The music changed from "Amazing Grace" and "The King of Love Mine Shepherd Is" to out and out dirges. I recognized Verdi's Dies irae from the Requiem Mass and some Bach. I felt the low notes more than heard them and was moved to tears. It wasn't that Lura and I were so close—we'd been acquainted for less than two weeks, but I felt uncomfortably responsible. If I hadn't accepted the case from her banker husband, Daniel Worthington, would he have killed her? No, this was naïve thinking. He had known where she was and had intended to kill her from the start. I'd been set up to flush her from the protection of her cousin, Senator Aguirre, before she connected Worthington to a major money laundering scheme.

I'd been chewing it over to the point of obsession for days. That is, in between mourning my broken seven-year love affair with Dexter Trouette and looking over my shoulder for Rodriguez's goons. I hadn't come to feel any more comfortable with the conclusions I'd drawn about what really was happening than before I'd drawn them, and as far as Worthington was concerned, his intentions had been lost the moment Anibal put a bullet through his head to save me from being murdered. It was all too bizarre, and now I was sitting in a pew in a colonial church in Mexico City mourning someone I barely knew as though I were one of the family—holding hands with her sister's husband and leaning on her cousin, her best friend—crying. Am I a hypocrite? I just wished it would end and I could go hug my dog and go home. But home would be so empty without Dex.

"Where's Pepper?" Anibal asked me sotto voce.

"In the combi. Is Coyoacán a safe *colonia*?" I replied under my breath.

"Depends where it's parked. This is a pretty wealthy district, but you're not safe anywhere in Mexico. That's why all these *ricos* have bodyguards." He laughed softly.

"It's on Xicoténcatl," I stumbled over the indigenous name, "just off Centenario."

"I guess it's safe."

"Pepper's guarding—he'll tear any carjacker's arm off and beat him with it," I said with more confidence than I felt. He didn't tear any arms off when Aguirre's thugs hijacked me off Ruta 200, even if he did tear a hole in my kidnapper's throat.

"Don't think about it, Jade, it'll just bring you down," he whispered, giving my hand a little squeeze.

How did he know?

"We're going to Aunt Lidia's after. You're coming, aren't you?"

"I don't think so, Ani. I need to get going. Find a place to sleep. I didn't have a very restful night."

"You'll stay with me. I've got a house in La Condesa. There's a great coffee house nearby, La Selva. We'll go read international newspapers and drink espresso in the morning."

Anibal's warm smile and gorgeous coal eyes looked inviting. I was sorely tempted.

"Uh-uh, no way, José." I drew my hand back into my lap and shifted toward the aisle to focus on the mourners coming forward. Was he crazy? With what his family thought of me? Anibal slumped away, his jaw tight.

Two men in dark glasses, trailed by their burly boys, headed the column of people approaching the casket. They glanced side to side as if looking for someone. Anibal stiffened, and I studied him from under my too-long bangs, hoping he wouldn't notice I was watching him. As the men came even with our pew, Anibal turned abruptly toward me and sank his head into my chest, making sobbing sounds, and I found myself staring into my own eyes mirrored back at me from the closer man's sunglasses. He had a sneering little mouth under a scraggly mustache and beard, and I could feel the hatred he projected toward me. Or was it toward Anibal? The look chilled me to the bone.

The men passed on, tapped the coffin, and moved off toward an exit. I watched until the door closed and whispered, "Okay, Anibal. What was that about?"

He sat up, stopped his phony sobbing, and shifted away from me.

"I mean it, Anibal. What's going on?"

"I miss Lura so much," he said, voice catching on her name. He gave me a sad sack smile.

"So do I, but why don't I believe that's the whole story here?"

He turned back to me with an angelic expression, "I don't know."

"Yes you do; you knew those men. You didn't want them to see you," I accused. As if anyone in the church hadn't seen us up here on display in the front pew.

"Who are they, Anibal Aguirre?"

"Shhhh. I'll tell you after" —*on the way to Aunt Lidia's*, he mouthed, rolling his eyes in a feeble attempt to indicate he didn't want the others to know this big secret.

I sat back and shut up. How much longer would this go on? I couldn't see any way to get around it—I was going to be properly introduced to Lura's family soon. The heavy atmosphere weighed on me like water. I didn't want to meet the Aguirre-Laylors, that was for sure. Not if Aguirre had told them what he thought about my involvement in their daughter's death. It wasn't true, but I felt so conflicted. Did I give myself too much credit? Aguirre probably wouldn't speak my name. And he'd never say anything to his brother, Lura's father. Neither would Ani speak to Aguirre. And the events leading up to her death came so fast and furious, Lura wouldn't have had time to talk to her sister. I rationalized and let my tense shoulders slip from around my ears. These folks didn't have a clue who I was, and I'd keep it like that.

I slid closer to Anibal and perched on the edge of the pew. "I've gotta go, Ani. I wish I could visit with your family, but I just don't think now's the time."

"You can't go, JadeAnne. We're expecting you," he replied a bit too loud.

"I'm sorry, really. Please pass my condolences on to everyone, especially your aunt and uncle, but Pepper has been in the bus too long and it's warm. I've got to take care of him." I started to collect my purse and get up.

"Jah-dey, please," he whined. "You can't leave now."

"Leopoldo, control that ill-mannered boy," a reedy voice quavered.

Startled, I looked down the row. Aguirre faced his mother. "Yes Mother, I'll take care of it presently." He turned toward me with a look that could kill. I shrank back into my place and pretended to concentrate on the priest who had reappeared into view now that the mourners had said goodbye. Good, we're getting out of here.

"Anibal, you are disturbing your aunt's peace. Please be quiet," Aguirre whispered in his ridiculous formality. "Oh, and Miss Stone, my mother wishes to have your company at our gathering. I hope you won't disappoint her."

I smiled weakly and shook my head. Beyond him, I saw the old crow nodding, one bony hand clutching at her Leopoldo.

"Nuestro padre, que arte en cielo. Santificado sea nombre thy. El reino de Thy viene, thy será hecho—"

The padre led the remaining congregation in the Lord's Prayer. Few remained in the cavernous church. Mostly old ladies in black mantillas, Lidia's friends, no doubt. Squirming around, I couldn't see any men in sunglasses and it came to me that I didn't feel like I was being watched anymore.

"—y nos perdonan nuestras infracciones mientras que perdonamos a los que violen contra nosotros..."

Maybe that's what I was supposed to do—forgive. God was telling me right there at Lura's funeral, I had to forgive. But whom? The list was long.

"And deliver us from evil for thine is the kingdom and the power and the glory, forever and ever."

Okay, I'd forgive myself. And then I'd let the Aguirre family forgive me, too. Amen.

ABOUT THE AUTHOR

Ana teaches creative writing and autobiographical writing in California's wine country. She is the founder of JAM Manuscript Consulting where she coaches writers, assists in developing projects and copyedits.

When Ana isn't helping other writers, she posts book reviews and tips on writing craft and the business of writing at www.anamanwariing.com/blogs/Building a Better Story, and produces the North Bay Poetics, a monthly poetry event. She's branded cattle in Hollister, lived on houseboats, consulted brujos, visited every California mission, worked for a PI, swum with dolphins, and outrun gun totin' maniacs on lonely Mexican highways—the inspiration for The JadeAnne Stone Mexico Adventures. Read about her transformative experiences living in Mexico at www.saintsandskeletons.com.

With a B.A. in English and Education and an M.A. in Lingustics, Ana is finally able to answer her mother's question, "What are you planning to do with that expensive education?" Be a paperback writer.

If you had as much fun reading this book as I had writing it, please consider leaving a review wherever you purchased your copy.

To find out about new books and upcoming events, please take a moment to sign up for my newsletter, Writing on the Wall: http://www.anamanwaring.com.